TREACHEROUS TRADE

A FIONA MAHONEY MYSTERY

· *USA Today* Bestselling Author ·

KERRIGAN BYRNE

0 9 8 7 6 5 4 3 2 1

Cover by: Maryna Zhukova

Published by Oliver Heber Books

Chapter One

❧❧❧

A *prostitute.*
      Murdered.
      In Whitechapel.

Inspector Grayson Croft had spoken the only concoction of words with the power to thwart the confession perched on the edge of my lips. One moment it had been waiting to dive into the cozy darkness between us, shattering the life I'd built for myself.

Until he'd interjected—as men like Croft were wont to do—and I swallowed the incriminating admission so quickly, I nearly choked whilst forcing it past the lump of emotion in my throat.

To be fair, his entire sentence had been "I've come to accept that if a prostitute is murdered in Whitechapel, there's nothing I can do to keep you from the investigation, short of locking you up and losing the key."

However, I only marked the important bits of this statement.

I knew Amelia Croft, a woman I'd never met, was his sister. Indeed, I knew more about her than I wished to.

Secrets that would tear this tidy home down to its foundations.

I'd come here to do that, I supposed. Not purposely, but I was swiftly realizing that if I made my confessions to Croft, one of them would devastate this little family of his.

Blast, but it was easier to think of Croft as an adversary before I'd sat by his fireplace in this masculine study, next to stately bookcases, whilst sipping strong, sweet tea he'd prepared to my liking without even consulting me first.

I couldn't remember ever telling him how I took my tea.

He was a detective, after all. I supposed it was his job to pay attention to details.

I took a sip, then another, buying myself time to process these new deaths. To consider how they changed everything about what I was going to do next. "I've not read anything new in the paper," I said breathlessly. Surely two murdered women in Whitechapel would create a stir.

"I'm unsure of how long we'll be able to keep it from the press." His lip lifted in a semblance of a snarl. There was no love lost between Croft and journalists.

"How is your sister mixed up in this?" I asked.

"Did she not mention in her letter?"

I made a negative gesture. I'd never received a letter. I'd come here on my own business, but I'd be damned if I allowed Croft that information before I gleaned what I could from him about this timely bit of news.

"She knew the victims." He studied the hemmed cuffs of his trousers as his hard jaw worked over something that might have looked like shame on features less brutal than his. "From earlier days."

The inspector's mossy gaze did its best to lock me into the chair he'd placed next to the fire in his study upon my arrival. I'd been grateful for it at the time, as I'd traveled from Chelsea to Lambeth through the frigid early London morning to unburden myself.

Feather-sized snowflakes had begun to collect coal dust from the January air, dispelling a bit of the post-holiday gloom with a mist cold enough to freeze your lungs to the bones of your ribs.

The cozy, golden-hued Croft residence had been a welcome sanctuary from the pall of grey.

Leaning forward, if only to prove that I could beneath the intensity of his regard, I returned his flinty glower with one of my own. "Tell me *everything*."

At my command, Croft hesitated.

Though he'd been glaring at me since I arrived, he finally took a fraught moment to truly assess me. And because I detested his penchant for mercurial appraisals and monosyllabic answers, I returned the dubious favor by raking him with my own rude stare.

But for green eyes, we shared exactly zero physical traits.

If God made man of clay and earth, he picked the most stubborn stone from which to chisel Grayson Croft. Something abrasive and volcanic like a pumice, constantly grating at the fibers of my nerves.

He was too large to be graceful. Too square-shaped to be elegant. Too hard-used and disgruntled to be considered handsome, at least by my standards. Though he secured his inky-dark hair back with pomade and a fine-toothed comb, his undignified jaw always wanted a shave.

Sometimes I itched to pin him down and do it myself, if only to know what he'd look like without a perpetual shadow. Though a razor wouldn't quell the ones in his deep-set eyes. Those shades were created by something far more sinister than time and neglect.

"You look terrible," was his eventual verdict.

"I meant, tell me something useful and relevant, you addlepate." I pushed myself from my seat and turned my back on him, stalking to the bookshelves that dominated his walls.

Were I a hedgehog, my quills would have stood on end, and I did everything in my power to advertise that I was prickly with impatience and *not* self-consciousness.

I crossed my arms over my tender middle and gave his enviable collection of fiction undue examination.

Croft and I had been at odds ever since he'd held me captive, spitting and screaming, as I discovered the mutilated corpse of my dearest childhood friend, Mary Kelly. He'd objected heartily when the landlord offered me money to clean Mary's blood and offal from the anemic, moldy rooms off Dorset Street, once her body had been carted away by the coroner.

And he'd renewed those objections as I built my career doing that very thing for so much of the greater London area for nearly three years now.

The dead often left a terrible mess behind... and I could get blood out of just about anything.

One would think I'd be used to Croft's brusque brand of brevity after so long. And yet I'd allowed him to provoke me with this opportunity afforded by a murder in Whitechapel, and also by a droll comment on my dreadful appearance...

Of course I looked no better than ghastly. In the past handful of months, the love of my life had been stabbed to death in front of me by a man well-deserved of his vengeance. On top of that, Jack the Ripper—my sworn nemesis—had taken to sending me cryptic letters from his throne in Hell. One such missive solved the murder of several copycat killings in his name. Another had been attached to a journalist the Ripper claimed to have butchered for *my* benefit.

Now, only I and two other souls knew the perpetrator of the three officially unsolved Ripper-esque killings, and evidently I was the only one of the trio cursed with a conscience.

For months I'd been nothing but a creature of

grief. But eventually, guilt had seeped through the mortar of my melancholy, and driven me out onto the cobbles in search of the absolution that only came to a true-born Irishwoman, such as I, through confession.

It'd be a cold day in Hell before I confessed to a priest again, but I'd truly planned to unburden my soul to one of Scotland Yard's most relentless detectives. I'd come to inform him that my business as a postmortem sanitation specialist wasn't the sole reason I could afford my lovely rowhouse in Chelsea. Indeed, my skills had been conscripted for one of the most notorious criminals of the London underworld, "the Hammer," and his prolific assassin, "the Blade."

Inspector Croft had three open murder cases I could close with the whisper of one name.

A name it would kill me to malign.

But I'd come to do just that, ready to consign my fate to his large, square hands—astoundingly callused for a man with a desk job, I noted.

However, he'd ruined my plans to do so by intimating that more dead working women in Whitechapel had invoked the terrifying name at the top of the suspect list.

The Ripper. The man I'd vowed to search for while I still had breath in my body.

And instead of granting me the subsequent details, Croft told me *this*?

That I look terrible?

Did he assume I didn't own a mirror? That I couldn't see for myself that my auburn hair had lost its luster? That my wan flesh merely haunted my skeleton because grief had frozen my blood as sluggish as the Arctic and stolen my appetite for living, let alone food? My lips had drawn thin, and color deserted them. Freckles that had once danced across my nose paled, lending doubt to the notion that the sun ever kissed me at all. Dimples had lengthened to lines, bracketing an ever-present scowl.

Even my fashionable dark woolen winter gown and velvet cloak couldn't hide how bitter and brittle I'd become. Yes, I knew all this, and I didn't bloody care.

"Is it him?" I asked the tomes, wishing I couldn't feel his eyes on my back. "Is it Jack?"

"Fiona, if it were, don't you think the city would be on fire with the news of it by now?"

How would I know? I had no idea when the murders had occurred. Yet he seemed to think I might. He'd intimated that it was his sister who'd summoned me.

But I'd found him home alone.

A strange coincidence, that.

"Where is Miss Croft?" I queried. "Should she not be here?"

I wouldn't mind a reprieve from being alone in the inspector's lair. The rest of the house boasted a decidedly feminine touch, enriched by the aroma of vanilla and baking bread. These scents permeated the study as well, intermingled with a darker spice and the clove tobacco the inspector was so fond of.

He took this scent with him into the world, and it had always befuddled me because it matched him not at all... and somehow simultaneously complemented him.

Which was irritating in the extreme.

"If two... ladies of the evening are dead in Whitechapel, it'll only be so long before the press catches wind of it, and they will set the city ablaze like it was sixteen sixty-six," I reminded him, gathering myself enough to turn and face him. "So, you might as well give me the details now." It took everything I had not to fidget with my hair, to smooth my dress or pinch my cheeks.

It wouldn't make me look less terrible.

One dark brow lifted. "Did Amelia explain nothing?"

I was still working on becoming a convincing liar, so I told the truth. "Most people tend to impart details to me in person."

"I'm surprised she didn't just summon you to Fleet Street."

"I'm sorry, but why would I go to Fleet Street when the murders were in—"

"Because the women only *reside* in Whitechapel," came a husky feminine voice from the doorway. "But they work in the same brothel on Fleet Street."

It wasn't the wealth of onyx hair, uncommon height, or sturdy jaw that pegged the woman as kin to Croft, so much as the matching Northern accent and the same haunted gaze as her—I realized with a jolt of surprise —*younger* brother.

"*Worked*." Amelia Croft's eyes were a great deal softer than the inspector's as she corrected the tenses of the women who were now in the past. "I wanted to engage your services, Miss Mahoney, because the coroner has yet to come for Jane Sheffield, who was gruesomely murdered at the very brothel in which I used to ply the trade."

Chapter Two

Amelia Croft cut a figure every bit as striking as her brother's, even bundled as she was in a frock coat and winter trappings. With a gleaming gold rose brooch on the lace collar of her modest, high-necked gown, anyone would have placed her as matron of a respectable household, rather than a spinster former prostitute.

I remembered, not long ago, Inspector Croft intimated that he and his sister had resorted to less-than-reputable trades as destitute orphans from Northumberland. I never judged nor censured him for it, and yet a stain of color crept from beneath his high collar at the indelicate mention of what his sister used to do for a living.

As suddenly as she'd appeared in the doorway, she swept away, her boots clicking with brisk efficiency on the floorboards.

Inspector Croft and I blinked at each other for a moment and, in a strange syncopation, mobilized to follow her. Abandoning my tea to a table, I trailed him down the long corridor toward the front of the house and nipped at his heels like a small—no doubt irritating—dog as he hit through a door into an impressively large kitchen.

"Amelia, I *specifically* remember telling you *not* to contact Fiona Mahoney on behalf of your friend." He annunciated every word through gritted teeth, as his sister bustled about the kitchen, tying a brown-paper-wrapped package with some twine. "Did I or did I not declare it too soon?"

Too soon? Did he mean after Aidan's death?

Croft had added his name to Inspector Aberline's flowers and the brief note of condolences for the death of the man he'd known as my priest and close confidant. But I couldn't think why he would ask Amelia to wait longer than a handful of months to contact me after Aidan's loss. Most people did not grieve for their friends and ecumenical leaders as long as they did their spouses or their kin.

Father Aidan Fitzpatrick was none of these to me...

But he was the man I loved. The man I'd *meant* to marry before he took on the cassock.

He'd not initially been forthcoming as to why he'd bound his life to the church rather than to me. I hadn't known it was to bury a guilty conscience in the service of God. Before he died, Aidan said he'd loved me too much to stain me with the blood on his hands...

And once I'd learned his sins, I was grateful.

Broken, but ultimately relieved.

What if I found out what he'd done after marriage? Children?

I'd never spoken of my emotional attachment to Aidan, least of all to Grayson Croft, who held nothing sacred but the law and his own honor.

"Of course you instructed me not to, Gray, but what good has ordering me about ever done?" Amelia moved from the counter to a round, heavy table that might have comfortably seated all twelve of King Arthur's knights. It dominated the room, and yet seemed to belong there.

Who else met at the Croft table? I wondered, as it

9

was a ridiculous piece of furniture for two unmarried siblings. In the center, a large arrangement of dried lavender perched in a crystal-cut vase bent as if waving in a perpetual breeze.

Several bundles of herbs hung upside down, suspended from the cupboard above the washbasin. I could only name about half of them, but then again, I was never any good in the kitchen or the garden, much to my mother's dismay.

A kettle simmered and steamed on the iron cookstove, in which a fire crackled, and several more jars of herbs and loose-leaf teas perched upon the shelf above. I squinted through my spectacles at the tidy script on the jars, but at this distance, the neat scrawl remained difficult to make out.

"Surely this isn't your idea of an introduction." A sharp look accompanied the curt rebuke, as Amelia removed ermine gloves to affix a ribbon to the small package. As she turned to me, the lines of censure smoothed from her forehead and the long owl feather in her cap bobbed as she nodded a belated greeting. "Miss Mahoney, it is so lovely to finally meet you. Grayson speaks of you so... Well, he speaks of you."

Did he?

I didn't dare look in his direction just now.

She couldn't bring herself to say he spoke highly of me, nor did she intimate that he spoke of me often, so I could only imagine in what capacity he discussed me with his sister.

Very probably as a workplace grievance.

"I confess, I'm surprised." I hoped my self-effacing smile didn't appear as much of a grimace as it felt. "I am the lowly cleaning woman that too often shows up to get in his way."

The wisp of an amused smile touched her lips aged with fine lines that hardship must have turned into grooves. I'd never asked Croft his age, though I'd put him somewhere between thirty and forty.

Which meant Amelia, at ten years his senior, would be glancing at fifty within the next few years. "There's nothing lowly about you, dear. You're a vision of elegance."

She was being kind, but I appreciated it.

"And here I thought I looked terrible." This time I *did* peek over at Croft, who made no move to meet my eyes, as it would keep him from boring divots into his sister with the force of his glare.

His jaw locked with such intensity that a muscle jumped at his temple, which told me I'd hit my mark.

Surely he'd known better than to tell me how awful I looked, even if it was the truth. He'd behaved badly, and would be rightly recriminated by his sister if she were aware. Luckily for him, Amelia had not been privy to his assessment of my appearance earlier, and seemed ignorant of the tension between her brother and me. "I've just come from the chemist's and chocolatier to procure some medicines and sweets for Bea. She's been unwell and is so distraught, I'm worried she won't care for herself. Jane was special to her."

Croft made a sound that landed somewhere in between a scoff and a lament. "A damn shame about Jane."

"Did you know her?" I asked him without thought.

He shook his head. "But women like her, that do... what she does... they're..."

I waited for him to produce the word he so obviously sought.

"They're brave."

"Brave," I echoed, convinced I'd misheard.

"Ladies who—give the business... are subject to more brutality than just about anyone alive. Coppers, soldiers, criminals, and laborers—we're trained to expect violence. To return it in kind." He shook his head, his sledge-hammer-sized fist flexing in frustration. "But women..."

I couldn't have been more astonished. Not only because Croft rarely, if ever, revealed an entire paragraph of words, let alone an opinion. But because he'd always seemed so conservative and principled, so disapproving of all things, that I imagined surely whores were among them, regardless of his sister's past.

I caught the look Amelia sent her brother, something fond, colored with a darker brush. Shadows of regret and a pain so brilliant it suddenly hurt to look at her.

Because it was to her he referred, of course. About her that he thought... the men who might have harmed her in the past, and the fact he'd not been in a position at the time to stop them. To protect her.

If I stayed here much longer, I might do something I regretted.

Like respect him.

Or like him.

And neither of us wanted that.

All thoughts of confession had dispelled into the miasma of misery in which I'd lingered for months. Something like verve suffused me as I realized I had a chance at rejoining the living and was reminded of my reason for doing so.

"I am sorry about your friend, Miss Croft." I stepped forward and retrieved Amelia's glove from the table, just as she wriggled her capable fingers into its mate. "I will be happy to go to work for you." I offered it to her, dusting off my rarely used smile.

I wanted to see where this Jane Sheffield had died. Needed to check how her body was placed, and to breathe the air in the room, hoping to maybe detect the Ripper in the stench of death a working woman left behind.

"Thank you, my dear." Amelia took the proffered

glove and caught my hand to give it a grateful squeeze. "No one looks after us, and no one seems to mind when one of us goes missing, or worse. And to be killed like Jane was... so... dreadful."

"How was it done?" I asked, doing my best to keep the curiosity from my voice. I *was* truly sorry for Jane. For Amelia and her loss...

But I'd had a friend butchered as well.

And I'd made a blood vow to Mary Kelly that I'd find Jack the Ripper and give her justice.

"It's not him." Croft's hard voice landed like an ax between my shoulder blades.

A crease brought Amelia's dark brows together in confusion. "Him? Oh yes, Gray told me you were something of a Ripper aficionado." A light went on behind the idea. "What if it *is* the Ripper? Gray can't confirm or deny; he hasn't seen the body."

"I know it is not. Trust me."

He'd said that before. And he'd been right.

But I couldn't believe it until I saw for myself.

If a prostitute was killed in Whitechapel, then Jack the Ripper would certainly take notice, if only to be displeased with another impersonator, perhaps. Which meant he might be lurking close.

Close enough to catch, if I were clever enough.

If I could remain the cat rather than the mouse.

"How can you know it isn't him if you won't go to the crime scene?" Amelia snapped at Croft, igniting an argument they'd obviously had before.

Croft ignored the question. "Who is the detective inspector on Jane's case?"

"Orson Davies—do you know him?"

"There are a hundred inspectors in the city, Amelia. I can't know them all."

"Then why are you being so stubborn in your refusal to at least take a look?" she asked. "It's not like you'll be upsetting a friend and colleague."

"Because it's not my division—I've told you this. I could be heartily reprimanded."

I snorted. "You mean to tell me the indefatigable Grayson Croft, the man who will leap in front of bullets and run into burning buildings, is felled by the threat of a mere reprimand? Your superiors must be terrifying, indeed."

Croft stomped to the stove and fiddled with a loose burner, stoking the flames beneath it as if overtaken by the urge to stab something. "*If* this were a Ripper murder—which it bloody isn't—Frederick Aberline would have been called down from Scotland Yard. The Ripper would have claimed it by now. He'd have made certain the press was notified and his ego was stoked by the furor of it all. Furthermore, neither of you would be going to the scene. I'd not allow it."

If it was the Ripper, I'd be safe at the scene. I'd be safe from him anywhere. Because the Ripper had killed *for* me.

He'd done it quietly. He'd cleaned up after.

And no one had leaked it to the press.

I'd—almost accidentally—caught the Ripper's copycat last year, snagging his attention and... possibly his admiration.

Neither of which I wanted.

However, if the Ripper watched me, I might catch sight of him as well. It was the only thought that kept me going some days.

"I'd like to see you try to stop either of us from attending to Jane." Amelia drew abreast of me, linking our elbows in feminine solidarity. "Besides, I don't know why you assume you have an opinion in the matter. Fiona will come without you having a say. Now get out of my kitchen."

Croft set his hard jaw into an obstinate expression that peeled a good twenty years from his face. "Gladly," he spat, before turning to slam out the same door we'd entered and clomp back to his lair.

One might almost call it a retreat.

I stared at Amelia in open-mouthed shock, as if she'd performed a miracle.

"What?" She lifted a glove to her face, as if checking the corner of her mouth or her cheekbones for a smudge or imperfection that would cause me to stare.

"It's only that... I've never seen another soul speak like that to him." *And live,* I added silently.

Amelia tossed her head back and made an almost equine noise of mirth. "I maintain that if I washed his sheets when he wet the bed at five years old, then I can talk to him however I like."

Pressing my lips together, I suppressed a hysterical little burp of mirth. Had I really been about to giggle? On a day like this?

I was literally unable to recall the last time I'd laughed... "I can't believe Croft permits it."

"As you see, Gray doesn't have the luxury of *permitting* me anything. I all but raised that boy, and I'll be damned if he orders me about."

Boy?

At well over six feet, and with a bit of grey dappling the perpetual shadow against his jaw, it was nearly impossible to summon the image of Inspector Grayson Croft as a hapless child with chubby limbs and a round face.

He must have been a difficult lad, to grow up to be such an ever-present thorn in my side.

I did let some of my amusement escape on a chuckle.

Oh Lord, but I was happy to have met Amelia Croft. "Please tell me you've done this in front of his peers," I begged with a wicked sort of glee. "I'd love the men who fear him to see him batted around thus. It was better than any Christmas present I've ever received."

"Oh, tosh!" She laughed right alongside me, though hers was in no way impeded by my sense of propriety or care for the dead. "People fear him because of his size and his gruff exterior. But they do not know him. Gray has always been such a gentle soul..." Her smile died on her features as they melted into something distant and melancholy. "It's why I did so much to protect him."

Far be it for me to argue the fact, but I wondered if she knew her brother at all.

Did I?

Many people had good reason to fear Grayson Croft. I'd seen him break a man's bones for no greater crime than disrespect.

"Shall we be off, Miss Mahoney?" Amelia gathered up her package and bustled to the door.

"Indeed." I took up my own coat, hat, and gloves, thinking of all I had to do. First, send a message to Hao Long, my assistant, to bring my cart and supplies and the coverings, should the job be extra complicated.

At least I didn't have to change frocks... I'd been wearing nothing but black for months.

Amelia was the first to speak, once we crunched over the cobbles to the high street in hopes of hailing a hackney. "I do wonder what brought you here," she said blithely, adjusting her cap.

I stalled, nearly slipping on a slick cobblestone. "Pardon?"

"You know, I didn't summon you." She slid a side-long glance in my direction. "Grayson didn't lie when he claimed to have told me you were in mourning. And though I don't have a tendency to obey him, of course I'm going to respect your own tragedies and losses. So, I am curious, Miss Mahoney—what brought you to our door? I could tell right away that you needed a reason to find yourself in my brother's presence, and was happy to let him think you were called by me because I *am* in need of your services. Still... it seems like an interesting coincidence, don't you agree?"

My mouth dropped open. I could not think of a single thing to say.

"It's all right." She gave me an unsettling and rather cryptic smile and a friendly wink. "I won't make you tell me your secrets just yet."

I thought of the secret of hers I held in my heart. As a teenaged prostitute, she'd given an unwanted child up for adoption to a woman named Kathrine Riley.

Katherine Riley, I'd recently found out, took money from desperate women with a promise to place their children for adoption. She dazzled them with stories of childless couples of the middle and upper classes, where the children could be fed, educated, and given opportunity.

Katherine had pocketed the money, and... the babies never went to families.

They never made it out of her home alive.

The Croft siblings had been searching for Amelia's child for some years now. And I was possibly the only person who knew where the innocent bones were buried alongside innumerable others.

I knew that Katherine Riley had been a worse killer than even Jack the Ripper.

I knew that Katherine Riley had met a terrible end. One she deserved.

I *could have* confessed that to the intrepid—no, *infuriating* Inspector Grayson Croft and his nameless nebula of a sister.

But now that I'd met them in their home, been engaged by her as a client, laughed at her antics, and appreciated her affection for her brother—no matter how misplaced it might be—I knew that it would be another painful truth I might have to take to the grave.

Now that I knew Inspector Croft had a heart, I couldn't bring myself to break it.

Chapter Three

❧❧❧

It had long been my opinion that places selling sex or alcohol seemed deeply melancholy in the light of day. They emanated a sort of desperation and loneliness I'd often ascribed to their customers.

I was intrigued to find out such was not the case with The Orchard, Amelia's former place of nocturnal employment.

She had shocked me by instructing our hackney to turn onto Fleet Street, the city's premier business thoroughfare, chiefly associated with publishing houses, the printing trade, and newspapers with mind-boggling circulations. Mounted signboards protruded in competition with one another, advertising the enterprises above stately doors.

Such frantic industry called for other supportive companies to be interspersed between the buildings and flourish even in the alleys and passageways off Fleet Street proper.

Indeed, we passed cafés, pubs, inns, solicitors, and clerks before we disembarked our hackney cab on the corner of Fleet Street and a narrow alley called Orchard Lane.

The office on the corner belonged to Beckett, Gallway & Sons, Full-Service Clerical. The façade was nothing but a wall of large leaded windows, framing rows of men in dark suits pecking away at typewriters.

I rudely gawked at them as we rounded the corner, appreciating the percussive sounds of the machinery. What caught my eye, though, was a lone woman sitting in the very back of the sea of men. But for her frizzy hair pulled into a tight knot, she was almost indiscernible from the rest, unless one looked beneath the uncomfortable-looking desks to see a skirt around her legs rather than trousers.

She had a dark jacket, high-necked white blouse, and commensurate black vest and tie. Her fingers, gloved against the winter chill, danced over the keys as swiftly as her compatriots'. Perhaps more so. Her pile of work, I noted, was taller than the rest.

A female clerk, I marveled.

I suddenly wanted to know everything about her. Did she go to school, or was she raised in the business? What battles had she fought for that seat behind the fifth row of Beckett, Gallway & Sons, Full-Service Clerical? Was she paid as much as her masculine counterparts?

"Here we are," Amelia said loudly from down the narrow passageway between the clerk's and a pub named the Nock and Quiver. She impatiently waited for me to cease dawdling and join her at an inconspicuous, but tastefully appointed door, above which a single sign advertised THE ORCHARD in elegant, decidedly feminine script.

One might miss it if they weren't looking, as soft greens and golds were all but lost on a street where every sign was as large and loud as a crier peddling his wares in Piccadilly.

Such a business needn't compete for attention, I supposed. The demand was—and ever would be—great. Meanwhile, the customers would pay extra to *not* advertise their patronage.

As nondescript as The Orchard might be, if one knew what trade was plied behind the door, they'd recognize it as an obvious reference to "getting Jack in The Orchard," a common slang in London for sexual intercourse.

Clever.

Better still to attach such a business to one more socially acceptable, like a pub or an inn.

It reminded me of my sometimes-employer, colloquially known as the Hammer, who owned an establishment little more than a stone's throw to the west, where Fleet Street morphed into the Strand, a more fashionable and upscale part of town. His gaming hell and brothel was famously christened The Velvet Glove, and was situated in a part of town where haberdasheries, tailors, and seamstresses indulged the wealthiest of customers.

The Velvet Glove, as one might imagine, was a rather tawdry synonym for the very female flesh for sale at said establishment. Somehow, the Hammer got away with being so cheeky. Perhaps because he catered to half of Parliament and most of the Queen's High Court.

Amelia knocked on The Orchard's door, the cadence a strange staccato of two sharp raps, and a long pause between three more.

The door swung inward to a long and purposely gloomy hallway, papered with a dull and faded arabesque design that peeled at the corners and above the wainscoting.

Amelia followed a large, stone-faced, pale man down the hall in silence, and I trailed them both with no small amount of apprehension.

"Why do you suppose there isn't a police guard at the door if a murder victim is waiting to be taken away?" I whispered.

"Because the police think we are a waste of their resources," Amelia answered, apparently not compelled, as I was, by the eerie, empty silence of the place to keep her voice low.

We, she'd said.

I understood she hadn't worked in this capacity in a very long time... Did she still identify herself as a prostitute? Or was it perhaps that anyone who might have known what she did for a living would always define her thus?

A gasp escaped me as we stepped out of the hallway and into a room that might rival any great hall or coveted solarium in a mansion in Mayfair or Belgravia. Large, welcoming furniture covered in gemstone velvets and silks were strewn about with lively cushions. Lamps were placed high and turned low so their flickering would not only cast a flattering gold, but create concealing shadows as well. The room itself was four stories tall, and a chandelier that might have once belonged in Buckingham Palace shimmered so high above, I had to tilt my head all the way back like a gapmouthed tourist to properly appreciate it.

Flights of spiraled staircases attached balconies to each of the four stories, from which the tenants of the chambers could step out and observe the goings-on of the great room. The walls all boasted either three or four doors, depending on the direction.

If one accounted for hallways or back stairs, I assumed, women gave the business in approximately sixteen rooms.

I hadn't time to do the impressive maths of possible income potential as we were led through the open door, down a short passage, and past a modest flight of back stairs. The butler let us into a small sitting room, done in pastels that felt rather muted and uninteresting after the vivid jewel tones of the gathering room.

Or perhaps it was the woman in the midst of the wicker and lace that put the background to shame. She was unlike any bawd of my imagination. Not only did she have the style and sobriety of any society matron, but a wealth of steel-colored hair and a build of bosomy practicality I'd not at all expected. Tall enough to be considered statuesque, she emanated an atmosphere of formidable brilliance and brusque insouciance that must alternately intimidate her customers as well as put them at ease. If *this* woman gave one's perversions her permission for a price, then all desires were acceptable, surely.

She and Amelia held their arms out, greeting each other like old friends with a warm kiss on the cheek and a hug that clung too long, belying any pretense of composure.

"I cannot tolerate such loss, pet," the lady said, in a surprisingly sophisticated accent, as she wiped beneath her eyes with a bent knuckle. "Not my girls. My family. In my own house, Amelia. This was no back-alley violence... but an execution. I will spill blood for what was done, so help me God. I—"

The woman bent at the waist for a moment as a few bone-racking coughs stole her breath and therefore the wind from her sails.

Amelia took her elbow and settled into the deep corner of a lavender wicker couch, perching next to her and keeping one hand enfolded in her own. "If someone is after the girls, I will do everything I can to help, sweet Bea. Where's your medicine?"

"Oh, it's just my asthma. It's always worse when the winter inversion keeps the coal smoke in the air like this." Bea waved her away with a flick of a lace-lined handkerchief she produced from her sleeve. From it, a medicinal, camphor-like aroma permeated the air.

"Did you bring that brilliant brother of yours, Amelia? My old eyes could stand the sight of him on a day like this." Eyes so light blue they might have been silver searched the doorframe behind me, somewhere above my head—which was where she might have found Croft if he'd accompanied us. "Protective brutes often irritate me, but I suppose they have their uses," she finished, laughing herself into another bought of coughs.

Amelia shook her head. "Grayson cannot investigate in a borough to which he is not assigned without being requested or obtaining permission... and you know what a stickler he is for the rules, God love his stubborn, principled hide."

"He's always had a bit of that in him, I suppose," the elder woman responded fondly. "Even when he was at his worst."

This bawd knew Croft?

From before?

I supposed she would, being his sister's former... employer and all. Though it appeared she had a more recent interaction with him as well.

Not for the first time, I wondered where Croft, an unmarried but worldly man, warmed the sheets with women...

Here?

I thought about the brothel and its opulence, where all doors were visible from the gathering room, and so, too, would be the persons disappearing behind them.

Something about The Orchard didn't feel like Grayson Croft...

It was too open here. Too visible. Or was it vulnerable?

Surely he didn't fornicate sharing walls with others. Nor would he be led up those spiral stairs by a pretty doxy with a flirtatious smile.

He was a man who took his pleasures in dark, smoky corners with a hand over his mouth to dispel the wicked sounds he might make.

I blinked and gave a cough of my own, choking on my wicked thoughts.

Where in Blighty had that come from? I gave my

head a good shake, dispelling Croft like smoke from his pipe, the alluring scent of which still clung to my high-necked wool bodice.

"I've brought you something, Bea," Amelia said, reaching for the wrapped gift she'd set on the chaise behind her.

At that, Bea raked her gaze over me once, twice, and then dismissed me with a little *harrumph* that stung more than it should. "I'm too distraught to consider a replacement for the girls just now, Amelia. I'll grant you, she's a pretty thing with elegant tastes and a sort of... wholesome appeal. But she looks like a widow in mourning, and I don't think I am in need of that at the moment. Besides, she's no match for the two beauties I've lost. I could still pass Jane for a teen, and I'd eat my hat if this one is under four-and-twenty."

She cocked her head to the side as blood rushed from beneath my collar into my cheeks. I knew that I could remain stoic when need be, but my Irish skin always gave me away, because emotion splashed me with a blush so intense some might call it a rash.

The bawd gave me a second look, this one slower and more insultingly thorough. "Her hair is a sensual garnet, though, and those breasts could—"

"You've got it all wrong." Amelia surged to her feet and crossed over to me, her package forgotten on the chaise. "Beatrice Chamberlain, allow me to introduce Miss Fiona Mahoney, London's *premier* postmortem sanitation specialist. I've brought her here to help with poor Jane."

"Oh. Indeed?" Without any sign of remorse for her unkind assessment of my appearance, Beatrice stood and held her hand out, encouraging me to cross the room to take it. She shook with the firm confidence of any man, her grip warm and strong through the thin lace of her glove. "It always gladdens my heart to see a woman at the top of her field."

"It's easy to be the best when you're the one and only." My modesty was far from false, as I'd come up with the title all on my own. Very few others performed my sort of services, mind, but I couldn't imagine what they called themselves.

I'd never met one.

Mostly it fell to family members or property owners to clean up after their dead.

"Even so, what you do is most necessary." Passing her hand down her bodice in a tense gesture, Beatrice checked a watch chain on the vest of her velvet, grey-and-green striped gown.

"I—er—I'm not a woman with a delicate constitution, Miss Mahoney, but I'd rather not go back in that room the way it is, if it's all the same to you."

"I completely understand, Miss Chamberlain. That is what I am here for," I said, forgiving her immediately for any insult I might have taken from her appraisal. To be fair, at nine-and-twenty, I'd be aging out of the profession, as they'd say.

"It's *Mrs.* Chamberlain," she corrected absently, her eyes drifting to the door.

"Oh, forgive me." I'd not assumed a woman in her line of work would be married.

More fool, I.

"You take your ease," I suggested gently. "Once my assistant arrives with my implements, I'll get right to work. Until then, do you mind if I... assess the scene?"

"You'll not want to be near that room yet." The cloth went back over her mouth and nose, and she took a few bracing breaths. "Jane is still—she's in there."

No, she wasn't. Only the shell that once housed Jane was left in that room. Just flesh and bone, organs and offal... along with blood and such I'd have to erase from the rugs and floorboards. Or the walls, furniture, *et cetera*.

Amelia reclaimed her perch in front of Beatrice. "I

25

learned of this tragedy a good hour-and-a-half ago. You're saying the police have *left* poor Jane here?"

"They've come and gone, mostly. Just waiting on the coroner's cart." Beatrice cast an apprehensive glance in the direction of the business proper. "Apparently, it's been a busy morning for corpses."

Though I understood her consternation, I couldn't believe my luck. I needed to get into that room with Jane. To confirm if my fears were founded. To assess for myself if Jack touched this corpse, or another copycat... or if perhaps this was simply another terrible and unavoidable violence against a vulnerable woman.

"Mrs. Chamberlain..." I hesitated, making certain to phrase my question as gently as possible. "Can you tell me in what... what state you found the—" I paused. The what? The body? The victim? The woman? "How was poor Jane situated? Er, or—could you ascertain how she died?"

Judging by the way Beatrice and Amelia stared at me with matching censorious expressions, I deduced I'd still managed to ask the wrong question, despite my best efforts.

"I understand it's an indelicate matter," I said. "But I-I'm only trying to determine how many chemicals will be necessary along with protective coverings and what have you. Is it a—fairly grisly scene?"

"Isn't every murder scene grisly?" Beatrice pressed her lips together in stern approbation.

"Most certainly," I said. "But some have more... fluids than others, to be sure."

"You'll forgive Fiona's frankness, Bea," Amelia swiftly interjected. "But think of it this way: To her, death is like sex is to us. A trade. Something she deals with daily and is rather inured to. She famously cleaned the Mary Kelly scene during the Ripper's autumn of terror a couple of years back, or so Grayson told me. I understand once you've seen such a horror, no other murder can quite compare in its gruesome nature."

"You make a living cleaning up after murdered whores, then? Why—to make a name for yourself?" Beatrice didn't pause to allow me an answer. "Do you tell yourself it's to help the unfortunate and disadvantaged? Because you will not find such women here, you see. The Orchard is a place where women are proud to work, and until recently it was one of the safest and most lucrative establishments in the city." The proprietress had given me an entirely new assessment. This time not as a prostitute, but as a professional of a different nature.

Something in her eyes compelled me to speak a truth very few people on this earth knew. "Mary Kelly was my friend since before we could walk. After my father was killed, I emigrated here from Ireland to join her. To work with her in a place very like this. But by the time I arrived... it was too late. The Ripper found her first."

Grayson Croft had been there at the scene, holding me back as my heart broke over her ghastly remains. He'd seen me at my very worst. My most feral.

What had he told his sister when he arrived home that day? What else did she know about me from his perspective?

Beatrice's eyes changed then. Softened, if only from steel to iron.

"I found another way to make a living, ma'am," I continued. "But I do not presume it is a better way. Furthermore, I respect the remains of all people equally, but it is important to me to find the Ripper. And so yes, I look for him in every violence done to a woman, especially women who... Well, I find that most women who work on their backs do so to avoid scrubbing on their knees, as I must. And I'm certain many find your trade much more agreeable than mine. However, both services must be performed in order for society to work, would you not agree?"

At that, she melted like warmed butter, just as I hoped she would. "I suppose it makes sense. Two of my girls are dead, and you're here looking for the Ripper. That said, I don't think you'll find him here, love. Being the purveyor of goods and services that I am, I followed that case with avid interest... Jane and Alys were not killed by someone with such crude and violent proclivities as his."

"Alys?"

"Alys Hywel," Beatrice said. "A beautiful bird from Cardiff. Worked here only two months before they pulled her blue body from the river in Whitechapel three weeks back."

"I'm so sorry," I murmured. "Was she drowned?"

"So says the final report," Amelia said, her lip curling with distaste. "Suicide, the coroner called it, despite my adamant protestations. Lazy git didn't want to perform an autopsy on a prostitute, is all, and had no patience for my belief." Beatrice made a crude gesture and rolled her eyes. "Just another reminder that having a cock somehow makes your opinion twice as important in this bloody world."

I agreed with the sentiment, but wisely didn't mention that, in addition to said sex appendage, coroners were also in possession of a medical degree and no little amount of expertise. I was lucky enough to be acquainted with several, and my opinion of them was by and large favorable. Especially of Dr. George Bagster Phillips, who was often my partner in business... as well as a little bit of crime.

"With your permission, Mrs. Chamberlain," I said. "Might I peek in on the scene?"

The color of her eyes changed from frosty to downright frigid. "You won't be needing my permission so much as from that lackwit Orson Davies, who fancies himself a detective inspector. He's as corrupt as he is ugly."

"I can hear you, you know."

I jumped at the sound of a waspish, masculine voice as it was thrown down the stairs just outside of the open door to the parlor.

"I'm painfully aware of the acoustics of my own establishment, thank you," Beatrice said, with such vexation that I almost wanted to duck to make sure the venom in her tone didn't splash all over me.

Swift, angry footsteps descended toward us.

I stepped to the side to make room for the squat, red-faced man who charged through the door, his balding head down like a Spanish bull.

"I should arrest you for a bawd, Beatrice Chamberlain. See if I don't put you in chains one day." His accent was as far from highborn as Whitechapel was from Buckingham Palace, so to hear him talking down to the erudite, elegant women in front of him was right peculiar.

Beatrice stood, drawing herself up to her full height, which was a good several inches over his. "I invite you to try, you lackwit. You know as well as everyone that this establishment caters to more than half the papermen and publishers in this town. One more threat from you and I'll make certain you'll be immortalized in the press, Inspector Davies. Imagine, if you will, the things I could have written about you. Things done in this very place."

"I'll sue you for libel, you harpy," he growled, through teeth as crooked as a stool pit rat's.

"Find a solicitor or advocate who isn't indebted to me, I dare you."

"A challenge I'll have to accept at some point, *madam*." He spat the word, leaving no mystery to which way he meant it.

Turning on his heel, he faced me, dismissing the two

women at the couch by giving them his back. "I've heard of you, Miss Mahoney," he said, his tone changing from one of conflict to conviviality in the space of a blink.

The fleetness of emotion left me a bit dizzy.

"I sometimes enjoy a round of golf at the club with Inspector George Aberline and Dr. Doyle, his optician friend, who is a crime writer of some growing consequence," he bragged, hooking his thumbs in his vest pockets.

I darted a glance over his head at the ladies, knowing I needed to play nice with him, but also not wanting to incur their wrath.

"I am a great admirer of Inspector Aberline's," I said carefully. "We work together often." Aberline was the original inspector on the Ripper case, and had engaged me several times since then. He was a wonderful advocate of my position.

"I thought it right strange what you do at first, scouring up organs and whatnot and scrubbing up murder scenes of people that i'nt your kin." He grimaced in such a way that made him impossibly less attractive than before. "But Aberline, he helped me to see it's a kind service you perform for the grief-stricken."

"That was lovely of him to do so." For as long as I could, I would refrain from complimenting this blighter. I disliked him intensely.

"You met on the Ripper case, then, eh?" he asked with avid interest.

"Indeed."

"Gave you a soft spot for whores, you was saying... Can't blame you for that. You've a kind heart, an' all." His eyes were glued to my chest, with little to no interest in the heart that beat there.

I proffered him a smile I hoped was both shy and winsome, even though Croft's words from this morning still echoed in his voice, like smoke snagging over shards of cut glass.

You look terrible.

At least the lighting in the place was meant to be as kind as possible to a spinster like me. Because even though I found the man in front of me insufferable in the extreme, I needed his good graces to get what I wanted. So I did what I did with all detestable cretins like him when I needed their permission: I appealed to his ego.

"It seems, Detective Inspector Davies, you're the man to talk to about gaining access to Jane's room?"

"I am the *very* man." He beamed, casting a glance over his shoulder as if to check if Mrs. Chamberlain was taking notes on how to address him.

"Would you very much mind if I poked my head in to see what I'm up against? It's easier to prepare my delicate constitution, you see." I cast my gaze downward, but not so quickly to miss that his own eyes narrowed in such a way that I worried I might have laid it on too thick.

"It's against protocol..."

"When has protocol ever meant a lick to you?" Beatrice snapped. "You've set bedposts to knocking against the walls in this very place while you were supposed to be on duty."

"You're on dangerous ground, woman!" he roared.

I rushed around to stand between Beatrice and him, blocking his view of her with my body, hoping to disarm him a bit. "Inspector Aberline never mentions a protocol when I'm assisting him." I put a finger to my mouth, tracing the ridge of my lower lip—the one that might have been described as "pouty" a time or two. "But then, I suppose he's at Scotland Yard's main branch now, and likely has the sort of influence and seniority that can make such calls—"

"Well, if it's good enough for Aberline." He offered me his arm. "I'll supervise the scene, of course."

"Of course." I tucked my arm in his, casting a commiserative glance over my shoulder at the two women, who wore wide-eyed expressions of surprise and admiration as the irritating inspector conducted me *exactly* where I wanted to go.

We climbed two flights of back stairs and emerged on the second-floor balcony.

"Prepare yourself, Miss Mahoney. It's not for the faint of heart."

"Thank you for the warning," I demurred, more for his benefit than mine. For indeed, Amelia had spoken true when she intimated that once I'd been inducted into my business by the macabre, hellish chaos that was Mary Kelly's murder scene, very little caused my heart —or any part of me—to feel faint.

It wasn't that I was cold to suffering and murder, but it wasn't the sight of the dead that I found most difficult.

It was the pain of those left behind.

The vision of Jane Sheffield, however, was alternately better and worse than I'd expected. Worse, I thought, because of the rather macabre beauty of the tableau before me.

Her chamber was done to look celestial; the presence of death seemed almost like a prologue to some sort of spiritual ecstasy. The darkest color surrounding us was the cream damask pattern against the white walls, or the silver of the candlesticks. All else was ivory, iridescent pearl, and white, from the fluttering bed curtains to the pallor of the corpse positioned oddly on the floor.

This was not an atmosphere rendered at all sensual, in my opinion.

And then I remembered what Beatrice had said when I was naught more than a possible employee.

Jane could have passed for a girl in her teens, and judging from the white-pressed, shapeless gown and the suggested purity of the room... I suddenly wanted to shrink from the fantasy being portrayed within.

Youth—girlhood, even.

Innocence. Virginity.

Something to be corrupted.

"Poor lamb," I whispered, meaning the sentiment with my whole self.

"That bit—er, bawd *would* spread lies about me," the inspector griped, apropos of nothing. "I dinn't never buy one of these whores like she said... whilst on duty. Never would. Never did."

I made an appropriate noise, too absorbed by the scene before me to much care about his sexual proclivities at the moment.

Or ever.

I did note the wording of the denial, in that it wasn't one. Not really. *Whilst on duty* was quite the modifier to his claim.

"A right eerie sight, i'n'it? I'll see that face for weeks in me nightmares." Davies drew abreast of me, peering down at the body with rank distaste. "I hope you are not likewise troubled, Miss Mahoney, and too many hours of sleep stolen by horror."

"I shan't be," I murmured. My nightmares only contained one demon...

One victim.

They didn't leave room for Jane, though I understood why the rat-faced inspector might be thus afflicted.

It wasn't the amount of blood from the corpse I found troubling, as I'd scoured up at least a lake's worth of the stuff by now...

It was the way the substance had left Jane Sheffield's body.

Prostitutes were often found murdered in some sort

of terribly sexual fashion, I'd found. They were frequently the embodiment of what society hated about a woman with additional sins piled on her shoulders. The Ripper wasn't the only killer of whores who invariably left his victim's legs open. Who tore their clothes away, stripping them of their dignity—their humanity—in the process.

There were usually egregious, violent wounds. Penetration of some terrible sort with a weapon.

Blades, bullets... body parts.

Men were possessed of so many body parts that they easily could—and frequently did—turn into weapons. I found it a wonder they needed to mechanize even more to extend their violent reach.

Jane was the first murdered woman I'd ever seen with all of her clothes on, and this realization made me more disgusted than I'd ever been at a murder scene.

All but Mary's, of course.

Her arrangement wasn't at all sexual, but... sepulchral. The body was stretched as long as it might be in a tomb, covered with the modest nightdress, feet only slightly splayed as if relaxed in slumber. Her arms were crossed over her chest, but not precisely in the way of those being prepared for burial. Because her fingers stretched and strained, even in death, as if reaching for her neck.

Even that unsettling sight wasn't the eeriest part.

I could find no evidence of stabbing in the pristine white of her garments, nor were there ligature marks on her slim throat, nor joints or bones out of place suggesting violence. I could find no bruises or abrasions on the skin that had once been alabaster and was now iridescent with death.

Blood oozed like tears not only from her eyes, but from her ears, nose, mouth. Indeed, every visible orifice *wept* thick crimson rivulets.

Because she lay on her back, the streaks from her

eyes ran into her ear, or caked into the fair wisps of curls at her temples. The river from her nose found the curves of her lovely cheekbones and streaked down her neck into the girlish plaits of her hair.

The volcano of blood streaking from her lips flowed down a slim, smooth neck to find the ivory carpet beneath, pooling into misshapen stains.

Drying blood rarely stayed vivid, which meant she hadn't been deceased for too long.

I wondered if she bled from anywhere else, from other orifices. I considered asking Davies, but I didn't think that would ingratiate me to him very much. Even homicide detectives seemed to shrink from what I did, or rather, they were repelled by the fact that I didn't shrink from it myself.

I supposed I'd find out when the body was claimed, judging by the substance of the stains left behind.

Beneath what looked like a mask of pagan war paint, Jane's dark eyes were not only open, but peeled wide with a desperate terror I'd never seen on the face of the dead.

Most corpses appeared lifeless, stiff, and often at peace. Even murder victims.

But Jane, her mouth twisted into a grimace of agony... I half expected her to spring to life and flee.

The hairs along my arms and down my shins prickled and tingled as I stared at the ghastly, sinister representation of pure, unadulterated dread on such an angelic beauty. It was no wonder at all that even a hardened woman like Beatrice couldn't bring herself to look upon it.

"What did you see before you died?" I wondered aloud. *Or whom?*

Not Jack, I knew that much.

As much as I hated for Grayson Croft to be right, I couldn't attribute this murder to the Ripper.

"I've never seen anything like it," Davies admitted,

sticking his pinky in his ear to alleviate an itch before flicking at the nail with his thumb.

For some reason, I found the sight of such behavior more distasteful than the corpse, and had to smother all wrinkles of disgust from my features.

"She looks like she suffered, don't she?" His irritating voice smoothed a bit with some semblance of pity, and I found myself glad he possessed a modicum of humanity at least.

I shook my head absently as I studied the unsettling expression. "She looks more frightened than in pain, I think."

He grunted, though whether in agreement or argument, I couldn't tell. "Jack the Ripper liked them to suffer, eh? He done ghastly things, like take out their organs and slice up their... more sensitive parts."

I rippled at the macabre curiosity in his voice, the same tone I heard from so many when they discovered I'd seen the real thing.

They didn't know the half of the horror, and if they'd been there, their curiosity would have turned to aversion.

"Actually, no," I replied stiffly.

"No?"

"Any indignities the Ripper victims suffered were postmortem. He slit their throats first, two clean cuts. They all died almost immediately."

The subsequent humiliations began with nine-and-thirty stab wounds to the face, body, and genitals of Martha Tabrum, and ended—so far as anyone knew—with the physical and sexual dismantling of my best friend.

"Oh. I thought you'd only been to one Ripper scene." Davies didn't seem to like that I knew more than he did about the case. That I could impart to him information he wasn't already privy to.

"Aberline let me peek at the other case files," I said,

crouching over Jane Sheffield's body to take a closer look at her hands. "As a favor."

Her nails were discolored, the joints and knuckles stretched and stiff. What had she been reaching for? In what position had she actually died before someone staged her like this?

"Do you think she was poisoned, Inspector Davies?" I asked. "I've been told that horse-loads of arsenic might make one's nose and ears bleed thus. Or was it strychnine?" Suddenly, I couldn't remember which toxin begat which symptom. Standing, I looked about the room for a dressing table or a medicine cabinet. Both of which were not a part of this particular setting, for obvious reasons. Young girls didn't apply cosmetics or administer their own medicine.

There was, however, a drink cart with several decanters and two glasses in the corner.

The irony galled me to the core.

The inspector was looking at me strangely, but to my surprise, he answered. "I'll know more when the autopsy is done. The attending coroner, Dr. Bond, said it could have been ratsbane, and I have seen a man once bleed from both ears after arsenic poisoning... How would you know that?"

"I work with an overabundance of chemicals, Inspector, and I do very meticulous research into all of them before handling. For my own safety and that of my employees."

He eyed me warily. "Never heard of arsenic being used as a cleaning agent, Miss Mahoney."

"Well, it isn't. But, as you said, it's very useful for getting rid of vermin. And vermin famously tend to make a nuisance of themselves in proximity to the dead."

Case in point, the inspector himself.

At that opportune moment, the scuffle of steps and the drone of masculine voices announced the arrival of the coroner's cart. Which alleviated stress for both the inspector and me, as we seemed to have mutually tired of each other's company.

I made myself as invisible as I could as the men cleared the body away, and bade goodbye to Davies by asking him to give my best to Aberline at their next golf outing.

Remaining in the room, I studied the soiled carpets as Davies and Mrs. Chamberlain held a vitriolic conversation elsewhere below stairs. I didn't catch every word, but I did hear the proprietress demand to be updated on the investigation.

It wasn't difficult to guess at Davies's reply based solely on his tone.

Whilst they bandied insults at one another, Amelia appeared at the door. She gazed down at the few stains on the pale carpets with dismay, and I thought we were both sorry to note that poor Jane had bled from every place a person could possibly do so.

"This gentleman is here for you, Miss Mahoney," she said after several attempts at clearing her throat. "He is carrying a great deal of supplies."

She opened the door wider and stepped aside to let in Hao Long, the dark-eyed Chinese immigrant who'd been my assistant for nearly two years now.

"Thank you, Amelia. I will come to find you and Mrs. Chamberlain when I'm finished here." I tried to inject gentle dismissal into my tone. If she were distressed by such an inconsequential amount of blood, then I was glad she hadn't seen the body. The horror of Jane's features.

"I hope you've brought my sodium hypochlorite powder," I said to Hao Long as I moved to help relieve him of his burden of several baskets.

He had a perfectly mobile cart full of supplies he would retrieve from storage once I called him to a death, and a deft pony to pull it. However, it seemed very few people died on the ground floor here in London. And I gathered from the strands of silver threading into his blue-black braid, and the lines branching from his eyes, that Hao Long was a man much older than I'd first assumed.

His movements muffled by the flow of ebony silk, Hao Long fought for some breath as he frowned at the carpet.

I wondered, for the first time, if my assistant was in need of an assistant.

I'd always spoken to him in my language, and he spoke to me in his. Neither of us understood much of one another, but we both got along well enough through nonverbal modes of conversation. Hao Long could scowl in any dialect, and I often knew what his gestures and expressions conveyed without needing clarification.

For example, this scowl told me he was insulted that I even showed up to this job, as it was so small. He could have taken care of it himself and pocketed a greater share of the bill.

"I know," I said, unable to communicate the story or my reasons for being here. "I'll leave you to it and I'll send you the commissions."

He nodded, shooing me toward the door like an ornery parent.

I allowed him this, though I turned when I'd almost reached Amelia, who still remained in the doorway.

"I want to thank you, Hao Long, for doing so much of this work while I've been... While I've been unable to."

Mary Jean, my housekeeper—for lack of a better term—had been coordinating with him when a job would land at my door. This was much to their mutual frustration, I'd gathered, but I'd been too caught up in Aidan's loss to much care.

39

I'd need to make certain they were both compensated, for keeping my business alive without me.

Drenched in shame, I realized that without this profession, Hao Long—a once widower and father with a lovely if alarmingly fertile second wife—would be out of a job. It wasn't well done of me to lose myself in the death of a beloved, and endanger the livelihood of all those who depended upon me for survival.

"It won't happen again," I promised.

His response was an extra shooing gesture, but one of the swats on my elbow might have been a pat of consolation. That was how I determined to interpret it, at least.

A dazed Amelia and I wound our way back down the stairs toward the parlor, where we found a fuming Beatrice Chamberlain pacing in front of the fire.

"I see you and the detective inspector are still at odds," Amelia said, going to the sideboard and retrieving a crystal decanter. Holding it up, she silently offered the amber-colored liquid within to both of us.

Beatrice accepted. I declined. I almost never drank. Especially at work.

"Orson Davies is little better than a stain on humankind," the flinty-eyed madam spat. "His father should have spilled him on his mother's back and wiped him away with a towel to discard in the laundry."

"Goodness, Bea, descriptive as ever, I see." Amelia paused in her pouring to cast a nervous glance in my direction, no doubt to gauge a reaction.

I pressed both my lips between my teeth, suppressing my second inappropriate giggle of the day.

"Where are the other girls?" Amelia asked. "Are they being questioned?"

Beatrice accepted her drink with a sad but grateful smile and squeezed Amelia's hand. "I told them all to stay home today. They shouldn't be privy to... No one should have to see a friend—done like this."

"That was kind," I said, then I had a thought as I checked the watch affixed to my own bodice. "Did Jane live here, Mrs. Chamberlain? Or had she stayed very late?"

"Neither," the older woman answered. "She came in very early, before we open for business at eleven. It was poor Bess who found her."

"The cleaning woman?" Amelia asked at the same time I said, "In the *morning*?"

Amelia didn't seem inclined to comment further, so I finished my thought. Sort of. "Eleven seems awfully early to... well, to... pay for..."

Amelia and Beatrice shared a look at my expense before the bawd drained her liquor and stood to refill her glass. "As you've noticed, we're situated in a rather hectic business district. The men here are not like dock or factory workers, using their bodies until they give out. They don't have foremen keeping their nose to the grindstones, as it were. You'd be surprised how many men who work office jobs pay for a bit of slap-and-tickle during their lunchtime or before they go home to their wives."

"Of course," I said, because I couldn't think of any appropriate reply to that bit of information. "So, do you have other employees who reside here full-time?"

Beatrice shook her head. "My rooms are not generally used for sleeping. There are occasions my girls are engaged for an entire night, or perhaps multiple nights. And there are men who like the homemaker treatment, feeling for a few days like they've a wife to come home to. In those cases, I'm happy to oblige. However, most of my girls aren't tied to one bed, no pun intended. Part of the fun is that a customer can select a woman *and* a place in which to enjoy her. As you may have noticed, the rooms are themed."

I *had* noticed, and was still uncertain how I felt about it.

"My poor girls... I worry that they'll never feel safe again," she said. "I pride myself on how protected The Orchard is for those who work here. I employ security. I don't allow mistreatment, or violence, or even job dissatisfaction. There are so many men who would take what we are selling, or force more than is sold... I am strict about the discipline of those men. Those criminals."

"Any men recently giving Jane or this... Alys any trouble?" I queried.

"None that I can remember, but I'd have to check with my security, as I'm not always informed of every incident."

I found it odd that was the case, as I knew the Hammer had an establishment twice as large, and no one seemed to take a breath within shooting distance of The Velvet Glove without him knowing about it.

I wisely decided not to press the issue and instead asked, "So... did Jane have an early shift?"

Beatrice stalled, then swallowed as she paled. "No. No, Jane wasn't due in until this evening. I don't know what the devil she was doing here."

"Did she have a key?" Amelia asked.

"No."

"Then she either came in early or stayed late... Or I suppose she might have—" I swallowed my next conjecture until both women speared me with glares of demand.

"Or she what?" Beatrice asked.

"Was someone paying for the rooms overnight?"

"No one." Bea shook her head.

"Then if she didn't have a key, she'd have had to... break in. Yes?"

Beatrice sat heavily, as if the starch had been let out of her knees. "It's the only possibility."

"Can you think of any reason why she'd do that?"

"No... I... I mean, only one reason. If she wanted to meet a client here, without giving the house its cut."

"*The house* being you."

"Yes," she said, her demeanor toward me decidedly chillier.

"She could have been looking for information about Alys," Amelia cut in, very obviously reaching for another explanation.

"Alys." Beatrice's eyes fluttered and she rubbed at her temple. "That rat bastard Orson Davies didn't even ask about Alys..."

Amelia shook her head. "Doesn't even want to consider two girls have been killed in a month? That's a nearly impossible coincidence."

"Is it?" Beatrice pressed the cool glass of her drink against her forehead. "In our line of work? It's hardly unheard of."

I turned to Amelia, whose face was set in a very familiar, very Croft-like scowl of determination. "You don't believe Alys committed suicide?"

"Categorically not. She was a bright young thing. Thought too much of herself to do something like that, all told. Was looking for a rich protector, and would have found one, too. She was a consummate professional and popular with her clientele."

"Yes," Beatrice agreed softly. "Alys could have been the realm's most celebrated courtesan someday. She had some very important customers. All she had to do was get out of her own way."

They could have been speaking about Mary. She'd been a lovely friend, but one with more vices than scruples. Some people believed that meant she deserved to die.

"Bea," Amelia said gently. "Do you think your enmity with the detective inspector is an impediment to the case? Should you perhaps request another one?"

"Don't you think I did that with Alys?" Beatrice said with an acerbic bite. "That man, Davies, was one of Alys's most faithful customers before she got too choosy for him. The way I see it, some might call that motive. But do you think his sergeant listens?" She made a bitter noise. "It's all the same. Men all like whores until they're dead, then they kick them aside like rubbish."

"Not all men," Amelia said. "There are a few good ones out there. Grayson is a notable exception."

Bea pressed her lips together, and this time it was she and I who shared the speaking look.

Was Croft really so different than his masculine counterparts? He'd worked tirelessly to save his sister from such a profession. He was ashamed of her past. He'd treated me with disdain, and I often thought it was because of my decision to become a prostitute before this career chose me in the nick of time.

"*Men.*" Beatrice tossed back her second drink and slid a yearning look to the sideboard before a bout of coughs seemed to pin her to her chaise. "They think so much of what's between their legs... Why then, I ask you, is a woman worth less the moment he puts it into her? And the more men she allows inside of her, the more worthless a human she becomes in their eyes. It's one of life's more infuriating paradoxes... that one tiny organ can sully an entire human."

I thought about that. About Jack. About the fact that I was afraid to take a lover for that very reason.

Because he'd made it clear that my purity meant something to him.

He killed whores because he hated what they did.

Beatrice set her glass on the table in front of her. "I do know that you think Alys and Jane's deaths are connected, Amelia, but the truth is, there's just as great a chance that they are not. I think Jane was seeing someone outside of The Orchard, which I absolutely do not allow." She speared Amelia with a look so full of meaning that the other woman's eyes skittered away. "And whoever this person was should be the prime suspect in this murder inquiry. Whereas Alys... She might have been another tragic victim of Whitechapel's violent streets."

"Anything's possible." Amelia shrugged, obviously unconvinced.

"Could you not ask the other women in your employ?" I suggested. "One of them might know more. Might be willing to say what secrets the girls were keeping, now that their lives might be more at stake."

Bea shook her head. "The girls don't talk to me of secrets, I'm afraid. I'm not their friend; I'm their boss."

"But Fiona's right," Amelia said. "They *do* talk to each other... keep their secrets among themselves. So many of them have no one else."

"True..." Beatrice drew out the word.

Amelia tapped the air as if plucking an idea out of the space between them. "What we need is someone on the inside, as it were. Someone who they could learn to trust. Someone clever. Who would ask the right questions."

In an eerily synchronized motion, both women's heads swiveled to look at me.

"No." I put up both hands. "*Nonononono*. I'd make a terrible—I mean—That is—No one would believe I—"

"Because you're a virgin?" Beatrice's head cocked to the side as if it were an affliction she pitied.

I lifted my hand to my own forehead, wondering if I had my virginity scrawled there for worldly people to read. She'd not been the first person to guess I'd never taken a lover, and certainly not the first pimp, I was ashamed to note.

"No! Because I'm nearly thirty and—let us kindly say—well fed."

"You are lovely, Fiona Mahoney," Amelia replied, with genuine emotion and a sparkle in her eye. "Any number of men would pay a pretty penny to warm your bed."

I gestured to Beatrice. "That is decidedly not what she said when she thought you'd brought me here to work for her."

"I was distraught." Beatrice shrugged, raking me with another assessment, this time with a more favorable eye. "With a bit of color in your cheeks and the right clothing, you could sell the devil out of the reluctant mistress, or perhaps the buxom and desperately lonely widow. Oh! The curious and tempting spinster schoolteacher. Not the innocent ingenue, per se, but still a sort of woman so many men would just kill to corrupt."

"Oh yes!" Amelia clapped her hands together. "That would be splendid... Large, sad eyes. She can keep her spectacles on. Show plenty of ankle and tits. I have just the costume to accentuate all the right areas."

I put my hands over the pertinent areas, as if they might see through my many layers of clothing with their unrelenting gazes. "I'm happy to help the two of you in any way I can, but my job is to clean up the blood, not solve the crimes or gather the information."

"But we *have* no one else to solve the crimes." Amelia put out her hands to show how empty they were of solutions. "There is no justice for women like us."

"Just like there was no justice for Mary," Beatrice said—the one thing that gave me pause. Had I not devoted my life to her justice? Just how far would I go to find it for her?

Did Jane and Alys deserve any less?

"I am not losing my virginity in a brothel," I said. "I'm sorry if that offends you, but it's not something I'm willing to do to solve a crime."

"Of course not!" Beatrice stood and sniffed, lifting a stubborn chin so she could look down upon me like an imperious dowager. "I'm offended that you assumed that was part of our discussion. We'd give you Alys's old room, of course, as I've not yet replaced her. She was more like one of the mistresses of Versailles holding court than a proper whore. Her time was engaged in advance, and her clients were spirited up the back way through the inn. The girls will be told this is also the case with you, and won't be privy to the comings and goings—or lack thereof."

I pressed my lips together against a *no*, and then castigated myself for even considering it. "I'm sorry," I said firmly. "There's nothing you can say to talk me into this. My answer will forever be *absolutely not*."

Chapter Four

❧❦❧

"**A**bsolutely not!" Grayson Croft roared. He stood like a sentinel, alternately scowling and roaring at the very idea I'd allowed his sister to break to him.

It irked me that I'd said the same thing, and through some technique of trickery and magic manipulation, I'd been brought around.

Judging from the thunderous look on Croft's face, he wouldn't be so easily persuaded.

Not that I blamed him. It had taken me the entire hackney ride from The Orchard back to the Croft residence to figure out just how I'd come to be influenced myself.

As I stood in the aromatic kitchen with the siblings at each other's throats, I was surer of my decision than I'd ever been.

Because chief among my reasons was that Jack the Ripper wouldn't like it.

These deaths had forced me to recognize that, though the Ripper had been pulled out of his hellish hiding hole to answer back for the perceived insult of imitation, he'd gone quiet again for the months I'd taken to mourn Aidan.

Which was both a blessing and a blight. Because he

made himself known by taking a life, which I absolutely didn't want...

And yet I still needed to find him.

This way, perhaps I could provoke him to come after me, rather than another hapless woman. And when he did, I would do everything in my power to be ready to face him when the time came.

I saw this in my future, the Ripper and me. Two of us facing each other, dueling to the death, as it were. I'd make him hate me before the end... I'd crush whatever fledgling admiration he'd talked himself into on my behalf, and I'd make sure the fire of loathing was mutual before we did our best to tear each other apart.

He had more practice in that respect.

The tearing.

The ripping.

But I had the rage of millions of maligned and murdered women inside of me. I could feel them in my quiet moments, urging me forward. Perhaps I'd had enough taken from me that I was no longer afraid of what the Ripper could do to me.

And that came with its own form of strength.

Another reason I'd been swayed was, to no one's surprise, the similarities between the victims in this case and those of the Ripper.

Prostitutes.

I saw Mary in so many of them. Even Jane. Though Mary Kelly's curls had been dark and shining to Jane's pale, coarse locks, their figures were both trim and delicate, their bones sharp, and their features unbelievably youthful.

It was all of these reasons, along with the reality of injustice for Mary and women like her.

It was because men like Croft were angrier at the fact that *I* might become a prostitute—or pretend to be one—than he was that two of them had been killed.

"You are *not* dragging Fiona into one of your lost

causes, Amelia. I forbid it." He swiped his hand through the air as if that punctuated the end of the discussion.

"It's as adorable now as it was this morning that you think you can forbid me anything." Amelia reached out and patted his cheek with both affection and condescension.

Though it didn't surprise me that Croft caught her wrist in his hand, I still jumped at the swiftness of the motion. "I mean it, Amelia. I really must put my foot down."

Jerking her hand back, Amelia snatched an apron from a hook on the wall and pulled it over her head, careful not to disturb the flattering coiffure. "Then do so! Put your bloody foot down, and then do it again, and again, and until they carry you somewhere else, preferably out of our way, because Fiona and I have work to do."

Croft turned to me with a look that landed somewhere between consternation and supplication, as if he might find a modicum of sense in my direction. He was visibly diminished to find me leaning on a countertop, endlessly amused.

"Surely you're not going to... to *work* at The Orchard," he said. "To take men as—as *customers,* for the sake of some bloody amateur investigation?"

"Don't be daft, Gray. She's taking Alys's old room."

"Is that supposed to mean something to me?" he growled.

"It was if you listened to a blasted word I've said during our dinners. Alys worked with private clientele on an appointment-only basis. Fiona will be doing the same, except there will be no true appointments."

His deep ebony brows fell as he thought about that. "No one will buy it."

"That's for us to worry about."

"What about your business?" he asked me, and I realized I'd not spoken a word in my own defense since we arrived. I needed to own this decision every bit as much as Amelia did.

"*My* business is none of *your* business," I retorted. "Besides, you have made it no secret that you detest what I do for a living—"

"I do not detest—that is—" He threw up his hands. "These hijinks you two are cooking up won't be profitable financially, nor will your ill-conceived investigation."

"I beg your pardon!" I snapped.

"Beg all you like—this is a harebrained idea at best, and dangerous besides. You're waltzing into the lion's den, Fiona, with no one there to protect you, and for what?"

"For the restless souls of two murdered women, you churlish brute. Women who have little hope of seeing justice otherwise." I stabbed a finger at his chest, stopping well short of actually poking it, as I'd made that mistake before and nearly crumpled my joints. "Beatrice Chamberlain employs rather burly men for security at her establishment."

Verdant eyes darkened to obsidian as he glared down at me, and his voice smoothed from thunderous to hot and volcanic. "And yet her employees keep turning up dead."

"Out! Don't make me tell you again, Grayson. Get out of my sight or you won't like what happens next." Amelia stepped in front of me and pushed—*actually pushed*—her brother. She planted her palms square on his chest and shoved with all her sturdy might.

I'd have been a bit less shocked had he not taken a step or two back, retreating a little beneath her tiny onslaught.

Amelia had the look of a dark Valkyrie as she advanced on her stymied brother. "No one asked your permission, and now I'm regretting giving you the information, so unless you're going to help find this killer, you can fuck off, because your kind are not welcome here."

"My kind?" He suddenly stood fast against her onslaught, advertising that it was his natural way to allow Amelia the illusion of her physical dominance.

But in reality, her strength against his was nothing more than a whisper in a windstorm.

"Men!" she said acidly. "Forbidding men who think they know better. None of us would even be in this jam without the likes of you lot. So get out!"

Croft held up his hands, his features rearranging from forbidding to cajoling. "I already told you, Amelia, I'll look into things at the Yard. I'll call in some favors and do what I can to..."

"That's not enough. Now stop being useless and go fetch my trunk from the attic. The one with the blue lid." Amelia snatched a towel from the handle of the oven and swatted him with it hard enough to make a sharp sound.

"Why?" His surprise melted into an oddly boyish confusion. "What's in the trunk?"

"Never you mind. Just fetch it for me, you overgrown dolt, and put it over by that screen there."

I promised myself that one of these days I would cease being astounded when Croft obeyed his sister's edicts. But that day was not today.

Having rid us of him momentarily, Amelia muttered a few curses as she bustled and banged about, putting the kettle on, retrieving a stockpot and several sharp knives then lighting two burners on the cookstove. "Cook isn't back from visiting her family for the holidays, so you'll have to suffer my culinary inadequacies, I'm afraid. I have a few decent recipes I picked up here and there—"

"You needn't make anything on my account," I said, backing up until I ran into the round table. "I shouldn't stay long enough to dine."

"Of course you won't after that display," she muttered, pulling the long match from the burner and holding it to a fully packed pipe she retrieved from a shelf next to the door. "Stubborn cur seems determined to die alone."

"I'm sorry, what?"

Ignoring me, she took a pork loin from the larder along with some lard and bottled jars of potatoes. In irate, jerking motions, she plucked some herbs from this bundle and that, tossing them into a mortar. She'd taken up the pestle and ground these herbs into a fragrant powder by the time Croft descended from the attic, his footfalls impossibly heavier than before.

No one said a word to each other as he banged into the kitchen, set the trunk down by the window, and grappled it open with a screech of metal on metal.

Clomping over to his sister, he glowered down at her. "The hinges on your bloody trunk are rusted. I'll oil them before work tomorrow."

"Thank you," she replied sharply, still grinding at the powder as if it might be his bones.

"Don't bloody mention it." With that, he marched out again, slamming the door behind him.

Brothers.

I couldn't allow myself to think of mine, not without withering into a powder finer than in her spice bowl and blowing away in the winter wind.

One could only contemplate so much grief at a time.

Abandoning her work, Amelia took a cream linen screen from behind the cupboard and unfolded it to create privacy between the table and the far wall. "Change into this," she ordered me, retrieving a pile of silks and petticoats from the trunk and shoving it into my arms. "This will be perfect for what I have in mind, but I might need to make a few alterations. You're a bit shorter than I am."

Only this morning, the thought of undoing my dress at Grayson Croft's home would have sent me into fits of hysterical laughter. But here I was, ducking behind a screen and a window, cursing the tiny buttons on my high-necked black frock.

"You made this?" I asked, desperate for a distraction from my racing thoughts.

"I'd have been a seamstress if I could have afforded it," she said, over the busy clanging and clashing of her kitchen.

Amelia was incredibly talented with a needle. Even before I tried on the gown, I could tell how sumptuous and well-made it was. The fabric was costly and fine, not the cheap imitation so many costumes so obviously suffered. Once I'd stepped out of my frock and bustle, I peeked around the screen to look at her own bodice, which was bland enough to be considered serviceable. Not dowdy or old, just a plain peach taffeta with sedate pearl buttons, beneath a dark vest and well-loved apron.

"Tell me about Beatrice," I said when she caught me studying her, before I disappeared back behind the screen. "Did she work her way up in the business before she became the proprietress of The Orchard?"

"Quite the contrary, actually," Amelia replied with a warm sort of amusement. "Bea was a society wife, married to a wealthy solicitor who belonged to a family of some consequence. Apparently, she inherited a great deal of money when he passed away, along with a letter he'd left detailing how many 'houses of ill repute' he held accounts at. Instead of going back to church, she bought one of them, and has been in the business some twenty years or so."

At that I stalled, undoing the first couple of my

stays in order to get the garment on. "Then how did she..."

The door to the kitchen exploded open and heavy boots marched in, interrupting my question. "All right, you two, you win. I've decided I'm going to Scotland Yard to discuss this Inspector Orson Davies with Chief Inspector—" Croft suddenly went still and quiet for the space of several breaths before growling, "Jesus Christ."

At that moment, I realized the screen had been placed in front of the window, and the sun wasn't down yet.

Croft could see me stripped down to my corset, drawers, and stockings... or at least the shadowed outline behind.

"Get out of the kitchen, you rank pervert!" Amelia shrieked, striking him with something I could only assume was a wooden spoon, by the sound.

"What in God's name, Amelia?"

"She's trying on a gown I've made."

"Well, how was I supposed to know some woman would be changing garments in my kitchen?"

"In *my* kitchen," she corrected him with another loud swat. "Now stop staring and leave."

The sanctimonious Grayson Croft had been staring? I did my best not to preen at that information.

If someone thought you looked terrible, did they stare?

One would think not.

As he left, I forced myself to ignore his existence by conjuring the name of the man who made me forget all human emotion but for hatred.

The Ripper. He'd told me once in a letter that if I was searching for a killer, I'd find his motives if I investigated the victims. If Alys and Jane's deaths were related, what traits did they share? Other than their vocation, obviously.

"Amelia, you mentioned you were close with Alys Hywell? More so than Jane?"

"Aye," she replied, the spitfire draining out of her at the mention of her dearly departed friend. "She paid me to stitch her costumes. We spent a lot of time in this very kitchen, tittering and gossiping, when Gray was off at work."

"Why only when he was out of the house?" I wondered.

"He doesn't like to know how close I've remained to *the life*." That sisterly fondness crept into her smoke-cured voice once again. "Not after all he's done to save me from it."

"I understand that, I suppose."

"I do and I don't," she said. "I am a firm believer that all we once were informs what we become. Of course, we can change, we can grow, but to think ourselves better than anyone else because we're no longer as desperate as they are... Well, it's not right. Not in my mind."

"I agree," I murmured, because I did.

"Anyway, Alys... She was everything Bea said. Vain, self-involved, a little devious. But she was also lively and funny and very warm-hearted. Generous with her compliments and her money and, of course, her favors. She was loud and bombastic, a notorious flirt. The lifeblood of any room one would find her in. And yet..."

Amelia broke away for a moment, the only sound the snick of a knife falling through potatoes. "There was a vulnerability to Alys as well. A sadness that I think she overcompensated for with all that gaiety. She was alone in the world, and so aware of it. No parents to speak of, or siblings. So many of us are orphans. Either without a family or... better off far away from them."

The bleak note in her voice squeezed my heart.

I thought about Mary, who'd had a cruel father, one she'd turned to *the life* to escape.

Then I thought of my kind da, and my six murdered brothers lined up in a row on cold metal tables. I'd been left with nothing. No money, no opportunity but for factory work, where two of my cousins had already been killed or maimed. Mary had sent me some coin and a ticket to London. She'd set me up with a madam in a very upscale establishment, one she'd been kicked out of because of her drinking and carrying on.

She'd be happy to see me doing better than she did.

That was the kind of friend she was.

"I was orphaned," I told Amelia, surprising even myself. "I was going to turn to the profession out of... financial desperation."

"I see," she replied carefully.

"Croft mentioned the two of you were also orphaned. Quite early, I gather."

"Not early enough, my dear," she said darkly. "We both preferred life on the streets to that at home."

"Oh, Amelia I'm so sorr—"

"Let's not, Fiona," she said, with an odd sort of cheerfulness. "I'd rather not."

To be honest, I wasn't in a place to lay bare the past either, especially when this dress left me so otherwise exposed. The tops of my breasts kept threatening to spill over what could have been a modest, plaid wool bodice, if it only had several yards more fabric.

Where a schoolteacher's dress would have eyelet lace or cotton frills, this one had sheer sleeves and was pulled up like a drapery at each thigh to show everything below the knee.

"I'm dressed now," I called to her. "If one could call it that," I muttered to myself.

"Good! Step out and let's have a look at you."

I tiptoed from behind the screen, tugging on the

bodice to make certain all the pink parts of my breasts stayed covered.

This time, I wasn't aware that Croft had opened the door again until the door handle broke off in his grip.

"What will it take to keep you away from here?" Amelia snapped.

"You said she was dressed!" He gestured wildly. "You bloody lied!"

"She *is* dressed—that's her costume." His sister's tone lowered from exasperated to entertained.

"Tell me you did *not* make that, Amelia."

"But I did."

"Well, you're not wearing it anywhere," he said to me.

"Oh, but she is."

"Like hell she is. She'd be arrested for indecency."

"*She* is standing right here." I gestured with my arms as if no one could see me, which drew a wild stain of color from beneath Croft's collar. He kept his eyes firmly glued to his sister, but not before he'd sneaked several glances at my boots, my stockings, and everything below my neck.

"It's not as though she'll be out of doors, you big dolt. She'll only wear it as a costume."

"But people will see her. *Men* will see her!"

"That's the idea."

"*No*." He whirled to face me, snapped his jaw, and then turned back to his sister. "No. And I say again... absolutely not. I came in here to tell you that I'm going to Scotland Yard today. On my one bloody day off, and I'm going to make sure this is solved through the *proper* channels."

"That would be much appreciated," I chimed in, because he wasn't the only one with scruples about me wearing this dress anywhere.

"Now, if I do so, can you two promise me that dress

goes nowhere out of this house?" He shoved a finger at me, still unable to look.

Amelia leaned against the counter, the gleam in her eyes as bright as the one on the sharp knife gripped in her hand. "You have two days. If these murders are not solved in the next forty-eight hours... Fiona is going *incognito*."

Chapter Five

❧❧❧

The peal of a scream poured acid on my frayed nerves and electrified my heart to give an extra kick against its cage.

I gathered up my skirts and half tripped, half ran up the steps to my Chelsea rowhouse and slammed inside.

"If you want it, you'll crawl on your knees for it," came the street-roughened voice from my parlor.

One belonging to a familiar female.

It became instantly clear the second scream fracturing the air contained more frustration than fear. Still, I didn't stop to divest myself of my winter garb before rushing to see what all the commotion was about.

My maid, Mary Jean McBride, was busy dusting porcelain and glass knickknacks over the fireplace. Her nine-month-old daughter, Teagan, kicked and yawped from her belly on a blanket in the center of the room, straining for a knitted red mouse about a pace beyond her reach.

Unfazed by my appearance, chubby little Teagan let out a screech that threatened to shatter the windows and let winter invade my domicile.

"Caterwaul all you like, you little miscreant," the lively Mary Jean said, in the particular singsong voice people saved for their infant children. In her own South

London patois, often the kindest words could sound like a slight, or a threat. "I'm not picking you up, and I'm not bringing it to you. I seen you crawl toward that cat in the garden yesterday, so I know if you want it bad enough, you'll figure out a way to get there, won't ya? Won't ya? You darling little fraud."

She turned to her child and tensed to find me standing in the doorway, looking, no doubt, like a wind-burned ragamuffin.

"Miss Mahoney!" Mary Jean's young and attractive face split into a genuine smile, revealing teeth that'd been stained by poverty, even at her tender age of one-and-twenty. "I heard you was dressed and gone before the 'ouse even stirred this morning." She bustled over to Teagan and swiped her from the floor, settling the baby in that crook on her hip that seemed made just for the child. "Now that you're 'ome, you want some tea or something to warm your bones?"

"Don't bother, Mary, thank you. You've your hands full here," I answered, perhaps a bit too quickly, as I'd rather leave her and the child's noise here at the front of the house and retreat to the relative solitude of the kitchens.

Besides, to call whatever abomination she dubbed "tea" was doing a disservice to the entire British Empire's beloved beverage.

I'd engaged Mary Jean as a maid-of-all-work on a sentimental whim upon meeting her at Katherine Riley's murder scene. The girl was widowed only a couple of days, as her young husband had perished in a factory incident. Destitute and desperate, Mary had taken the last of his earnings to pay Mrs. Riley in hopes of placing little Teagan with a family who could care for her.

Thank God the woman hadn't been able to add Teagan to the ashes of her previous victims.

The little nipper made enough noise to rouse both the gods above and the demons below, but she was a sweet child, all things considered, and the light of her mother's life.

Something in Mary Jean's predicament, in her heavy, dark hair, eyes, and lovely, high cheekbones, had reminded me of another Mary.

My Mary.

Mary Jeanette Kelly.

So, without thinking—without hesitation—I'd taken her in.

In return for her service, she had a fair wage, and the entirety of below stairs to herself, as I didn't have need of other staff. Furthermore, she was able to keep little Teagan with her when she worked.

I couldn't fathom what women like us, women who must rely on themselves for income, did with their children during their long days of employment. Where would Teagan go if not here? To a stranger? To a wet nurse? Who among the working or lower classes could afford such things?

I had days when I regretted my decision, days when even three stories weren't enough to separate me from the baby's constant din. It had also become immediately and abundantly clear that Mary's skills didn't reach into the realm of the domestic.

But in all, I enjoyed Mary Jean's company. And more importantly, she'd brought new life, comfort, and company to Aunt Nola. She was bright, capable, and willing to learn. I appreciated that she kept my house, my aunt, and my business from falling into disrepair whilst I wallowed in Aidan's death.

I blinked and hesitated, realizing I owed Mary an apology and an explanation.

"Well, don't you look better today after being in the out of doors?" she marveled, batting her lashes like a flirt. "Your eyes have a bit of life in them, miss. It's good to see that."

"Thank you, Mary. I realize I have not recently been

very present... or perhaps the word I'm looking for is *pleasant* in your time here. I want to say how very sorry I am—"

"You don't got to apologize, miss." She held up her hand to stop me, bouncing her baby on her hip with one strong arm, impervious to the stream of drool running from the child's mouth to the sleeve of her starched white apron. "I'm all sorts of aware just 'ow lucky I am to keep me Teagan with me an' all. Besides, your aunt Nola told me you lost your fella. That he was killed."

That same strange breathlessness overcame me whenever I thought of Father Aidan Fitzpatrick. A terrible mélange of hatred and hunger. Of regret and rage. "He succumbed to the St. Michael's Cathedral fire," I corrected her, my voice sounding queer even to my own ears. "And he was my priest, not my—"

She flapped her hand in an artless dismissal of whatever I'd been about to say. "I know you weren't married or nothing, seeing as how Irish folks don't let your vicars have wives, but you loved him, dinn't you?"

"I did," I whispered, wondering why I was suddenly telling this painful truth to someone little better than a stranger, and in the presence of her burbling baby.

"Then you lost him," she declared. "You grieved him. And grief is pleasant for no one."

I was silent, staring down at the black garb I couldn't seem to stop wearing. I knew all the reasons I shouldn't, but any other color just seemed sacrilegious, like a mockery of my despair. I hadn't merely lost the man I'd loved. I'd lost everything I knew about him. Every memory we'd made was now tainted by who he'd become at the end.

And I mourned that as much as I mourned the man. Perhaps more.

"I've decided to start working again," I told her. "So, you don't have to send for Hao Long by default anymore. I'm sure everyone thinks it's well past time for me to have—"

Mary stepped closer, smoothing a bit of Teagan's russet frizz to her round head even as a speaking look made me forget what I'd been about to say.

"If you don't mind me saying, miss, when me Joseph died..." She swallowed, then continued, "... people was always handing over advice like I asked for it. And I know it was kindly meant and all, but... I secretly hated 'em for it. And here I go about to do the same thing."

She screwed up her courage, looking so vividly young, even though we were a scant handful of years apart. "I realize there are rules around what you're supposed to feel about the departed, and for how long. But whoever came up with them was a right git, if you ask me. The way I sees it is... you feel what you feel because that's what you feel."

I felt my tense face crack into a smile. The whole of her philosophy was charmingly, absurdly simple, and yet infallible.

"You mourn for as long... or in my case, as short as you do," she continued. "I loved me Joseph with all me 'eart, but we 'adn't known each other long enough to build a life or even many memories, past the notches we put in our bedpost and the chaotic merriment of my pregnancy with Teagan. He was gone after little more'n a year together, and I'm supposed to be wearing the mourning garb and casting me eyes down for more than the whole of the time we even knew each other? Seems a bit loony, don't it?"

It did. I had to admit.

"And since Joseph went so young, all I can think is, what if I died, too? What if I died before I never learnt to smile again? I *need* Teagan to grow up with smiles and laughter. With a mother wot's a whole woman, even though a part of her has been cut out. That's important to me. I can't make myself be sober a whole year or more. I weren't really built like that. I'm silly and ridiculous and I find the world all sorts of funny and strange. I have to laugh at it."

She paused to coo at Teagan, who wrapped her fist around the maid's cap and tugged at the lace, pulling it askew. The young mother pried it from her daughter's grip before turning sage and solemn eyes on me. "Me father used to say that some people were built to carry sadness in 'em. And I say, if you don't want to give that sadness to God or to the gutter, then you carry it as long as you feel it. And bugger all who tell you when and where to put it down."

"Thank you..." I managed, feeling as if my dark heart had been poked with a cauterized needle, allowing a pinprick of her light and warmth to permeate the gloom.

Drawn by the adorable, if bulbous, spherical impossibility that was Teagan's head, I avoided the dribbly bits by tracing my fingertip down the bridge of her nose. She rewarded me with a sopping smile and the view of two little white ridges in the bottom pink of her gums.

"Oh my, she has some teeth in there," I said, avoiding the grateful emotion threatening to close off my throat.

"And sharp little buggers, too," Mary complained with her customary good nature. "It's why she's been an absolute monster of late, and will be for a few weeks longer, I think."

I found a sudden and fervent gratitude at the prospect of spending the time away, even if it would be at a house of ill repute.

How did I couch this to my household, I wondered? I couldn't very well say I was on my way to pretend to be a prostitute in order to help catch a killer the police didn't seem in any hurry to find. That certainly wasn't in my *curriculum vitae*. In fact, it might be altogether il-legal. I wasn't sure.

Croft had said he would use his connections, of course, and if anyone had the ability to mobilize the powers at Scotland Yard to link two murders when one was already marked as solved on paper, it was him.

But my father had a favorite saying: *It'd be easier to get blood from a stone.*

And as many stones as Croft could break with his bare hands, I doubted he'd squeeze much blood from them, metaphorically speaking.

I'd vowed to let him try, but I wasn't holding my breath.

"I suppose I should warn you now, Mary, but I might be gone on a long... position for a few evenings come this Thursday. Nola would need some extra care, and someone else to tend to the evening meal. Should I hire Mrs. Shively to cook for the week?"

"It is *you* who will need the extra care, *Fiona*," shrilled a voice from behind me.

Startled, I whirled at the threshold of the parlor to see the slight and unsettled specter haunting the bottom step of the ornate staircase.

My aunt, Nola Mahoney, lifted a gnarled hand to pull back the black lace she often draped over her fea-tures. The veil was to help her walk among her spirit guides more easily, she claimed, to make them feel as though she belonged in their realm without fearing her.

But what had the dead to fear from an enfeebled old woman?

No, I thought that she wore the shroud so that when she heard the disembodied voices echoing through her troubled mind, she wouldn't have to look up and see that no one was there to make the sounds.

Her veil created shadows and shapes where none ex-isted, and therefore, when the voices came, she could pretend they were merely otherworldly company. Not malevolent demons, as she'd once assumed.

Or worse, her own mind turning on itself.

It was kinder, I thought, to let her assume this. Kinder than the hellish asylum I'd found her underfed and unwashed body wasting away in some years ago.

And certainly kinder than the truth.

She was, indeed, losing a bit more of her mind with each passing year, and there was nothing I could do to stop it.

"Aunt Nola." I steadied my alarmed breaths as much as I could, before addressing her odd outburst. "What do you mean, I need to take extra care?"

"*Betrayal*, Fiona. *They've* told me. Someone close to you is going to betray you... or worse. You are going to betray them. Lovers, I think. Your lover? Or maybe someone you love? Someone will be in love, and then... *treachery*. Treachery will tear them apart."

I heard Mary gasp behind me and had to suppress rolling my eyes with such fervency they might have gotten lost in my skull.

If I were a superstitious woman, I would argue that it had already happened. That the man I loved had betrayed me. That his treachery had been against every living soul.

Even God.

But I wasn't one for the occult any more than I was one for religion these days. Indeed, I didn't think Aunt Nola nor her spirit guides could predict the future any more than I believed that anyone could predict whether a soul had gone to God or the Devil.

All I could do was clean up what was left of them when they were gone, and accept that we'd all find out eventually, when it was our time.

Pinching the bridge of my nose, I did my best to gather the lost vestiges of my patience.

I loved my father's sister because she had helped to

raise us after my ma died. And I loved her because she was like him in so many ways, my da. The same strawberry hair, the same flakes of ginger and cinnamon flecking their translucent skin. Same shrewd gaze and generous heart.

Except now, her eyes were ever more often clouded.

I made to go to her. "Nola—"

"The dark squares!" she shrieked, which set poor wee Teagan to answering in kind.

I noted, unkindly, that if the child were so disturbed by the sound of a screech, one would have thought she'd take pity on *us* from time to time.

"Of course, the dark squares." I didn't think I was able to keep the exhaustion out of my voice, but still, I stopped short. Bending my head, I lifted my hem, if only to be certain my heels touched the darker squares of the fine entry floors as I made my way to Nola.

It was a fixation of hers on what we called her "bad" days. She became convinced that if a light square on the floor were to be trodden upon, the sky would fall. The streets would be overrun by brimstone. London would burn.

Again.

And so we did this dance for her, to keep the End of All Things at bay. To save what little we could of her sanity.

I'd reeled in some of my vexation by the time I reached her. Enough, at least, to gently say, "Nola, please explain what you mean when you say *betrayal*. Is this another one of your card readings? Or did you hear something? Another letter?"

I asked, because once the Ripper had delivered me a note here, and she was the one to coax and comfort me as I very nearly lost my own mind.

She shook her head. "*They* told me."

They. Them. Days like today, I detested every last one of these invisible spirit guides, all of whom were silent until Aunt Nola needed something, or had a premonition of some awful kind.

All of whom cared nothing for my schedule or my own sanity.

They were not optimists, I'd gathered, nor were they omens of anything good. More like harbingers.

If *they* were here, then Nola truly did need more care than usual.

Mary drew abreast of me by way of the dark squares, shushing the baby by shoving a finger between her gums to gnaw on. "What did they tell you, madam?" she whispered, her voice lowered in reverence.

A believer, I thought, was Mary. But I hadn't the heart to ask her outright, lest she be offended by the skepticism I could not always hide.

Regarding me from beneath a veiled expression, Nola finally produced something from a pocket inside her bronze and black braided gown. Three cards. "All right, it *was* the cards they spoke through, but Fiona, it's one of the worst readings!" she insisted, as I clenched my hands into fists. "They told me to pull three for you because you'd disappeared this morning."

"I left a note," I reminded them both, spearing Mary with a quelling glare. "A couple, in fact."

"I showed you them, didn't I, Madam Mahoney?" Mary said, paling a little. "I told you she'd be back—we just didn't know when."

"I knew you'd gone somewhere dangerous." Nola's expression turned both wounded and accusatory, her ashen complexion made more so by the dwindling light of the dreary afternoon. She reached out to me, her claw-like hands gripping my arm with surprising strength. "You were chasing *him* again, weren't you? The demon in your dreams."

I did my best not to find it odd that she'd called the Ripper that, when I'd only just thought of him as such this afternoon.

The demon in my nightmares.

"Aunt Nola." I placed my hand over hers, gently prying away her bruising grip. "I was merely called to a murder scene to clean up after a body." I omitted my ill-advised attempted confession in Croft's home. She needn't worry about what might almost have happened. What had I been thinking?

I hadn't. Grief had driven me to the brink of madness…I was convinced of that now.

And blood had brought me back.

Most of me, anyhow.

"This time, it had nothing to do with the Ripper," I was glad to state.

Nola's eyes shifted this way and that, as if reading a book neither of us could see. The effect was unsettling in the extreme. "But he's nearby."

Despite my disbelief, fingers of dread—infinitely icier and sharper than Nola's—laced in between the knobs of my spine, gripping at my very soul.

"What makes you say that?" I asked, in a voice more unsteady than I'd intended.

"This," she hissed, shoving the card beneath my nose. I had to take a step back and adjust my spectacles before I could see it clearly.

A man lay on his face in blood-soaked mud with an abundance of swords pinning him down. I counted ten.

The ten of swords.

"Treachery!" Nola crowed, her own Irish accent thicker than mine, as two years in London hadn't had the same smoothing effect. "Treachery, betrayal, ruin, deceit, by someone you won't imagine. By someone you trust."

"I hardly trust anyone," I said a bit wryly, trying to dispel the eerie mood gathering around us. "So I don't fancy I'm in danger of that."

"But what about this?" she whispered, producing the second card.

More swords. This time eight. A woman was tied to a stake, the swords buried into the marshy ground around her, while in the distance, a castle loomed like Olympus on a mountain.

"What about it?" I asked, already dreading the forthcoming explanation.

"She's you, Fiona! This is *you*. Bound by your own fear and pain. Abandoned to it. It is this very lack of trust that will lead you in the wrong direction. Toward danger, rather than away from it. Don't you see? You could free yourself. So easily! Just like this woman here." She shook the card in frustration. "See how her feet are not bound, how there are these sharp swords everywhere? She could cut herself free. Run to the castle. To safety. Take off the blindfold so she could see clearly, but she won't. She awaits her fate like this, rather than fighting. Oh, Fiona, you have to stop this before it's too late."

I pressed my hand to Nola's arm. "All right," I said. "I'll do my best, Aunt Nola. I'll be careful, but I'll also fight. I'll cut free of the things that bind me..." I cast about in my memory for whatever else she'd been talking about, as I'd learned when she was this agitated that it was best to simply agree.

"What did you mean about the lovers?" Mary asked in a tremulous voice. "That seemed important, didn't it?"

Were I in possession of a temper like Croft's—and had she not been holding an infant—I might have given in to the overwhelming urge to slap her.

"The lovers." Nola produced the final card. "The lovers. I'm so sorry, Fiona. What terrible news. The lovers will be ripped apart. Betrayed. Oh, that's so sad. After Aidan and everything that's happened."

Living for as long as I had with Aunt Nola, I'd un-wittingly—unwillingly—picked up a bit of tarot knowl-

71

edge, and did my best to apply it here, if only to pacify her.

"Aren't the lovers a perfectly decent card?" I took it, looking down at the couple depicted there, standing in front of two trees, one the tree of life, the other the tree of knowledge, their union blessed by someone standing in the middle... I forgot who. An angel, perhaps? "You've told me previously it's an auspicious card, meaning commitment or happy choices, romance, or at least a flirtation." I waggled my brows at her.

"Sure, I did. I said that." Nola nodded, cocking her ear as if hopefully listening for good news. Her subsequent expression left no doubt they hadn't told her any. "But these other two cards surrounding it. They affect it, you see. You cannot pull so many swords and not be stabbed by them. I'm just sorry, Fiona. There is so much danger for the lovers, I'm afraid. Too many secrets. Too much betrayal. It's too, too sad. I can't..."

Her eyes welled with tears, and I let out a breath, pulling her in for a gentle hug. "There, there."

The eight of swords and the ten of swords? It seemed to me that someone merely forgot to properly shuffle her deck.

"I'll be careful, Nola," I continued, rubbing at her thin back, thinking she needed a large meal and a strong pot of tea. "Perhaps it's already happened... you think? Perhaps the reading is telling you the swords have already fallen, and now I must pick myself up?"

"No." She pushed back to look up at me, brandishing the lovers before me. "*They* told me that you are surrounded by men, Fiona. Wicked men and dangerous men. By men who would devour you, if you were easy to catch and tender to bite."

She wasn't wrong. No one needed the cards to see that.

"It's quite lucky I am neither of those things, then.

Tough and full of gristle is this hide." I smirked in spite of myself.

"One of them wears Jack's face," she prophesied ominously. Her eyes went even more glassy as she went deeper into her troubled mind. "I-I had a dream. That the Ripper was old. He had a wrinkled face and knobbly hands. This means he is going to live long, Fiona. Or maybe that he already has. Perhaps you may not catch up to him. Perhaps... you should stop trying."

There was no chance of that, but I realized now what all this hullabaloo was about.

Nola was worried for me.

She'd been aware of what happened to Mary Kelly. To all of Jack's poor victims. She'd seen what a letter from Jack, peppered with words of admiration couched in thinly veiled threats, did to my composure. How it had threatened my sanity.

She was afraid for me.

For the danger I put myself in, not only when I worked my own trade, but when I searched for a killer in the blood of the dead. Anyone might feel this way on behalf of a beloved niece.

"If Jack is old, Nola, then you won't have to worry about his overtaking me anytime soon, at least not before you pull me another reading, yeah? Maybe tomorrow the cards will be kinder. And I won't be leaving the house before then."

"It's the young and powerful you need to have a care for," she insisted, ignoring me altogether. "All these wolves at your door. Poor lamb. All these wolves and no one to kill them for you."

Finally, I decided I'd had enough of this nonsense. Taking Nola about the shoulders, I steered her down the last step and toward the back kitchens by way of the dark squares.

"Nola, do you remember back in Limerick, that wolfhound old Seamus McGrady had in his pastures?" I asked. "Big as a horse, he was, and I kept asking old man McGrady if I could ride the beast."

"Aye. I remember," she murmured, allowing herself to be led by me.

"What if we got a dog? Someone to keep you company and entertained. To keep the house safer from the wolves, as it were. Would you like that?"

"That dog's name was Lothaire, and he would take naps and accept treats as the O'Driscoll boys stole some of McGrady's ewes. Useless creature."

I sighed, settling Nola into a chair so I could put the kettle on. I wished I could tell her she didn't have to worry so much.

I already knew I had wolves surrounding me, and the way I survived was to become a member of their pack. I walked a very thin line, performed a very skilled and intricate dance to keep them at bay. To convince them of my loyalty and my discretion.

Lest they turn on me.

Chapter Six

❦

Was I going to go through with this?

    Was I, Fiona Ina Muerin Mahoney, going to don the uniform of a prostitute and join the denizens of the night?

Standing on the ledge off my back door that dared to call itself a balcony, I leaned on the railing and watched evening shadows elongate over my back garden. I suppose I should say it was Nola's garden, as she was the only soul who tended to it. Though it was a testament to her deteriorating state, I thought, that she'd neglected to clip the dead and frozen blooms this winter, leaving a strange bed of floral corpses wilting beneath overgrown hedges. I should pay someone to clean it up before spring, when I hoped that things would improve for us both.

Perhaps her distress, too, could be laid at my feet. I hadn't been well since Aidan's death, and her anxiety for me might have made everything worse.

Lord, but I was a fool. I needed to do better by her. By everyone.

Somehow.

I hunched over a large tin of tea, linking my fingers around it as if the warmth might spread to my core.

It didn't.

However, I would brave the cold for a moment of blessed silence in which to organize my thoughts. Or perhaps my feelings.

When confronted by the skepticism of others, it'd been easy to stand my ground and stubbornly debate the reasons I should be going to The Orchard to gather information.

But in my quiet moments, uncertainty leaked in through the cracks in my courage.

What business had I doing this? What expertise? What sort of trouble could I land myself in, either legally or otherwise, that would have repercussions on the people who relied on me?

Or... was I giving this entirely too much consideration? I meant no one harm, only my help, what little I could think to give.

And if I were honest, I felt I owed Amelia. If I couldn't bring myself to give her the truth that would break her, then I could at least help her uncover this one.

The screech of a wrought-iron gate broke my reverie, and I startled just in time to see a lanky form sauntering toward me, his hands lifted to his mouth as he lit a cigarette in a long, expensive-looking holder. His smoking jacket was the deepest, richest amber that brought out the garnet undertones in his whisky-colored eyes.

My neighbor was becoming rather famous, really. A conversationalist and a man-about-town, but not merely as a dilettante and social upstart. He was a journalist, an editor, a playwright, and most recently, a novelist. I became more and more aware of how lucky I was for the times we spent alone, smoking in our gardens and gossiping about our exceptionally dissimilar days.

He was another denizen of the night. One more soaked in absinthe rather than arsenic.

Yet we understood each other... and when we didn't, we delighted each other.

Trotting up my steps, he seized my face in both of his hands and noisily kissed each cheek twice. "I saw you coming home this very afternoon, which means you left early. Or at least before I woke," he announced, in an accent so entirely cultured, one might forget he was from Ireland as well. "Tell me you went to work today. Tell me *everything*. Who is dead? Anyone I know?"

"Good afternoon, Oscar," I said with mock censure. "It's lovely to see you again, as well. I'm faring slightly better, thank you for asking."

He wrinkled his aquiline nose and pursed lips entirely too full to belong to a man. "Oh *please*, do let us dispense with the pleasantries. Life seems as short as a winter's day, and if I'm honest, I have so much to tell *you*. But I want you to go first." Flapping the hand with the cigarette holder at me, he motioned for me to begin. "I demand you reveal what job was interesting enough to pull you out of your self-imposed sequestration."

In pure, smooth, Oscar Wilde fashion, he mentioned the fact that we hadn't seen each other in some months without quite mentioning it at all. There was a shadow of approbation beneath his ribbing, but nothing truly serious.

It was more fondness than frustration I released in my long-suffering sigh. "If you're bursting at the seams to tell *me* something, Oscar, why don't *you* just go first?"

He took a long drag and let the smoke escape with his words. "Because, darling, the suspense is terrible, and I need it to last."

"That doesn't at all seem practical." I wrinkled my nose at him.

"To the devil with practicality, is what I say." His eyes were brighter than usual, his energy almost frenetic. "Especially when anticipation is *this* delicious.

Now tell me what you've been about, and if it's not that riveting or salacious, then fill in those parts with fiction."

I snorted. "What use has fiction in this case? Practicality is what keeps the world turning. One must think realistically to survive."

"No, *you* must think thus to survive," he corrected me with a grand flourish. "No great artist ever sees things as they really are. If he did, he would cease to be an artist. Reality is ugly and rude. Therefore, fiction is necessary for a reason, my dear, and I must live in a bit of whimsical fantasy if I'm to continue to create."

"I don't suppose I can argue with you there."

"Of course you cannot. Besides, I'm not here to argue. I'm here to listen. Now tell me what you're up to. I shan't ask again."

So I did.

Leaving out names, of course, I regaled him about Alys and Jane, how they'd lived and how they'd died. About their distraught madam. And about Amelia, the former companion who wanted nothing more desperately than to help.

Oscar's eyes were as wide as a barn owl's when I revealed our plans for me to establish faith with the working women, and learn what I could about the victims, so I could help to find their killer.

Once I finished, I felt quite incredible that I'd made Oscar Wilde, one of London's most loquacious raconteurs, speechless for a full minute.

He finally said, "In my experience, the world is divided into two classes, those who believe the incredible, and those who do the improbable. You, my dear, are an alluring and alarming concoction of both."

I blinked twice, wondering if he'd complimented me or not. "Thank you?" He didn't elaborate, so I went on. "I'm not doing anything unheard of. I'm merely spending a few nights at The Orchard in order to ask pertinent, if somewhat indiscreet, questions."

"Questions are never indiscreet, though answers sometimes are." He studied me for a moment longer, as if debating saying his thoughts out loud.

"You think they'll see through me?" I asked, voicing my own secret anxieties.

He dipped his cleft chin. "I think you'll need to be careful how you approach this. You, my dear, are not the kind of woman who works in these places, and I'm more worried about the men who frequent them than the women. I mean, I would take one look at you and know you aren't a whore."

Suddenly terribly glum, I picked at a fleck of peeling paint on the balcony. "I made that very argument to the bawd. I'm too old to pass for a courtesan, aren't I? Too freckled and bespectacled and plump and—"

"Fiona!" Oscar seized my shoulders and gave me a little shake, spilling some of my tea. "No, that's not *at all* what I was implying. Lord help me, but I'm nothing if not an aesthete. I choose my friends for their good looks, my acquaintances for their good characters, and my enemies for their intellects."

"And unfortunately for you, one can't pick one's neighbors," I teased.

He slid me a wounded look. "Surely we are friends first and neighbors second, are we not, Fiona?

"Of course we are."

"There. Then your loveliness is uncontestable. I can't abide ugly friends."

That drew a dry wisp of a chuckle, much unused, from my throat. "You are kind. I've been told I look terrible today."

"Well..." He drew out the word. "No object is *so* beautiful that, under certain conditions, it will not seem unattractive. You, however, have a beauty of spirit that shines through despite the pallor of your skin, the lankness of your hair, and the shadows beneath your eyes. What you need is some sunshine, fresh air, a good laugh, and a better drink."

"Then I am doomed." I motioned to slate-grey skies, sooty air, and frigid wind.

"Well... I can help with the laughter and drinks in any case." He nodded toward my door. "Invite me in."

"So we can drink from *my* stock?" I slapped his shoulder with no real strength.

We went through to the kitchens, and I poured him a cup of my best brandy. We sat at the café table in the breakfast nook, sipping and looking out the large window framing my abomination of a garden. He chatted in his lively manner, making the kinds of gestures that might knock things off their shelves were he not such a graceful man.

I laughed for the first time since Aidan.

Oscar knew who Aidan was—who he'd been to me. But he never understood the depth of my pain in that regard. Or my sense of betrayal.

I planned to take that information to my grave.

"Oscar," I said during a lull in our conversation. "I'm sorry I haven't been available for you. For this. I feel like the world's most terrible friend."

"I understand, darling. Grief makes one's world very small."

"I'm sorry I let it do so these past few months. And I shan't in the future."

"Oh, but you already have. You have for ages, and will for an indeterminate time yet."

I tensed as he gave me a speaking look over the rim of his crystal glass. "I-I'm sorry?"

"Your world, fascinating as it is, is already small, Fiona. It is *him*. The Ripper. You've lived your life in grief for a girl years dead, who might not have deserved such a gift as your obsession."

Hurt thrummed through my blood, protected by a

quick spurt of temper. "What do you mean about deserving?"

"Well, the bloody obvious, of course. Mary was a friend to you, but you'd lived apart for some years, knowing each other only through correspondence. Writing is hardly a truthful medium, dear, believe me. She could have only presented to show you the most wholesome parts of her life, whilst subsisting on a completely different reality. I mean, we both know what she did for a living—not only that, but how far she'd fallen before—"

I set my glass down heavily and laid both my palms flat on the table. "Are you intimating that Mary's profession—that her weakness for drink—made her life less meaningful?"

"I was not," he replied, eyeing me with wariness. "But I'll dare to intimate it now, because it's the sad truth of things. In the eyes of polite society, whores are barely humans. Just a set of orifices to penetrate. When they die, no one cares."

He'd not been the only person to say this, but hearing from him, from a man who should know better...

"*I* care," I spat at him. "People certainly *cared* when Jack was slaughtering prostitutes in the streets! They rose up on behalf of those women, created militias to patrol their neighborhoods. They looked for him for ages. Longer than any murderer in memory."

"Yes, but don't you think that was due to the salaciousness of the deaths? The sheer audacity of them. Leaving women slaughtered and carved in the middle of the streets. The subsequent frenzy of journalists, *et cetera*. Just think, if it'd been five or six of *you* dead... don't you think the Ripper would be swinging by the neck already?" He held a hand up to stave off my tempestuous reply to finish, "There is no justice for women who work the night—that's all I'm saying. So why do you persist in looking for what doesn't exist, when you could be moving on with your life?"

"Because that is the most ridiculous thing I've ever heard anyone say, Oscar Fingal O'Flahertie Wills Wilde!" Hands still splayed on the table, I pushed myself to stand, and then marched to the opposite window to glare out east toward the city.

"Look at what we've done as a species." I motioned to the lights in the distance. The smokestacks, and bridges, and churches. "Behold what we've built. Once, there were no engines or steel. No gas lamps nor electricity. No wires. No telephone lines. No heated water and sewage pumps. None of these existed until someone imagined them into actuality. Once they were nothing better than an idea. Then they were a toil. Very probably a failure. Many failures. And then... and then a reality. So maybe I'm looking for a justice that doesn't yet exist... but the idea of it does. The *need* for it does. And maybe I'll just have to make it my own bloody self!" With that, I turned my back on him. "If you'll excuse me, Oscar, I have work to do."

Behind me, his chair scraped against the wood floor moments before his large hand enfolded mine. "Please don't be cross with me, Fiona," he begged, before pressing a fervent kiss to my chilly knuckles. "I'm so clever that sometimes even *I* don't understand a single word of what I'm saying."

The desperation in his tone didn't only cause me to pause, but also poured a salve on the heat of my surly mood.

"You *know* I think that people who sell sex and companionship sell a *much-needed* commodity. I truly don't look down upon them so much as others do. I was only lambasting society itself. Surely you can attest to that, being the practical woman that you are. It's a travesty, certainly, but a reality nonetheless." He'd trapped me with my own words, and I put a hand over his, though he persisted. "It pains me to see that you've taken the mantle of justice on your shoulders, when it shouldn't belong to you. It's too much for one lady to bear."

I knew this. I saw the truth in his earnest eyes. "Forgive me my temper, Oscar. I'm... I'm a bit overwrought from the day."

He dropped another kiss on our joined hands. "*Of course* you are, my darling. Let us never quarrel. You are one of my nearest and dearest. And of course, I am a true friend, Fiona, and I have learned through painful experience that true friends stab you in the front. So, if I am blunt with you, it is because I care so much. But I didn't mean to be insensitive. Not when your heart is so full of love and loss."

I conjured a smile for him. "My heart is full, but not of love."

"Then you must change it, Fiona. A life without love is like this." He swept his hand toward the window. "A sunless garden where the flowers are dead."

He was not wrong.

"How did you get to be so wise?" I asked, resting my head against his shoulder.

"Experience, my love," he said, petting my hair. "Experience is one thing you can't get for nothing."

"Experience is the one thing I lack in this regard," I lamented.

"You mean... sexually?"

I nodded, unable to say the word, let alone look at him when he said it. "I don't know how everyone seems to be able to tell! What is it about me—you know what, don't answer that. What can I do to hide this from the other women?"

He tutted, shaking his head and snapping a forelock of hair out of his doleful eyes. "Don't worry about the other women. Worry about the men—they're the ones you need to secure. If you do so, the women will believe your truth is actually a façade."

I eyed him balefully. "I don't follow."

"Give them what they want, Fiona." He turned me to face the window, and I watched our reflections as he drew my scarf from my neck and held it up like a veil over my nose and mouth. "They want fiction. They want anonymity. Man—and woman, I daresay—is least himself when he talks in his own person. Give him a mask, and he will tell you the truth. You understand?"

"I think so?"

He dropped the scarf, studying me for a moment. "I have a scrap of lace I've worn as a mask to some very indecent clubs. I will get it for you."

"Oscar, your face is gigantic next to mine."

He drew back, pressing a hand to his wounded chest. "Have a heart!"

"No! I'm not being cruel. I simply mean it won't fit."

"Oh." He dropped his hand, his mischievous grin returning. "I'll make adjustments, of course, and while I do, I will tell you of this extraordinary person I just met. Fiona, I'm nigh frothing with incandescence."

"Person?" I echoed.

His eyes became serious for a moment, not losing their sparkle, but covering it in meaningful caution. "Don't let's use names. Or even pronouns. Just sensations and feelings and kismet and desire. I promise the story will be just as good."

"How can it be just as good if I'm not to know who this mystery person is?"

"I know it's terribly unfair, but I'm afraid this person will have to remain invisible. A mystery. You love a good mystery, don't you?" He raised his eyebrows over a cajoling expression, blinking his unjustly long lashes at me.

"Mysteries are meant to be solved," I reminded him.

"The true mystery is the visible, not the invisible. And even then, it's all perspective."

He left me to contemplate that load of malarkey as he loped next door to retrieve the mask.

I watched him go, a bit troubled over this development in his relationships. He resided next door with his wife, Constance, and his children, Cyril and Vyvyan. He did his best by them, which was not as much as they deserved. Because his true heart loved other people.

Other men.

He'd confessed this to me before, and then rarely brought himself to say so again. For this was a dangerous knowledge. One that could land him in prison, if not worse.

Once he'd retrieved his mask, we found a place to work in front of my dressing table. He set about snipping ribbons and threading them through a lovely lace confection whilst securing it to my features. All the while, he spoke with unabashed animation about someone who turned his entire expression luminescent.

In my state of mind, as fractured as my heart was, I thought I'd find it jaggedly painful to hear about someone falling in love. Because Oscar truly was falling, if not already deeply in love.

And I did.

However, I forced myself to ignore the pain, because I knew that no matter whom Oscar fell for, the relationship was doomed.

We both knew it.

And so, because I loved him, I could pretend that this story he told with such verve had a happy ending.

I wasn't marvelous at pretending, but Oscar had been right about one thing—this filmy lace covered me from forehead to nose and hid the worry and pity for his future from him as he chattered away like a woodlark.

Looking at myself in the mirror, I saw someone I didn't recognize. A woman with salacious secrets, ones that were less painful than mine, and more tempting.

Me, a temptress? I could half believe it like this.

Yes, this would work perfectly, I thought. It would be the very thing that could hide me from those who would see the truth.

So that I could find it in the dark.

Chapter Seven

❧

I wasn't afraid until the moment I disembarked the hackney at Orchard Lane.

If I'm honest, I was delighted just to be getting out of the house. What with Teagan teething, Mary's frenetically chipper overcompensation for the noise, and Aunt Nola's portents of doom, I was ready to beg Croft for a night or two in a cell for escape.

Also, as much as I hated to admit it to myself, seeing Oscar radiant with a new love might have been the worst of it. For which I felt terribly guilty.

I should be glad for him. And I was. But something about that the brilliance of his smile only illuminated the yawning chasm of my loneliness. It dug at wounds still tender with scabs.

At least here at The Orchard, almost no one knew me. I could truly become someone else.

More specifically, Viola Montague. A *nome de théâtre* of sorts, selected from both my most favorite and least favorite Shakespeare plays.

Or perhaps I meant *nome de guerre*.

I tried to become Viola as I bustled through the frigid late-winter night, my head hidden in the fur hood of my floor-length coat. Not only against the bite of the wind, but to conceal the scrap of lace across my features from the evening inhabitants of Fleet Street. I'd bought the coat, a full and feminine confection of ermine and midnight-blue velvet, for this very place. Its length and abundance hid the lack of adequate skirts underneath.

I hesitated at the entrance to The Orchard, grappling my anxiety with both hands and some stern inner monologue.

Who was I to do this? What sort of sex and sin would I be subjected to? Could I truly pretend to be immune? Death was one thing, a realm in which I felt comfortable. Well, knowledgeable, at least.

Sex? This was a universe foreign unto me.

Not by choice, exactly, but because I'd spent most of my life in love. In love with a man who'd promised to marry me and spoke in whispers about the love we would make. He'd kissed me often, and passionately. His hands had become familiar with my skin, dawdling in places they ought not to find.

But he'd never ventured inside me with any part of himself. Even though I would have let him. I would have let Aidan do anything he wanted to me.

Maybe because I knew he wouldn't. Because he respected me as much as he loved me, and that had meant something for so long.

Once I lost him to the church, I'd done my best to move on. Partly because he awakened yearnings within me I'd wanted to explore.

But no other man who'd kissed and groped at me came close to making me feel like Aidan had. To making me want more than what they took without asking... a hand in my bodice or a tongue shoved into my mouth.

And then I'd lost my entire family in one night, and struggled to survive. I didn't visit those dark months after, but romance had been the furthest thing from my mind.

When Mary invited me to join her in London, she'd given me the price I could charge for my virginity, and it was often more than most people I knew made in an entire year.

And after her blood-soaked tragedy, well... I'd retained my virginity whilst building a business, because it almost seemed like more trouble to find someone to relieve me of it then I wanted to bother with.

And so, a virgin I remained.

What was worse, everyone seemed to be able to tell.

Dear God, I was making a mistake, wasn't I? Anyone could take a single look at me and *know*, regardless of the mask across my features. I still felt so uncovered. Exposed.

Above all that, would I be spending my evening with a murderer? Did the Ripper know I was here?

As was my recent habit, I searched my vicinity for him, understanding how ridiculous it was to do so. I had no idea what he looked like. The only people who did were in the ground.

Sometimes I hunted for that man in the papers, the one with the shifty eyes and hawkish face, clad in a dark, tailored suit and top hat. A creation of the press, but an evocative one, nevertheless. The only visual representation that we as an empire possessed.

There were so many men who fit exactly that profile to be found here in London. It would be easy to find Jack in the eyes of any random gentleman.

However, the only other soul with me in Orchard Lane was, to my surprise, another woman. Dressed in a long overcoat, much like mine, she floated rather than walked down the narrow alley, almost like a disembodied torso in a cloud of frothy pink skirts.

Approaching me, she affixed a pleasant—if practiced—smile to her rouged lips and even performed an actual curtsy. "Hello there," she said in a velveteen voice with just the slightest trace of Cockney peeking through the cultured affectation. Her hair was pulled back from her face so tightly that her eyebrows sat unnaturally high on her head. But for that, she was a lovely girl. Perhaps my age, I was pleased to note. "No need to fret, love—just tap on the door there and Butler will help you pick from the stock. It's a lovely night for a warm cuddle, is it not?"

"Oh, erm..." Caught entirely off guard, I stepped away from the stoop, creating distance from the very idea. Remembering myself, I affected the cultured British accent I'd practiced with Amelia. "No, I'm sorry. I am one of the stock. That is... it's my first day—er—evening. I'm Viola. Viola Montague." I held out my hand as if we weren't meeting for the first time in an alley in front of a brothel.

"Oh!" Eyes as blue and unburdened of intellect as little Teagan's lit with warm welcome. "I'm Isabelle James. Pleasure to meet you, Viola." Every elite thread unraveled from her accent as she shook my hand with great vigor for such a tiny creature. "I s'pose no one told you to come in through the entry at the back of the alley. It's better the customers don't see you arriving to work. Bea says it shatters the fantasy for them. Strange, innit?"

Threading her arm through mine, she gently tugged me deeper into the lane, the wisps of her skirts creating a lake of pink around us both.

"I mean, where do they think we go when we're done with our shift? Do they imagine we're stored in a cupboard until we're needed again?" she continued, without waiting for any sort of response from me. "Indira says they don't think of us at all once they've spent their load, and she's right, of course, she's always right. But I've never been like, *Oi there, a doctor is unlocking his surgery, now I can't imagine him healing me with his instruments because I watched him fiddle with his keys.*" She giggled at the ridiculousness of it all.

"Well, I—"

"Where were you posted before this?" she asked, as if we might have been governesses or companions rather than whores. "I went to live with me aunt Belinda once me mother died. And she put me to work on the docks in Southwark when I was a girl. I moved to Wapping for three hellish months, until I found Bea. I used to think that these upper-crust houses were the dream, but these days I'd take a dirty dock worker over some of these fancy fucks, and no mistake. Don't read me wrong!" She clutched at my arm with her other hand, as if she'd read the astonishment my mask was unable to hide. "Some of these young clerks and bookish boys are so sweet, but journalists and businessmen? Genteel lords with bleeding bank accounts and too much pride to work an honest day. They're the most twisted of them all. Or worse, *tourists*."

She sniffed and spat on the bricks at the end of an alley before tapping a staccato rhythm on an ancient brown door, a rhythm I committed to memory immediately.

"Are tourists particularly"—I searched for the word —"depraved?"

She looked at me askance. "No more than usual folks, I suppose. But you know"—she tipped her head toward mine, glancing up the alley as she did so—"*foreigners*."

The word escaped her like a curse, and I wondered if she'd consider me such a tainted thing. An Irishwoman from the wrong side of the war.

Turning to me, she petted the fur on my collar and exclaimed, "This is real, innit? And you talk like you've an education. From further west, are you?"

I'd prepared an answer for this, though I was so overwhelmed by her vigor that I'd lost it in the chaos. "I—"

The door swung open, saving me from having to reply.

Isabelle shoved me toward whoever stood in the shadows beyond. "This is Viola Montague, a new girl Bea must have hired to replace poor Jane." She commandeered the introductions, and I was all too happy to allow it, as she propelled me through a short entryway and into a large, disorganized dressing room nigh exploding with color.

"I'm replacing Alys, actually," I blurted, instantly imagining that I might have just made my first mistake. A new employee might not know the particulars of the tragedies so recently experienced by the women here. "Wh-who is Jane?" I asked, clumsily doing my best to recover.

"She used to work here," Isabelle said. "She—um. She died... quite recently."

"How awful," I said, not needing to portend my distress. "How did it happen?"

No one seemed in a hurry to answer as I scanned the room in front of me.

The dazzling array didn't merely belong to the silks and petticoats and underthings exploding from every cupboard and trunk, but to the women themselves. It seemed someone from every corner of the Empire's overreach paused to stare at me.

An astonishingly dark and lovely African woman rested her delicate bare foot on a chair and adjusted her garters under a pale green gown. She had a riot of ribbons threaded through a braid of full hair crowning her regal head. She might have been a princess rather than a prostitute.

Seeming to misread my enchantment as antipathy, she dismissed me with a roll of her eyes before resuming her ablutions.

Two women with long, silken black hair and skin the color of treated teak conversed in the corner. One was draped in the vibrant saris of India; her wrists, lobes, and even her nose glinted with bangles and jewels.

The other was blindingly, ethereally beautiful, and had donned a gown that would have been unmistakably British, if the folds of fabric over the cage of her bustle weren't translucent enough to advertise that she wore no drawers beneath.

I looked away to avoid gawking at the cleft of her behind, and quickly realized that the attire I'd borrowed from Amelia Croft was sedate in comparison to most of the women here.

In the blazing light of several gas lamps, I noted that Isabelle's hair might have been gold when she was a young girl, but was muddied to something a little more akin to honey now. She unpinned her trifle of a hat and checked that several hot-ironed curls hadn't been too damaged in the wind.

Another beauty with tight ochre curls stood with her knuckles perched on her hips. "So Beatrice thinks *you* can replace Alys?" she asked, in a Continental accent I couldn't place. Somewhere between Italian and Spanish, I thought, but was scarcely sophisticated enough to know. She had skin the color of the southern sand once the pull of a wave had abandoned it, and I wanted to test the satin texture.

"I-I'm only here to do what Mrs. Chamberlain hired me to do." I spread my fingers in a gesture of confusion. "Is there something I'm missing?"

"*Who is Jane?* this one asks," said a Rubenesque brunette from a dressing table where she arranged her hair in only her corset and drawers. "Let's see if Miss Montague survives the Brothel of Blood."

"Aye, though business is scarce enough as it is," piped up a Scotswoman from over by the door, the only other redhead, as far as I could tell. "That Bea would even consider employing someone else when we've

93

barely enough work to go around is a load of ripe shite, if you ask me."

A chorus of agreement dropped my heart into my belly. The sinking realization that Isabelle was the only welcome I was likely to get had me struggling not to turn on my heel and flee.

It was the image of Jane's blood-streaked features that kept my boots planted to the plank floors.

Brothel of Blood? Did that have to do with the recent deaths? Or was there something more sinister at The Orchard than I'd been led to believe?

"Well," Isabelle said from beside me, "if she's taking Alys's place, perhaps that means she comes with her own private clients, don't it, Viola?"

"It does," I said with a smile I hoped appeared less brittle than it felt. "You shan't be asked to share your wages with me. I very much wish us to be friends rather than competitors."

The striking African woman cackled at this, and several others followed suit.

"That's Ekyate." Isabelle pointed as if the woman had not given me her back as a sign of disrespect, her bare shoulders still shaking with mirth. "We call her *Kya* here. And over there are Indira and Brinda." She motioned to the Indian women, who continued to stare.

Gesturing to the olive-skinned Continental woman, she said, "That's Isobel with an O, and I'm Isabelle with an A. To uncomplicate things we call me Izzy, and her Belle, because she's such a beauty."

That didn't uncomplicate things at all, what with the spelling and pronunciation changes, but I wasn't about to mention that fact.

"Then there's Morag, Katherine, and Penelope..." She pointed at several others I hadn't time to commit to memory, then checked the few shadows and corners of the room. "Anyone else is probably already either left for the day or working."

"It's a pleasure to meet you all," I lied, receiving very few, if any, replies.

I hadn't the slightest idea if I'd be accepted among these women, but I certainly hadn't expected such a blatantly chilly reception.

Deflated, I considered my future had Mary lived. She'd said she'd set me up with a job in a house very much like this. Would just such a welcome have been awaiting me then? Would I have failed utterly and ended up like her, a Whitechapel street doxy, calling out on the streets for customers in order to afford her dingy rooms for the night and enough gin to keep the tremors at bay?

I'd planned to save her from all that... to figure out how to find us something respectable.

"Don't mind them," Isabelle hollered, not at me, but in rebuke to her silent, inhospitable colleagues. "We've had a hard go of things this last month, and it's made us all *bloody impolite*, evidently."

No one responded to her, but neither did they rebuke her.

"It's been a devastation, to lose two of us in just over a month," she explained, her empty eyes suddenly brimming with unshed tears.

"I can only imagine. I was told Alys drowned in the Thames," I said somberly.

"She didn't drown. She *was* drowned. That's the way of it," Kya said, her voice smooth as glass and her words sharp as cut diamonds. "Alys wouldn't have sullied her corpse in the Thames. *If* she'd killed herself, it would have been something more dramatic than another body being dredged out of the river sludge."

"No one knows that for sure," argued the Scot, who I remembered was named Morag.

"No one *knew* for sure," corrected Isobel—er, Belle. "But after what happened to Jane... It's hardly a coincidence, that's all I'm saying."

95

"What happened to Jane?" I asked, as if I hadn't seen the gruesome aftermath of her death.

As if I wasn't here on her behalf.

Either Indira or Brinda—the one in what I'd be forced to call a gown—glided to the middle of the room, flipping a feathered fan open to brush it against her glowing skin. "Jane's body was found upstairs a couple of days ago," she informed me in perfect English, with a haughty glare of abject disapproval. "Some of the girls think she was poisoned, but we have *no* proof of that." She sent a quelling look to the women gathered around, and they each ducked their heads in what seemed to me a deferential manner.

"Dear God, I'm so sorry for your loss." I meant every word.

She lifted a lithe shoulder and smoothed her hand down hair as shiny as a slick of ink.

"Doona tell Indira ye're sorry," Morag crowed. "She hated Jane."

It took everything inside of me not to ask why. Now wasn't the time. Not yet.

I took in the impossibly perfect symmetry of Indira's features with a more assessing eye. Could all that haughtiness contain hatred? Enough hatred to kill?

Glaring over at Morag, Indira said, "It isn't speculation regarding Alys. The coroner said she drowned herself in his official report. We should leave all of this unpleasantness to the experts and the lawmen rather than indulge in foolish theories and reckless suppositions, don't you think?"

"I very much agree, Miss, er..." I held out my glove to her, hoping to offer the respect of a proper introduction.

"Just Indira." She frowned at my hand as she nodded to me. "You would not be able to pronounce my surname."

"Fair enough." Dropping my hand awkwardly, I

turned to Isabelle, my only ally. "Is there somewhere I can put my things?"

She looked around us, seeming as stymied by the chaos of the room as I. "If you're to take Alys's old room, then I s'pose you can have her trunk over there in the corner as well. Though..." She paled a bit. "I think it still has a few of her things in it."

"Oh." I swallowed hard, wondering how to side-step this mire. I wanted a moment to look through those things, but absolutely could not in present company.

Besides, I was still uncertain what I'd be searching for.

"Well... perhaps I'll ask Mrs. Chamberlain if she might send Jane's effects to her next of kin." I followed Isabelle as she navigated around some of the chaos to a hook over a trunk in the corner nearest the door I assumed led to the establishment.

"Do you know when Bea might arrive to show me to my room?" I asked, after finally gathering the courage to undo my coat and hang it.

Peals of feminine laughter erupted from every corner.

"Oh, *la!*" Someone taunted from behind me. "Has the Queen her own self descended from Buckingham Palace to consort with Bea?"

"Need an attendant, do ye?" Morag quipped. "Doona look to poor, dull Izzy. She'd lose her way with a map and a guide."

"Izzy is one of *us*," Indira snapped.

Meaning *I* wasn't.

As an interloper who'd already secured a position of importance, *of course* I wasn't well received.

I turned to face them, and was saved from having to address this as their mirth swelled to hilarity.

It took every bit of willpower not to cover my exposed shoulders and breasts by crossing my arms. Or better yet, to throw my coat back around myself and sink into it until I disappeared.

They were all laughing at me. At how I looked.

All but Indira.

Indeed, her gaze was so hard it could have been chiseled from marble.

"You *wore* your costume here?" Belle drawled between chortles.

I couldn't imagine the reason for their glee as I glanced down at the skirt drawn to just above my stockinged knees. I'd been pleased with what I saw in the mirror before I left my home.

"What is the matter?" I queried. "The long coat with the cloaked hem and train protects me from any bother about indecency by the police. No one would have the slightest idea what I wore beneath."

Kya snorted, draping an arm around Morag. "She's certainly from the West End if she's never been bothered by the police."

"They bother me plenty," I said truthfully. Just not in the way in which they referred. My vocational complaints with the law differed in almost every respect to theirs, I imagined.

Not for the first time, I truly realized how little I understood about the plight of these women. How dangerous and incomprehensively inhumane their conditions were without willing police to protect them.

Though the profession wasn't illegal, per se, neither was it sanctioned socially. After two deaths—possibly murders—they still came to work here. Still kept a very tightly woven fidelity to one another.

Like Croft, I found them brave. Unkind and unwelcoming, but brave.

Belle stretched her lithe form and stood, stalking toward me with a feline curve of her hips. "Tell me you're not going to wear that lovely, expensive gown home once your customers have spurted their leavings all over it. My God, I can't imagine."

Isabelle wrinkled her nose. "You didn't bring *anything* else to wear?" Suddenly, she covered her cheeks and addressed my tormentor. "Oh, Belle, what if that's the only gown she's got? Need to borrow something of mine, love?"

Stunned, I shook my head. Dear Lord, there was so much to this I hadn't even imagined, let alone prepared for.

"No," I said, then held both hands up in a protective gesture against both their misplaced pity and their malice. "No, I... I don't generally keep the skirts on long enough to soil them. This is for the advertisement of services, not the application of them."

"Listen to her." Morag tossed a thumb at me. "*The application*, she says. I'll try that on for the next time I'm feigning a come. Oh, yes, ye big lad, *apply me, apply me!*"

Their laughter set my skin aflame with wrath, and I did my best to rein it in. What a piss-poor time to realize that I'd spent very little time in the company of other women, especially in groups. Growing up with only a father and six brothers, I'd learned how to interact with the world through their tussles and torments.

I drew upon those lessons now. Throwing my shoulders back, I pulled a few pins from my hair and let it fall down past my shoulders until it tickled my elbows. The scent of my rosewater pervaded the atmosphere around me as I pulled off my spectacles and glared through the mask I'd nearly forgotten I wore. I hoped to capture some of the fearless wit of the man who'd put it there.

I found the eyes of every woman in the room and counted to three before moving on to the next. Four of my six brothers had been taller than me, and I'd had to learn to wither them down to my puny height with naught but a look. "*My class* of clientele appreciate a bit of erudition and conversation before the business. My *company* comes at every bit of a premium as my *cunt*. So, if you *ladies* don't mind, I'd like to see my room before I have to entertain my first appointment."

There. That'd produced the desired effect of their silence. If my voice shook a bit, I hoped they assumed it was from anger and not anxiety.

I needed to escape. To retreat and regroup in peace so I might better prepare my next strategy. But I'd be goddamned before I backed down to this room full of vicious harpies.

This had been an absolute disaster, and I certainly wasn't making any friends now.

"Never you mind," I said to the frozen tableau in front of me. "I'll find it myself."

"All right, Viola. Put yer hackles down. I'll show ye," said Morag, her full lips pulled into not exactly a chastened line, but certainly a less caustic one. Both Belle and Izzy joined her, along with Penelope and Katherine, suddenly keen to make my acquaintance.

Well, I thought, letting out a relieved breath. Now we were getting somewhere.

I followed their frilly convoy through a short, wood-paneled hallway that could either be followed straight into the gallery room or branched left past Bea's sitting room and up the back stairs.

We angled left, and I noted that the door to Bea's sanctum had been left ajar, though the woman herself was nowhere to be found. I'd been told that Amelia would visit tonight in the wee hours to see how our scheme had fared.

It didn't seem like I'd have much to report, I thought grimly. Only my staggering failure.

"Bea usually shows you about your business in the off hours before you start working." Izzy's sudden appearance behind me startled me out of my skin. "But she ain't been the same since Alys has gone. Now with wot's happened to Jane. She doesn't seem well at all."

"Yes, I noticed she's afflicted with a terrible cough," I remarked, turning away from the door and back toward the stairs. "Was she particularly close to Jane and Alys?"

As she considered the question, Izzy screwed up her face in such a little-girlish way, I felt a little squeeze of fondness in my chest. "Jane, maybe. They were thick as thieves, but I think Alys was too spirited for her tastes. Those two were both some of her best earners, next to Indira and Kya, if I can say so. Bea is well mad at what happened to them. And some of the girls been saying she's had money troubles since—"

"Quiet, Izzy, ye daft cow," Morag growled from the landing of the stairs above us. "Bea would cane yer hide for spilling her business to a stranger."

Flushing as pink as her petticoats, Izzy cast me a chastened look and gestured with her chin toward the stairs, flanking me as I climbed.

"Don't you fret, Viola," she soothed. "Bea and the boys that protect us are never violent. She's a firm madam—strict, some might say—but a kind one. She expects loyalty, but only because she gives it so easily. It's why we all stay in this house, no matter what. She keeps us safe from the worst of it out there, and she never demands us to service her, like the pimps are wont to. Oh, and she doesn't take too much for the house."

"Her business practices are what drew me here," I said, glad to have made Izzy's garrulous acquaintance. I peeked down at her bodice, even more revealing than mine. The shimmer of a dress that, had it been more substantial, could have been a proper ball gown. "Is this not your costume?" I queried in confusion. "You wore this here as well."

"Oh, this? Well, I had a bit of an appointment before I came here." She tittered, gathering her skirts as we climbed. "Don't tell Bea... she don't like it. I've plenty costumes to change into before I'm due in the gallery."

Though Beatrice was technically my client, I decided I would keep Isabelle's confidence. In my opinion, what people did on their own time was no concern of their employers'.

"Oi, Viola, why the mask?" Belle asked, peeking over the railing from the floor above. "Katherine thinks you have been disfigured and now none of the places further west will have you."

"Actually..." I hesitated, the explanation I'd prepared suddenly feeling quite absurd. "My clients are partial to the mask; it helps them be more... revealing."

"Ah," Belle answered. "You're *that* kind of whore, then."

To what kind she referred, I had no idea, but I nodded nonetheless. Apparently, I was that kind of whore.

"Don't seem the sort," Izzy piped in from behind me.

"Well, you never know what sort people are until you have them alone and at your mercy in the bedroom." From where I drew that response, I had no idea.

And for the first time that night, the noises made by the women were those of agreement.

Progress, perhaps?

"Here ye are." Morag paused at a door to the third floor rather than the fourth, which was where I'd understood Alys's room to be situated. Or had I been misinformed?

"Butler will show your first appointment in when they arrive," Belle said brightly, as I passed her to where Morag held the door open for me.

Peeking inside, I noted that the trappings and

draperies were not as well appointed as I'd imagined. Indeed, not even as fine as the room in which I'd found Jane off the great room galley.

"Wait." I whirled around. "This isn't Alys's room."

"We know."

My head lurched painfully on my neck as Morag shoved me inside with all the strength of our barbaric ancestors and slammed the door.

I immediately whirled and seized the latch, panic ripping through my veins with a dizzying rush. Against the weight of three women—maybe four, if Izzy had betrayed me—it didn't budge.

Treachery. Nola's voice rang out in my head.

"Let me out!" I demanded, my Irish accent slipping into my diction as a creature of rage and fear rose within me. "Open this bloody door or I'll—"

"Listen," Morag hissed through the keyhole. "Someone like ye canna expect to be one of us if ye're never in the trenches with us. Ye understand? Ye'll do this job, and we might talk Indira into forgiving ye for stealing Alys's place out from under her, ye haughty trollop."

Indira—had she put them up to this?

Job? No. No. I couldn't do a job. Not here. Not in this room, where the work was *real.*

"Isabelle?" I appealed to my ally, hating the plaintive desperation in my voice. Hating that they'd revel in it.

"I-I'm sorry, Viola..." Izzy's voice sounded small on the other side of the door. "Just... just do it this one time. Well and good, all right. And you'll get out of there, no harm done."

What sort of man would these professionals foist on someone they didn't like? Surely this was some trial by fire.

I couldn't imagine it.

Or perhaps I could, which was when I became truly terrified.

KERRIGAN BYRNE

"No. No, you don't understand!" I banged on the door with the flat of my palm, ready to abandon the pretense altogether. "Please. Get Beatrice! You have to let me out."

Even through the shrill din of my horrified voice, I noted the soft click of a door on the adjacent wall.

My soul threatened to leave my body at the sound.

I jumped around, one hand pressed over my chest to keep my heart from escaping.

Two dark words wound their way to me from the shadows, traversing the space between us with a lethality that slid through my body with the precision of a blade.

"Hello, Fiona."

Chapter Eight

W hat surged within me at the sound of my name passing through those lips was not only indescribable, but unutterable.

The last time I'd seen this man, his hands were soaked in blood.

A primal protective instinct screamed at me to draw the knife I'd hidden in my boot. But what good would that do against a man known to all as the Blade? He'd earned the moniker by slicing a swath of blood through the ranks of his employer's enemies as one of the highest-paid assassins in the city. Perhaps the Empire. He was as likely to take my own knife from me and slit my throat as anything.

Emotion struck me like the sudden forks of lightning that split the sky as a portent to a devastating storm. A maelstrom built within me, around me, a chaotic tempest of seething rage and gratitude, sorrow and grief, shame and gladness.

I tumbled through the whirlwind for several breathless moments, not knowing where to land, unable to decide which sentiment to convey.

It was shock, apparently, that escaped without my permission.

"What?" The word contained every question I

couldn't bring myself to ask. Because I didn't know where to begin. I wasn't even certain that I believed my eyes.

Aramis Night Horse was a sight to behold in any environs. But against a backdrop of faded rose wallpaper and the lace curtains framing a window to the brick wall across the alley...

The length of time took me to realize he was *naked* spoke to the intensity of my disbelief.

Mostly naked. He still wore the dark leather trousers he was known for. Just nothing else.

What frightened me the most about Aramis Night Horse was that I couldn't read him. I could search the hard, marble-black eyes set deep beneath the slope of his proud brow and come away with more questions than answers.

I stared into them now, searching for something, for *anything*. Declining to look lower, though the entire awe-inspiring span of him remained perfectly, *infuriatingly* visible in my periphery.

I refused to let the long, lean, undulating muscle cresting beneath curiously hairless flesh intrigue me. I would not appreciate how he was gilded ochre and bronze by the lone lantern on the bedside table.

The bed being the only alarmingly inadequate separation between us.

Onyx hair with a length to rival mine was slicked back into a sedate queue at the base of his neck, revealing the beaded earring dangling from one lobe and the thick torque of silver at his throat. Serpentine, like the veins that wound down the strength of his arms.

Like the pit in my stomach, slithering with nerves.

He looked like the Devil's own nightmare.

In almost every culture I'd heard of, it was considered rude to stare. I didn't know if that was true for Mr. Night Horse's tribe, as he certainly had no compunctions about allowing his gaze to linger on every exposed bit of me without an iota of reluctance or apology.

"Fiona Mahoney." In a voice as smooth and dark as a moonless night, his American dialect, spiced with something just a bit more guttural, turned my name into an invocation. Whether a blessing or a curse, it was impossible to tell. "I hardly know what to think."

"What in God's unknown name are *you* doing here?" I asked in a rough whisper as I rushed away from the door, still painfully aware of the hostile women on the other side.

"That should be obvious, even to one far less clever than you." His gaze fell to the bed, and the wisp of a smile tugged at full lips that had no business near features so vicious.

"You—you shouldn't be here," I stammered, my mind still rejecting his presence. "Not when your boss owns The Velvet Glove. I very much doubt you are required to pay Jorah's rates for your... pleasure."

The suggestion of a smile vanished, prompting me to remember just how dangerous his displeasure could become. "The Hammer is not my boss. We have a mutual understanding."

"Does that understanding include following his orders in return for compensation?"

Lord, I should shut my gob. The last thing poor Bea needed was another bleeding corpse to haul away.

"He is 'Jorah' to you now?" I had the bewildering sense that this question meant more to Night Horse than the casual way in which he asked it.

Since Jorah David Roth, the Hammer, had given me leave to use his name after we were caught in a bloodbath of a gang riot together, he'd become more human to me.

But only just.

I referred to him by his name privately because it made him less of a monster somehow. I hadn't considered his leave to do so would be regarded as a novelty. Or a privilege.

"Does he not also give *you* compensation for following his orders?" the Blade asked when I didn't answer.

"He gives me corpses and bids me to make them disappear," I muttered, lowering my voice to be certain I was not overheard by the horde of females outside. "He gives me coin to scour up the rivers of blood he spills. To hide his sins. *And yours*. What he doesn't give me is a *choice*."

I spoke the truth. We both knew it.

After Mary's death, I'd been desperate and destitute, terrified of walking the streets with a butcher like Jack the Ripper after the working women of Whitechapel. I'd taken what the landlord at Mary's rooms paid me for that foul and soul-shriveling job and bought what few chemicals and cleansers I could find. Subsequently, I stationed myself outside the morgues, following the coroner's carts and boldly offering my services to the bereaved.

This was the state in which the Hammer found me. Half-starving. Homeless. Scraping together what I could to share rooms with other unfortunates in the common houses, stuffed to the rafters with those ready to slice you open, if only to get closer to the cookstove.

We'd met whilst I lingered at the scene of a suicide in Lambeth, crestfallen to be told that the body was hung from the rafters, and therefore needed no cleaning up after. Hating myself for feeling this way about the tragic demise of another human being.

The Hammer—Jorah—had offered me more coin than I'd seen in my lifetime to scrub out a room in the building adjacent to the one where the man hung. He was leery of the local constable and detective inspectors as they lingered over the suicide victim.

Much like that victim, I imagined, desperation had

driven me to agree, even when I noticed that the room had only one chair and buckets of blood beneath it.

That none of the blood on the Hammer's clothes was his own.

After that, he'd sent the Blade to "hire" me for other jobs, ones to which no police would ever be called. I refused, of course, and found out the hard way that I'd been employed by the *Tsadeq* Syndicate, a powerful gang operating under the guise of a fraternal order. A brotherhood of gang leaders who'd climbed high enough to not need dirty their hands anymore.

I'd sold my soul to man who vied with the Devil to own the sins of the city, and to refuse him was to bring my sense of discretion into question.

The only sin to the Syndicate was disloyalty. All else was vice, and vice could be sold at a premium.

At their head, the Hammer was named for one of their heroes, and he ruled with a velvet voice and an iron fist.

I had no idea how Jorah Roth and Aramis Night Horse had become associates, or how long they'd relied on each other... but when the Syndicate needed a job done with more silence and discretion than the Hammer could provide, they sent the man standing before me.

The Blade.

His sharp, unflinching gaze cut through me now, threatening to spill everything said and done between us onto the ground for the vultures at the door to pick through.

"He hasn't sent for you since... the night of the fire at St. Michael's," Night Horse said, resting his bare shoulder on the tall bedpost and regarding me with rank speculation. "You must be out of money if you're selling your—"

"I'll thank you not to say another word!" I rasped, holding my hand up against his—admittedly understandable—supposition before scurrying around the foot of the bed to his side.

He watched me approach with an avid interest that made me especially conscious of how little we both wore.

"Listen," I said in the lowest register possible. "My services were engaged by the proprietress of The Orchard after a woman was murdered here. I learned that Jane's death was the second within the space of a month. The local inspector is less than little help in the matter. And since the victim was likely poisoned, it is most probable she knew her killer. I am *supposed* to pretend to work here to gain the trust of the other women and glean what information from them that I can... and... well..."

He gestured toward the door with his chin. "And this is how it is going." His smirk first returned as a glint in his eye before it reached down to tug at his lips.

"They locked me in here," I muttered through a scowl. "I'm somehow supposed to prove myself by..."

"By fucking me." His left eyebrow rose as his finger traced the outline of my mask.

"Which I'm *not* going to," I said quickly.

"Pity," he said, his almost amiable demeanor never changing. "You are fortunate to find me in this room rather than a more... impatient customer."

"Yes, thank you ever so much for not raping me," I said, my voice dripping with sardonic distaste. Though I hesitated when the weight of his words hit me. Before I'd seen Night Horse, I was terrified of exactly what he mentioned—losing my virginity to a man who'd paid for it. Someone who'd been told he owned my body for the next half an hour and wouldn't take *no* for an answer.

I gazed toward the door, feeling some of my wrath for the women on the other side disintegrate. If only a little. This life they led...

Night Horse gathered a white shirt from where it

hung next to the washbasin and shrugged into it. I watched with curiosity as he fastened buttons from the bottom up rather than the top down. Was he leaving? Would he search for another place to take his pleasure tonight?

Now, when I watched the dark shapes of his arms beneath, I'd be able to conjure exactly what the ropes and cords of his sinew looked like.

I wasn't certain how I felt about that.

"You never told me why you prefer The Orchard," I blurted before I could think better of it.

He slid me a speaking glance. "I don't touch the women at The Velvet Glove. Neither does the Hammer."

I wasn't quite sure what to do with that information. It certainly created more questions than it answered. Of course I wondered *why*, but also how long he'd been coming to The Orchard.

And with whom he usually... visited.

Suddenly the image of Indira in his arms shoved its way into my mind's eye. An Indian and someone who had been mistakenly labeled thus, sharing their distaste for our pallor and our ignorance. Their lovely, tawny bodies tangled in the curtains of shining ebony hair as they moved in congress.

I reached for the bedpost, suddenly needing the support.

Without ceremony or self-consciousness, Night Horse wrestled the hem of his shirt into the snug waist of his trousers, and I found the sight oddly endearing and intimate.

What was happening to me?

"Why leather?" I wondered aloud, if only to fill the taut and strange silence between us. "Does it remind you of... where you come from? Of home? Surely it isn't more comfortable than linen, cotton, or even softer skins." I wisely didn't mention wool. Even most of the

Irish knew almost no one wore it for comfort so much as for warmth.

"I wear leather because it's what others expect of me," he answered.

"Odd, I didn't think of you as someone who did as others expected."

He lifted a shoulder. "It's easier to identify who—or what—I am. It disarms people from being able to do so."

I shook my head in disbelief. "I'd likewise never think of you as disarming."

As he glanced up sharply, I swore I saw something like a spark in his eyes before the cold darkness reclaimed them. "You don't think much of me at all, evidently."

"That—that isn't true." Was it?

Dropping his hands to his sides, he curled them into fists, studying me as if I were a conundrum that needed to be solved. As if I'd done something he couldn't begin to understand.

"I wouldn't blame you." He looked away. "You should hate me. I've half expected you to chase me into the shadows searching for vengeance, just like you do with the Ripper."

My every muscle tightened as my bones began to vibrate, the violent storm threatening the stillness of the night once again.

No. I violently rejected all mention of the past.

"We needn't speak of that night," I croaked, through a throat thickening with emotion.

"That night will fester like a boil if we do not lance it," he said. "I can see the fire in your eyes. Fire and my own darkness reflected back at me, even when you are civil. Do you not want to scream? Do you not want to slice and slash at me? Does your memory not burn with the sight of what I've done?"

I filled my entire chest with air until I felt as though

my ribs might separate. Slowly, deliberately, I released the breath.

So, we were going to do this here.

Now.

In the back room of a brothel.

What Aramis Night Horse had done.

For a bleak moment I was back at St. Michael's Cathedral watching in abject horror as Father Aidan Fitzpatrick, the love of my life, imprisoned the Hammer to his altar, and used a coal-heated knife to flay the skin from right below his clavicle.

For *days*, the police and I had been tearing the city apart, believing that Jack the Ripper had returned, as increasingly bloody murders imitated his own dastardly autumn of terror.

What I hadn't known until that nauseating moment was that Aidan had perpetrated the carnage himself, having taken on the mantle of an avenging angel. He'd learned of his victims' egregious sins and talked himself into believing that the voice of God granted him the power to mete out justice.

He explained to me in horrific detail just what had driven him to the brink of such madness, while wielding the knife against his next intended martyr.

Aidan had proposed to me before he left for America on a military errand, and returned to Ireland only long enough to announce that he'd vowed to become a priest.

I'd wondered why for years.

The night at St. Michael's, he revealed that he'd pledged his life to God out of guilt. Guilt for helping the army lay waste to entire villages.

Villages filled with people very much like Aramis Night Horse's massacred tribe.

After his confession, Aidan had expected me to join his righteous crusade against the evil infecting the Empire. He'd wanted me to wield the knife against Jorah myself.

It was join his holy war... or fall prey to it.

Aramis Night Horse had slithered into the shadows of the Sacristy, and with the fury of the damned, and the blood of unknown thousand screaming in his bereaved heart, he plunged his blade into Aidan's back.

Thrice.

"You must be so... appalled," I moaned, pressing trembling fingers to my lips. "Enraged, disgusted!"

"Fiona?" Suddenly he was there, towering over me, his hands encircling my wrists and firmly, gently, pulling them away from my face. "What are you saying?"

"I've wondered why I'd not been called upon by you for months. I thought it was because Jorah was recovering, but no. *No*, of course not. How could you stand to even look at me after...?"

Bemusement didn't sit easily on features as broad and sharp as his. "I didn't think you'd want to see *my* face," he said, suddenly releasing me. "I did not want these hands to offend you in your grief."

Hands now stained in the blood of the man I'd thought to be the love of my life.

For months I'd wondered what I'd feel in this moment. And for a split second, I'd felt it all... but now?

I took his hands in mine and turned them over to trace the crevices drawn into the skin of his palms. They were clean, unblemished, the flesh pale and pink, in direct contrast to the rest of his body.

"These past months, I did not grieve the man you killed. I grieved the man I loved, a man who perhaps never existed in the first place. You deserved the revenge you took, and so much more. I think a part of him knew that. And you saved my life in the process... though I somehow still find myself unable to thank you just now. I hope you can understand."

As stained with blood as his hands were, I could absolve him of this one deed. The rest he'd have to take up with whatever gods or demons received him in the end. That was no business of mine.

I finally gathered the courage to tilt my head up and saw something I'd never thought to find in his gaze.

Mercy. Compassion.

Humanity, even.

"I hated all Americans," he said. "I came here because I refused to die on the land that had been taken from me. Because I wanted to spill blood on the ancestral soil of the American machine. I thought I would hate all of you, too. That I would blame all of you."

"But you don't?"

He was silent a moment. "I don't blame *you*, Fiona. That is the only truth I can give you right now."

I nodded, both understanding him and not comprehending him at all.

"We bury this between us then," I proffered.

The dip of his chin sealed our agreement. "It is ash on the wind."

Just like the ruins of St. Michael's on the night Jorah and Night Horse had torched the cathedral with Aidan's corpse inside. He was forever canonized as a beloved priest who perished in a tragic fire.

"I'm sorry," I whispered, finally giving in to the blink that released a tear from my eyes.

His fingers closed over mine. "You should never have to apologize for being honest."

I sniffed, more aware of his warm proximity than I should have been in such a moment. "You obviously don't understand what it is to be British." I chuckled nervously. "Or Irish."

"No." He shook his head, still regarding me in that strange, soft way. "I can't begin to understand... but I do often find myself curious."

"About what?"

"Many things." His gaze snagged at the door, and he

squinted as if it might give him the power to see through to the other side. "I have decided to help you, but I want something in return."

"What is it?" I pulled my hands away from his, suddenly wary. There were only so many deals with the Devil one should make.

"I want to do something I never have before." He took a step closer, and without thinking, I retreated, his advance a waltz to which I did not know the steps.

"I—I couldn't imagine what that would be," I confessed on a shaking exhale. We stood in a room in which every conceivable thing was done for a price, and a few I was sure I couldn't begin to comprehend. "I told you, I'm not going to lie with you."

"I'm not asking you to."

"Then what could you possibly—"

He placed his fingers on my lips, pressing them gently as if testing their texture. "A kiss."

Chapter Nine

For the second time that evening, Aramis Night Horse had sent my heart galloping away from my chest in pure, unmitigated astonishment.

A kiss? Surely I'd misunderstood.

I jerked my head back, withdrawing another step to gape up at him with incomprehension.

His eyes remained on my lips, and my tongue tested them, unbidden, only to encounter the foreign flavor of salt and skin.

I swallowed, trying not to admit to myself that I didn't find the taste wholly repellent.

"Surely you're joking," I breathed in disbelief. "You've been visiting this place—this room—for who knows how long. And you're asking me to believe you've never—"

"What you believe does not change the truth," he replied with his commensurate indifference. "I require neither your belief nor your involvement or enjoyment. I'm only soliciting the experience."

He reached for his jacket and extracted a purse full of coin as I fought to overcome my crippling incredulity.

"Soliciting... the... experience?" I croaked, before clearing the disbelief lodged in my throat. "Surely you're aware that my—er—the *woman's* involvement and—dare I mention—*enjoyment* is rather the bloody point of the whole *experience*?"

"Is it?" He cocked his head to the side in a rather houndlike expression of perplexity. "So kissing is for the sake of the woman?"

"No!" I said, then paused. "Well, partly. It's for both."

"Then show me. And you can enjoy it as well" He offered me the purse of coin, the heft of which would likely cover a week of my regular sort of work.

I held up a finger against it. "No. *No*, this is not something to be paid for. Kissing is intimate. It is something people do when they—when they care for one another. When they want to show affection and veneration."

"I have had a wife, and I will not care again." His words hit like gunshots in the silence.

Suddenly so much about him made more sense. He'd told me he was hunting miles away when his tribe was slaughtered... He'd never said a wife was among the victims. I'd never asked.

"Don't say that," I said, mostly out of the manners instilled within me to say something encouraging after such a heartbreaking revelation. "You cannot know that you will *never* feel—"

"I know," he cut me off, his features a mask of stone and ice. "I have taken an oath."

"Oh." I wasn't at all sure what else to say.

"But still, I wonder..." He blinked back the void of wrath from his eyes, returning to the present conversation. "I have witnessed kissing. And my curiosity has—as you say—gotten the better of me."

"I'm astonished it's taken this long," I remarked. "I couldn't wait to kiss as a lass."

Aidan had been my first, though not my only, but I needn't think of that now.

He shrugged those wide shoulders, and I found myself lamenting the fact that he'd covered them up. "It is not something my people do."

"How odd," I murmured.

"Only to you." He raised *that* eyebrow. The one that often reminded me how truly narrow was my scope of understanding of the world.

"You're right, of course."

"My wife and I, we..." He stared at me, hard, before continuing. "We shared breath as we moved together. But your people, you close your eyes to touch mouths. I could not imagine doing so, not when the most interesting thing I can think of is watching."

I blinked several times, unable to conjure a reply, certain I'd just learned more about this man than anyone alive knew.

"Why me?" The question escaped on a whisper before the thought had fully formed.

His eyes touched me everywhere as he spoke, as if he picked the answers out of places never before exposed to a man. "There are reasons we kept our mouths to ourselves," he explained patiently. "So much of who we are—what we are made of—travels on our breath. Laughter and screams and threats. Disease and deceit. To my people, the idea of kissing is not only dangerous in that way but—" He searched for the word. "—unsanitary."

I hadn't realized that he'd glided closer until he was almost upon me, and I had to arch my neck up to see him correctly. "I'm amazed you'd want to try it at all, put like that." Come to think of it, I wasn't sure I wanted to either. "Especially with someone as... well, especially with me."

His gaze locked on mine, and I was mesmerized by the striations of mahogany and sepia in what I'd only ever thought of as the black of his irises. One would have to be this close to note the difference of the pupils.

To indulge in their secrets.

His harsh features softened in imperceptible increments as he towered over me. "When I thought of whom to indulge in this curiosity with, yours was the first name that came to mind."

I shook my head. "That makes no sense."

"It makes every sense," he insisted, lowering his head until the tip of his nose grazed my temple and the warmth of his breath stirred my hair. "I am never offended by your mouth. By the sight of your skin or the sound of your voice. Your scent is unique. Clean, even, beneath the rosewater you wear. Your teeth are well kept. Your breath... sweet." He inhaled, bringing the breadth of his chest only a whisper from mine.

I'd had decent poetry penned in my name. I'd been flattered by compliments, heartfelt and even improper. Some of them earning a kiss or favor to the presenter thereof.

And oddly, none of them had affected me with the depth of this artless honesty.

"One kiss. And I will make those women regret that they locked you in here with me."

I was nigh winded by the time I could summon an answer. "All right. One kiss only."

The words barely left my lips before he struck with the velocity of a viper. I was suddenly trapped between his body and the wall, my face captured between his terrifyingly strong hands. He angled his hard mouth toward mine, descending at a distressing pace—eyes wide open.

"No," I cried. "Wait!"

Reaching up between us, I clamped my hand over his mouth, wrenching my face to the side.

To my surprise, he instantly released me.

Sort of.

His palms rested against the wall near my temples, effectively still detaining me without technically handling me.

I wasn't the only one panting, I noted, as his breaths teased the tendrils of my hair.

I winced, realizing I'd quite literally slapped my hand over the mouth of the deadliest man I knew. I had to explain myself, and that explanation was going to be ridiculous.

But it wasn't murder I found in his gaze, as I'd expected once I gathered the courage to peek. It was something else. Something I had no name for. Something at once warm and bleak. Pensive and pleading.

His nostrils flared, and behind my palm, that full mouth wasn't dormant. It twitched and tested at my skin, which did utterly strange things to my insides.

"You have to close your eyes, or I can't," I insisted weakly.

He pulled his head back to stare down at me in that bewildered way I was coming to find alarmingly endearing. "Why?"

I lowered my hand to rest on his shoulder as I searched for the answer, realizing my reasons made no sort of sense. Until...

"Have you ever marked how a blind person makes their way through the world?" I queried. "How they rely on their other senses?"

He nodded, regarding me strangely.

I got to the point quickly: "Kissing is much that way, I've found. It's not an activity to watch. It's something to *feel*. To taste and breathe and hear."

"Hear?" he parroted, his forehead crinkled.

I nodded, trying not to be enticed by the warm scent of him, so dissimilar to anything I'd ever experienced before. There was leather, yes, and musk, but also something almost... epicurean in the masculine aroma.

Like buttered sweets baking, or a decadent roux being stirred over a cookstove.

Surely that was the only reason my mouth watered.

"Show me." He closed his eyes and awaited my demonstration.

I took a moment to process my position, to take in the length and width of the arms bearing his weight against the wall. The depth and breadth of his chest. The paradox of patience and anticipation tightening the skin over his sharp jaw.

He was the only man I'd ever met who'd asked me to teach him something. Who could admit, without a shred of ego or artifice, that there was a physical act he didn't understand, let alone excel at.

A deep appreciation for this very fact propelled me forward in that moment. A chance to kiss, rather than be kissed.

To take, rather than be taken.

The distinction was a first for me.

I watched everything his face did, every twitch of the eyelashes fanning across his dusky cheek and the flexes of his jaw that ran all the way up to his temple. My own eyes didn't close until I'd tilted my head and positioned it just right.

I exhaled a long, slow breath and fused our mouths.

His reaction was an immediate tension and a dramatic intake of air.

For an immeasurable amount of time, we stood without moving. All that existed in the world was the wall at my back holding me aloft, and the man hunched over me like a predator about to devour his prey.

But he didn't.

I was not even certain Night Horse breathed as the talk and tensions, the sins and sorrows that mortared the walls between us, fell to the ground, leaving only two people connected by very tender skin.

Without thought, my hands migrated across his

shoulder toward his neck; I was surprised to find him corded with strain when his mouth was so deliciously pliant.

I delved into the strength there, walking curious fingers against knots and sinew, kneading and pressing as my lips began to do the same against his mouth.

Muscle melted beneath my touch, his breath hitching on a dark sound.

I lost myself then. In sensation, scent, and the seductive heat of his vigor. Here, trapped in the enclosure made by his arms, his unyielding body, and the wall behind me, I felt something I hadn't been aware I'd been missing.

Safe.

Safe? Surely not here, where women were dying. Aramis Night Horse was many things, but *safe* was not one of them. He was the epitome of danger. The embodiment of it.

But as a creature of instinct myself, I sensed a shift between us. Something as tender as it was tantalizing. Something primal and protective.

I didn't know what I'd expected from him. An unbridled response, I supposed. Some sort of savage behavior more akin to the perceptions my people had of his.

Later, when my every sense wasn't overwhelmed by him, I would be ashamed of myself for even harboring such thoughts.

Night Horse, an apt and eager pupil, mimicked my movements at first, pressing and releasing my mouth. Then he grew bolder, testing the topography from corner to corner, glossing my lips with an intriguing, open-mouthed glide.

When I'd been kissed in the past, I often came away with abrasions of stubble, especially in the evening, when a man's shadow beard came in.

His cheek, however, was as smooth as mine, if nowhere near as soft.

Captivated, I shaped my hand to his jaw, charting my thumbs over the planes and hollows beneath his cheekbones. Enjoying the feel of his skin, the soft, damp sounds our lips made as they explored.

Pressure grew where we were joined. And where we were not.

While his hands remained firmly against the wall, I was hardly aware of how restless mine had become until they dropped to trace a line against the downy nape of his neck. I suddenly craved the smooth silk of his tresses between my fingers.

With tentative motions, I went to work on the thong binding his hair back.

The atmosphere between us changed, warning me only the space of a breath before the kiss deepened. Hardened. Became more carnal than curious.

He licked over the seam of my mouth, distracting me from the undulation of his body until I realized with a jolt that he'd pressed me into the wall with his entire length. My thundering heart suddenly froze as the evidence of his arousal ground against me.

Even as something low in my belly clenched in response.

In demand.

With a gasp, I broke the seal of our mouths, my eyes flying open.

The gaze that met mine surpassed the realm of dangerous to nothing less than fatal, containing a warning he manifested into words.

"If you untie my hair, you release my restraint, do you understand?" I'd never heard his voice so low. So lethal. "I will have you then."

I snatched my hands back to tuck against the safety of my own chest, my breath an unwilling prisoner in my throat.

Uttering a foreign curse, he pushed away from the wall and turned from me, dragging the sleeve of his shirt across his mouth.

A man of his word was Aramis Night Horse. He was right about how fortunate I was in that regard.

I didn't wipe him from my own lips, however. Partly because I couldn't move, and partly because he was flavored of chicory and something sharper. Like wine, perhaps.

I didn't want to brood on how pleasant I found the spice. Or that I'd enjoyed kissing a murderer.

"Was that enough?" I asked, in a hoarse voice I could hardly recognize. "Enough for you to keep your part of the bargain?"

He whirled and pinned me with glare, his ribs expanding with incredible gasps of breath.

In that moment, I recognized him not at all.

Before either of us could speak, he seized the wispy sleeve of Amelia's lovely dress and, with a quick yank, shredded it from my shoulder.

"What are you doing?" I shrieked, leaping away from him.

"Keeping my part of the bargain." Seizing my arm, he effortlessly pinned me into place. His free hand delved into my hair, without a hint of seductive intent, emerging with pins and combs until a half of the coiffure wilted down the right side of my scalp. Ripping off my mask, he threw it to the ground.

By the time I'd gathered my wits, he'd discarded the pins to the floor in a chaotic scatter and let out a sound so shocking in pitch and tone that I was struck dumb.

Something inside me cringed as he leapt onto the bed, bounding against the mattress in rhythmic jumps, emitting grunts and groans that set my skin aflame with mortification.

I'd never believe this if I wasn't witnessing it myself.

Aramis Night Horse, possibly the most stolid, enigmatic being ever to be claimed by the night, was jumping on the bed hard enough to rap the headboard against the wall. His feet bare, his shirt only buttoned to his sternum, he kicked at the covers and leapt from corner to corner.

When the provocative, guttural noises from his throat escalated, I covered my face with my hands and moaned myself.

Oh, my dear giddy aunt! Was this happening?

With a final howl, he dismounted from the bed and landed on the rug as silently as a cat, his dark skin glowing with the slightest sheen of exertion.

He looked the part of a man who'd enjoyed a boisterous tryst.

And I—I looked like the woman who'd provided him one.

Except he wasn't sated. Even someone as inexperienced as I could see that, plain as day. Hunger rippled along his skin and crackled in the air around him. He was a lion who'd not been fed.

And would now be unleashed into the night.

Where would he go, I wondered?

"I see what you meant about sounds. About the senses," he said blithely, striding to the foot of the bed as if he'd not just made complete chaos of the mattress. Bending, he retrieved an expensive, but well-worn pair of boots.

"I-I never would have guessed what talent you have for acting," I said, hoping to expel some of the strange friction inside of me.

One kiss.

I'd thought it a little thing. A harmless cost in the service of a greater purpose. I'd kissed before and had been affected physically. Or sometimes not, depending on the circumstance, or the kiss.

But this...

I was so often wrong about men. I had no idea one

kiss could change how I looked at an entire human. Could make me wish it would change how he looked at me.

But it didn't.

"You'd be surprised how much deception is needed to get close to a mark," he said, casually snapping his jacket from a hook adjacent to the headboard.

"I see..." Tucking my ruined hair behind my ear, I glanced toward the door. "Deception is uncomfortable to me. I fear I'll never excel at it."

"But your life is one of deception," he pointed out in a voice free of judgment or censure.

And still it cut me to the quick.

"Only because it has to be." My voice was stronger when I answered. Harder. My knees had regained some of their strength, enough at least to no longer need the wall to hold me up. "I wouldn't choose deceit, but it's the deal I made for that devil we both work for."

"The Hammer is not the Devil—he's merely the instrument he's named after." Night Horse flared his jacket behind him and slid his arms into it with animalic grace. "If people didn't give him their money for entertainment—if they didn't create secrets in his house and ask him to keep their sins against their god or their oaths against their debtors—he'd have no power. That is not the work of your Devil as I understand him, is it?"

I stared at the bed rather than meet his gaze, wondering if that was what the bedclothes truly looked like after a proper encounter with him. "No. You're right," I ceded glumly. "Sometimes I just wish I weren't drowning in lies."

As if he remembered something, he went to the basin and took a cloth from the hook. Soaking it in the water, he wrung it out and ran it over his face. "Lies are often kind," he said around the linen. "Lies are often essential. What is that charming saying of yours? They are a necessary evil." After blotting his face with a dry towel, he discarded both to the floor by the bed. Now it looked as if we'd cleaned up a mess.

"I don't believe in evil anymore." I told him.

"After all you've seen? Even after the Ripper?"

I shook my head. "I don't believe in good either. I don't know what we are."

What was it Oscar always said? *It is absurd to divide people into good and bad. People are either charming or tedious.*

Clever, and only slightly more facetious than my actual feelings on the matter. "I think there are people who hurt others, and people who are hurt by others," I said. "And, rarely, people who stand in between the two. Above that, who is to say what is good or evil?"

Night Horse looked at me with something very close to pity. "It is easier, Fiona, to see people for the animals that they are, driven by the baser instincts they try to ignore. Fear. Rage. Greed. Sex. Hate... revenge."

I pretended this last word wasn't pointed in my direction.

"Love?" I hated the hope leaking into my voice, an increasingly dim light flickering and dancing dangerously against the storm of sorrows that would see it extinguished.

That shrug again, one Gallic lift of his shoulder beneath the fine black coat. "Perhaps..." He stood against me once more, a pillar of inscrutable composure I could no longer read. "My hatred is commensurate to what my love once was. It is pure. And consuming."

How could he say such brutal things with such a beauteous voice?

Bending, I retrieved my mask from the floor with joints that suddenly ached with a familiar weight and pain. One that began in my heart and slowly spread through my entire body, like a spill of ink diluting water. "I do not think that love is the pure thing I once did."

"You were hurt by it," he said. "By the man who hid his evil behind God."

Hurt didn't seem strong enough a word.

"I might have been ruined by it." My face crumpled, and it took every bit of my pride not to turn away. For all the talk of lies, here was the truth I most feared. It was what had sent me to Croft's home, searching for some kind of absolution.

"I think... I think I'm broken..." I could say this to Night Horse. Because he was, too. The lone survivor of a massacred clan. A tribe, he called them. He now spent his life creating corpses in a foreign city. Not a man who waited for Hell to come for him, because perhaps he spent the rest of his life trapped in the abyss of his memory.

He regarded me in that detached, bemused way again, his head tipped to the side. "You do not seem broken."

I snorted, swallowing a flood of tears. "Women are better at hiding it than men."

Rather than handing me platitudes, he pondered this. "I do not know you well, Fiona, but I know this: broken men hurt others. Broken women usually hurt themselves. Or allow others to hurt them. But not you. You are scarred, but you are strong. You will not break."

I scoffed bitterly, crossing my arms and rubbing at bare shoulders suddenly cold. "I have you fooled. I am *utterly* weak." As evidenced by threatening tears searing the strength from my voice. "One tiny knock, and I'd shatter into shards."

Night Horse came to me, capturing my chin and smoothing away a wobble with his rough thumb.

It was at that moment I realized that kindness was its own form of cruelty, one almost more insidious than brutality. Violence and hatred broke upon one's fortifications, revealing where you might make them stronger. Malice taught you to harden yourself against it.

129

But kindness... it seeped into the weak places like a mist. Inescapable. Unstoppable.

I hated that I revealed myself to him. That I made myself vulnerable.

He read this in my eyes, I thought, and replied, "You are not so weak as you say. You feel fragile, but you will not shatter. If anything, you will detonate. I see your eyes when you are after the truth, and they are ruthless. Fragile people—broken people—don't want the truth. They usually create a story so they may live in a fiction that will keep them from their demons so they do not have to face them. But you, you chase your demon into the dark places, and that means you have courage."

Releasing me, he took up his purse of coin and left it on the bed. "Continue searching for the truth, Fiona. The search will keep you together until you are stronger."

I'd misjudged him again. He'd been neither cruel nor kind.

Just honest.

And it was exactly what I'd needed to hear.

Pausing at the door, he turned back to allow his eyes to linger over me in a way that threatened to melt the blood out of my body.

I thought we'd put our desire away, but an awareness had awakened between us. A knowledge that desire existed. That we enjoyed each other's flavor. That if I asked for another taste, he'd give it to me.

And more.

"Killing isn't all I know, Fiona," he said, his eyes so solemn I realized it was incredibly important to him that I understood this.

I had no idea what to make of it, so I merely nodded.

"My mother, she was a healer to my people," he continued. "She understood everything about earth and herbs and medicines. Knew everything that could be known..."

I blinked rapidly, wondering how his mother could have crept into our conversation after all that'd just passed between us.

"She taught me many secrets, my mother. Many things I would never share with your people, but I think... I think this will help you."

I stared at him, trying not to picture him as a curious, innocent, inky-haired little child at the elbow of such a learned and loving mother.

"What's that?" I whispered.

"A man will kill with his hands, with weapons, or with a command." He gripped the door latch and turned it. "But poison... poison is a woman's work."

Chapter Ten

❦

Woman's work.

I contemplated the words as he opened the door to reveal the handful of women lurking on the landing. They each tensed in surprise, poorly pretending they hadn't been listening to the humiliating commotion he'd made.

Were I not battling my own wretched vulnerability in the aftermath of our conversation, I'd have shared his cryptic smirk. Or perhaps succumbed to laughter at the comical display they made as he shouldered past them without sparing any of them a glance, let alone a pleasantry.

Once he'd disappeared, they tumbled through the door like a litter of unruly puppies, each spouting rapid-fire questions with simultaneous fervor.

What did he do to your dress?

Did he cut it with one of his famous blades?

What position did he put you in?

Was his sex as hairless as the rest of him?

Was it an extraordinary size in comparison, one way or the other?

Did he speak another language? Mark you anywhere?

To say I was overwhelmed by the barrage would be a gross understatement. My shock was almost matched by my temper. It was all I could do to not pick up the lamp and hurl it at their expectant faces.

Not only did I find what they'd done deplorable, but I was offended on behalf of Mr. Night Horse himself.

To them, he was a peculiarity. A curiosity. And not just because of his profession, but because of his origins. His skin. Because of the myths and superstitions perpetuated about his people. They'd used him as a punishment against me because of their prejudices against him.

Not only was Night Horse impossibly skilled in all ways physical, he was incredibly clever, wise, and not just literate, but learned.

I'd heard Americans called his kind *savages*... and I supposed he had an untamed element about him. But, by his own admission, he cultivated the effect to disarm others. In truth, Croft had shown more so-called "savage" behavior in my presence than Night Horse, who in comparison was a paragon of self-containment.

If one didn't count the murder part.

Which I didn't, as such, because I'd seen the remnants of his trade. Of all the kills I'd cleaned up after, his were the most precise. The least savage, as it were.

Lord, was I truly feeling protective of a murderer? Had one kiss muddled my morals so essentially, I could no longer find them?

Finally, it was Izzy who put her hand on the shoulder completely bared by my ripped costume, and asked, "Viola, are you all right? Did he hurt you too much?"

Her question snapped me out of my shocked, angry stupor. Because her question had not been *"Did he hurt you?"*

Because in this profession—to these women—pain was an expectation. A given. Men hurt women, especially during sex. And most especially the women they considered disposable.

"I'll survive." Summoning serenity, I pulled it around me like a shroud and decided that if I were ever to take advantage of a moment, this had to be it.

Even Morag's eyes glittered with a bit of guilt, and I planned to exploit it to the fullest.

"I've had worse," I lied, feigning a stiffness in my limbs as I went to where my mask had been discarded, retrieving it from the ground.

"Don't be cross with them. They didn't mean nothing by it," Izzy said, following me like a lost child. "We've all had to prove our mettle in one way or another, di'n't we, girls?"

I noticed the way she'd left herself out of the perpetrators. *They'd* locked me in... but she'd done nothing to stop them.

All right. I'd play along. This was some sort of initiation, and because of Night Horse's disconcerting—yet effective—performance, I'd passed muster.

Going to the bed, I snatched the purse he'd left and took a moment to reach inside, making certain to advertise the heft of it to the surrounding women. I didn't know exactly how much a week's wages were for prostitution these days, but this would more than cover it.

"Well, tell whoever's turn it was with him that I'll do the favor of giving them a night off any time." I drew the strings taut with an exaggerated motion. "The experience was well worth the compensation."

Morag's eyes became owlish over a nose that could kindly be called pert and cruelly compared to that of a certain barn animal with a tendency to find truffles. It was the one true hinderance to her beauty.

Like my bit of an overbite, I supposed.

"Ye're not saying he made ye come," she said in disbelief.

"Discretion is part of what I'm paid for," I hedged, hoping to keep the innate discomfort out of my voice. "But I will say... his taste was not *unpleasant*."

That part, at least, was the truth.

From the way they erupted with delight, I felt safe in the assumption that I'd truly taken a step toward being accepted among their ranks.

I hoped Amelia could forgive me for what was done to her lovely costume. Perhaps if I provided information along with the bad news, she'd not be too offended.

"Is he usually so generous?" I queried to the room at large. It seemed a miracle that any of these women would forgo such a payment in order to teach me a lesson. Especially if one went by how they all but salivated at the sight of the purse I still clutched in my hands.

"That's not generosity." Belle tilted her head toward the coin in question. "Alys's rates were astronomical, and she charged the likes of him double."

At that, I felt the blood drain from my face, taking any warmth regarding Night Horse with it. "He was a regular of Alys's?" I asked.

"Aye," Morag answered. "Occasionally Jane or Indira would have him if Alys wasn't working. Or sometimes all of them at once. I think the brute liked that Alys and Indira hated each other."

Izzy gasped, her hand going over her mouth. "And now... two of the three are... Dear, sweet God, you don't think *he* had something to do with it?"

I swallowed. Hard. I didn't know *what* to think. Night Horse was a killer by trade, but in the two years I'd known him, I'd never seen a woman among his victims.

Though it would be folly to imagine that I'd been privy to all his casualties, recent or otherwise. I thought of his features when I told him that two of the women at The Orchard had been killed.

He'd not asked their names.

He'd barely even flinched.

And then, with parting words, he'd pointed his deft

finger at the *women* surrounding the victims, casting suspicion upon them for Jane's poisoning, at least.

Continue searching for the truth, Fiona. The search will keep you together until you are stronger.

Had he encouraged me to search for the truth, assuming I wouldn't find it?

Suddenly the pleasant taste in my mouth turned to ash, and I couldn't swallow around the arid grit.

I shoved my reaction to this bit of information into a box and locked it away without taking the time to sort it out. I still needed to siphon as much as I could while I had these women enthralled.

"This Alys... she seemed to make enemies easily. What about friends? Did she have the same contention with Jane?"

"What's it to you?" Belle asked, deepening the already scandalizing cleft between her breasts as she folded her arms.

"It behooves me not to follow in her footsteps," I answered sharply, taking a page from their book. "If I avoid her mistakes, I am more likely to avoid her fate."

These women valued survival over social refinements, and under the circumstances, I could well understand.

"If I'm honest, none of us were close with Alys. She was... difficult to get to know." Izzy toyed with one of her honey curls, and I noticed for the first time she'd changed out of her frilly pink dress in favor of a shimmering cerulean gown, molded to her lush body. "But Jane was well liked by everyone," she added hastily. "Not an enemy in the *world*, our Jane."

"Except for Sophia." Belle smirked.

"Sophia?" I raked my memory of the introductions made below stairs.

Izzy shook her head. "You weren't introduced, and you aren't like to be, either. Moved up to The Velvet

Glove, did Sophia. She was the first to break poor Bea's 'eart."

"Lord, but this place be bleeding its whores." Morag crossed herself. "I suppose it makes more sense, Bea bringing ye on after losing three girls in such short order. She's hoping fresh blood will bring the wolves back to sniffing at our door and paying for a piece of the pink meat."

My brows drew together at her choice of words.

Belle chucked me on the arm that still held Night Horse's donation. "You don't want Bea to catch you with that. She takes the coin and gives your cut at the end of the night. She'll toss you out with the rubbish for handling the money yourself."

Surely Night Horse had known that. So why leave it on the bed for me?

"Better take it to her immediately," Izzy said. "And then we'll see if we can't find something else for you to wear before your appointment arrives, yes?"

"Of course."

We heard Beatrice before we found her, smoky voice filling the great room like that of a lieutenant colonel dressing down a cretin of inferior rank. Except, in this case, she flayed none other than a vicar with an outrage every bit as cutting as Night Horse's blade.

The portly man was tall as a Viking and built with the dimensions of a cooper's barrel, except rounder about the middle. He'd more hair coming out of his ears and nose than gracing his pate, and his skin was mottled so dark a red I wondered if he'd be left with a rash.

He clutched this morning's paper, the headline of which shouted Jane's untimely death in the boldest font imaginable. In the other hand, he brandished the Bible, from which he quoted with a fanatic's zeal. "Now the works of the flesh are manifest, which are these: adultery, fornication, uncleanness, lasciviousness—"

"Oh, stuff your gob, vicar." Bea puffed out her chest

and flicked the textured flesh of the Good Book. "Does not the verse right after the one you just quoted me have some strong things to say against 'hatred, variance, emulations, wrath, and strife'?" She lifted a carefully shaped brow. "Seems we're both sinners here."

The preacher sputtered and pulled the gold-leafed treasure in close to his chest as he searched the lavish great room for an ally.

Five men of various ages and states of *deshabille* sprawled about the chaises and chairs, caught in the middle of a smoke or a whisky. One fellow, doing his best to cover his youth with a golden mustache and long sideburns, had allowed the woman on his lap to undo his cravat and unbutton his shirt past his breastbone. They each sat frozen as a painting, apparently satisfied to let poor Bea fight this battle on her own.

"Listen, all of you!" the vicar beseeched the room. "The tragedies befalling this establishment are God's call to repentance. Do you not see? His retributions will spread across this city of sin, rippling out from this central spot like a drop on still waters. Washing the streets clean of abominations such as *her*." A long, gnarled finger unfurled mere inches from Bea's nose. "The abominable! Whoremongers, and murderers, and idolaters, and all liars shall have their part in the lake which burneth with fire and brimstone, which is the second *death*."

From beside me, Izzy seized my hand, and I read in her eyes the same thought that occurred to me.

What about the *first* death? Could this evidently obsessive vicar be responsible for the deaths of those he called abominations? Had he committed the same horrors Aidan had done, sending sinners to meet God before their time?

To my utter shock, Beatrice reacted to his threat with a very unladylike snort that dissolved into a chortle, and then an uncontrolled fit of laughter. "Sweet

Christ, Reverend Jewett," she said finally, wiping a tear of mirth from her eye. "Does it ever get lonely up there on the moral high ground? Come on, now. Why don't you go save the souls of those who are asking for it, and leave us sprightly sinners to our vices?"

"I'll thank you not to take the name of our Lord in vain." Vitriol squeezed his eyes so narrow that he could have been blindfolded with a bit of twine. "And it is my duty to spread the word of God to the faithless and the fornicators, the reprobates and degenerates. To bring them into the fold."

"Correct me if I'm wrong, but doesn't it say something in that book about 'if ye forgive not us our trespasses, neither will your father forgive yours'? If you want to take a seat for a minute, I could quote you passages on judgment, forgiveness, charity, love, *et cetera*. It seems to me you should leave the Lord's wrath to the Lord, and maybe take a page from his book and keep company with a few prostitutes and sinners before you condemn them to damnation."

I'd admit it was a decent attempt to defuse an explosive situation, but as I watched the large man step toe-to-toe with Bea, I knew it had failed.

A shadow moved, and the man they called "Butler" stepped into the light from the foyer, effectively flanking the vicar. One indistinguishable gesture from Bea froze him into an ever-ready sentinel.

Reverend Jewett lifted the Bible against Beatrice like a talisman, brandishing the paper behind it. "Keep thee from the evil woman," he sneered at her, at us, a dark hatred emanating from him. "The evil *women*! From the flattery of the tongue of a fallen woman."

"My tongue can do much more than flatter, vicar." Indira rose and ran the tip of her tongue against her wide, full mouth. "Why not pay a bob or two to find out?"

The scarlet of his skin deepened into a rather concerning shade of violet. "How dare you—"

"*Enough!*" Beatrice snatched both the Bible and the paper from the stunned holy man's grip and hurled them into the large, ornate fireplace. The patron's gasps barely had a chance to echo up to the third and fourth floors before her hand snapped back and slapped him with such force that his head wrenched to the side.

"How dare *you*, you sanctimonious bastard!" she bellowed at him, seeming to grow taller, or perhaps he shrank before the embodiment of her feminine fury. Either way, she was now—somehow—towering over a man a good head taller than she. "Do I go to your church and solicit customers? Do I come into your fucking house and bully you about your hypocritical heresy? Do I bother those men of the cloth who bury their seed in the bellies of *my* whores on Saturday night and then slander them at the pulpit on the Sabbath? *No!* No, I do not. But so help me *God*, if I see you anywhere near Orchard Lane again, no one—not even your Lord—will be able to save you from my wrath. Is that fucking clear, reverend? Now, Butler, throw this ass back onto the street so he can bray at his flock of sheep. I'll hear no more of it."

By the time she'd finished, I realized I was breathing as if I'd run a pace.

Not because I was afraid—quite the opposite. I was thrilled.

Something I hadn't felt in a long time gathered in my chest. A fervent, warm energy welled within me until I glowed with it.

Admiration, perhaps? Pride?

I'd bet my Mahoney name that somewhere in her veins ran the blood of an Irishwoman.

Before I had a chance to recover, an older man in an expensive grey suit and wearing a signet ring the size of a royal diamond set his whisky on the table with audible contempt. He stood, watching as the snarling vicar was "escorted" from the premises. "I say, Mrs. Chamberlain, certainly there was no cause for such flagrantly violent behavior. 'Tis unseemly for a lady to show such unbridled anger."

"I'm no lady, Lord Litchfield." Beatrice whirled on him, shaking her gloved hand as if it still stung. "I am a woman, and my anger is righteous. Besides, it is my duty to protect my employees and my patrons. It would be a shame if the reverend would take it upon himself to spread slanderous gossip to your constituents, would it not?"

He blanched, but rheumy eyes slid to the Bible smoldering in the flames.

What was worse to Lord Litchfield, I wondered? Blasphemy or scandal?

"It occurs to me, Mrs. Chamberlain, what with the lack of leadership of a man here... that duty does, indeed, fall to you... regrettably." Litchfield smoothed his hand down his vest and checked his watch nervously. "In that case, I have decided you're correct."

"I don't need you to tell me I'm right for it to be so," Beatrice replied.

His shoulders tensed as an outraged sputter filtered through his silver beard. "You are intolerably forward, madam."

"Or perhaps everyone else is insufferably *backward*," she said with a saucy toss of her head. "Now, I do believe you were here to take Belle upstairs and be about the business before you really aggravate me and I decide to reconsider your membership here."

Without waiting for his reply, she stabbed a finger in my direction, pulling my spine ramrod straight. "I'll have a word with you."

The hem of her dress swished behind her, making incensed, circuitous noises in the astounded stillness of the room.

With an encouraging little squeeze, Izzy dropped my hand so I could follow.

Even though Beatrice Chamberlain was neither my bawd nor my keeper, I still couldn't fight an absurd spurt of nerves as I approached her parlor. However, once I peeked around the doorway, I noted that her good spirits seemed to have miraculously returned as she rifled through her secretary drawers in search of something.

"Beware false prophets who come to you in sheep's clothing but in their hearts, they are ravening wolves." She chuckled a little as she extracted a long cigarette holder and a match. "His curate gets his cock sucked here at least twice a week," she quipped out of the corner of her mouth that held the cigarette stable.

I might have laughed if the trauma of my own brush with zealotry hadn't been so fresh. "I—I don't mean to overstep my bounds here, Mrs. Chamberlain—"

"Won't you call me Bea?" she asked, touching the lit match to the end of her cigarette until glowing embers crawled up the paper. "All my girls do."

I bit the inside of my cheek. "Yes, but... our employment relationship is a little different than theirs, and I was raised to be respectful of my—"

"If you say elders, I'm going to be cross," she teased. "And surely we are accomplices, you and I. Two businesswomen after the same thing. Revenge against those who wronged our loved ones. Justice for those girls out there who would find none without us. The wolves *are* at our door, Fiona, and I was not speaking out of turn when I said I consider it my duty to keep them at bay."

Strange, that the idiom regarding wolves had been used in my presence twice within the half-hour. And stranger still that those whom Beatrice considered wolves and whom the working women considered wolves seemed to be two separate species of male.

"I feel... prompted to warn you of those particular

wolves," I said. "History has taught us the dangers of Christian fanatics, and I've my own—Well, in my experience, they are the most likely to use the word of God as an excuse to do harm. To destroy without remorse. There is nothing so dangerous as a zealot who thinks he knows the will of a violent, vengeful God. I'd hate for you or your girls to be the one unlucky enough to garner their holy wrath."

She watched me for the space of a breath before silently offering me one of her cigarettes. I declined with a wave of my hand.

"Your concern does you credit, my dear," she finally replied. "But it is *my* experience that wolves don't kill unlucky deer. They kill the weak ones, and I'm anything but that. If a zealot wants to take me on, I'm happy to make him a martyr for his God."

Admiration at her ruthlessness welled within me. "Do you truly fear nothing?"

She threw her head back and laughed, making the violet feather in her coiffure tremble with her merriment. "Don't be silly. Only an idiot is fearless. But I've learned that if a leader shows fear, everyone beneath them—the ground beneath their very feet—will fall away."

I nodded, understanding her position. The same could be said for men in situations of power. I could only imagine how much more a woman must bear to keep her seat at the head of the table. How much more strength was expected of her.

Because no one respected softness.

"Is there a Mr. Chamberlain?" I asked, suddenly finding myself very curious about this woman.

"There was."

"You are... widowed, then?"

"Separated, actually," she said, without remorse or regret. "I realized early on in my marriage that I should not endure a man who would be ruled by me. Nor could

I endure the rule of a man. And so, marriage to one is not for me." She shrugged, moving to a sideboard to tap her cigarette into a crystal dish. "My husband is a good man, or at least he tried to be. But good people can still bring out the worst in each other..." Her eyes became distant for a moment, and she crossed an arm over her middle, a gesture I'd come to recognize as protective. "He resides somewhere in the South of France. Or Monaco, perhaps. I've no care to keep in touch."

"You do not seem to think very highly of men or their company," I blurted. "Not that I blame you."

She kept to her habit of laughing at the oddest moments. "Just because I do not pledge myself to one man doesn't mean I do not enjoy their company." Her eyes sparkled with mirth. "No, darling, quite the contrary. I am never lonely, and neither is my bed nor my heart empty. There are men I enjoy physically, socially, and even emotionally. I adore most men, in fact. However, the only time I want a man to think he is above me is when he's physically on top of me. Other than that, he can sod right off."

Little spasms of surprised delight escaped with the laugh I thought I'd lost. She joined me until we both sighed with the pleasantness of a controversial opinion shared in wicked feminine confidence.

"Do I need to be worried about what happened to you?" She flicked a hand in my direction, encompassing my ruined hair and Amelia's damaged dress.

"Erm..." I looked down and considered what I should tell her. I didn't want to get anyone in trouble, but nor did I want to lie to my client. "The girls... they didn't initially take to me as well as we'd hoped."

She made a rueful noise in the back of her throat. "I worried they wouldn't."

"You didn't mention," I said through a gathering grimace.

"Well, one never knows." She shrugged. "You're a

clever, endearing girl. I thought you had as good a chance as any. Do I need to intervene on your behalf?"

"No, actually, things worked out all right in the end. The girls had some rather interesting things to say."

She beamed at me. "I thought they might. I suppose I should have warned you... There's sort of a strange viciousness between prostitutes and courtesans. They're effectively the same trade; however, this is the only profession where the less you work, the more you can charge. Seniority and experience aren't as well respected as they are with other industries, and that creates an atmosphere of contention from time to time. Now tell me, what did you learn tonight?"

Even though I chose my words carefully, I could see the darkness gathering on her visage as I told her the pertinent parts about my interaction with Night Horse and subsequently the women in her employ.

"Surely you know some of this already," I surmised. "If Night Horse has been a patron here for some time, then you know that both Alys and Jane were particular favorites of his. And that Indira... well..." I stopped short, wondering if I should intimate that she might be next. Or that she might be suspected of the crime.

Beyond that, I had no evidence against Night Horse but a physical relationship with the two dead women.

And that he was a murderer by trade.

"If you don't mind my asking," I continued, "Night Horse is employed by a rival. Are you not afraid he'll... I don't know... sabotage you somehow?"

"Bah." She waved my words away with a quick flick of her fingers. "You know what they say: keep your friends close and your enemies closer. If Night Horse is a spy, all he'll learn from my girls is that they are successful, well trained, and happy. They know better than to share secrets, and their loyalty to me is appreciated both personally and financially."

Absorbing this, I said, "After tonight, I think it's safe to add the Reverend Jewett to our list of suspects."

Bea shook her head and claimed the chair behind her desk as if it were a throne. Or a strategy map in a war room. "If I know anything, it's men. And Reverend Jewett is all spite and no spine. I don't think he did this."

My brows slammed together. "But surely it's worth looking into—"

"Sophia," she cut in. "I think *she* is the thread we must pluck and follow to its source."

"Sophia," I agreed, though my suspicions about the vicar hadn't been satisfied. "Can you tell me why she left here for The Velvet Glove?"

"The Velvet *bloody* Glove." Bea slapped her desk with the palm of her hand as if the vicar needed another reminder of her rage. "I'd like to tear the face off that blasted blackguard. I'd give my eyeteeth to see him fall."

"You mean Jorah—er—the Hammer?"

Her eyes snapped to me, instantly alert. "You know him?"

I didn't think anyone alive *knew* Jorah David Roth. He was an extroverted enigma. All show and no tell.

But everyone who was anyone in this city knew to fear him. Including me.

"We've met," I said. "On good terms, I'd assume."

Her gaze went from keen to speculative as she templed her fingers. "Fiona Mahoney, you are a font of luck where I am concerned. Do you think the Hammer will remember you well enough to allow you to chat with one of his girls? I'd love to know what Sophia has to say about all this."

"It's certainly worth a try," I replied, which was the understatement of the century.

The Hammer would not only remember me—he owed me his life, after a fashion. A debt he said he didn't know how to repay. One I thought he'd rather forget.

"Seeing as how the night is young, I think you should make your way home to change, and then to The Velvet Glove. I doubt anything will be gained by your presence here."

"I agree." Standing, I tugged my ripped sleeve up my bare shoulder, feeling a sudden chill. "Oh, I just remembered. Night Horse left this. I'm told you're owed a cut."

"You keep it all, my dear." Beatrice heaved herself up and bustled to the door. "You've certainly earned it, and more. I'll add tonight's adventures to your fee, of course."

If I passed anyone on my way down to the dressing room, I didn't notice, as I was caught in a stupor of unexpected anxiety.

The last time I'd seen the Hammer, he was tied to an altar, the flesh being carved from his chest. He'd avoided me for these several months after, and I thought he'd prefer to continue to do so indefinitely.

After what he'd been through, if he pictured me at all, I was certain it was in his nightmares.

Chapter Eleven

❦

I f The Orchard whispered of sensual decadence, The Velvet Glove screamed it.

Beatrice Chamberlain had to keep the entry to The Orchard meticulously subtle so as not to advertise the proclivities being paid for inside. She relied on discretion and even shame to make certain her business was never fodder for public outcry or police attention. Tucked away beneath the veneer provided by a respectable inn, she existed for those who would maintain the illusion of decency.

The Velvet Glove dimmed the stars—even the moon—as it brooked no competition for attention. Shining like a lighthouse, a beacon against the night, it bade the denizens of the midnight hours to lose themselves in its magnificent menagerie of pleasures.

To partake. To indulge.

Music spilled onto the Strand along with the golden light from the open doors. The sprightly piano and fiddle beckoned to me as I stood out in the grey of the midnight hour, feeling anything but merry. A patina of frost covered the cobbles and glittering crystals of moisture hung in the air, as if decoration summoned for just such a night.

I did my best to blend with the revelers, wrapped in

the height of fashion, drifting toward the place like the keenest of moths to a flame. They made artful poses for a handful of journalists and photographers before allowing the brilliance of the grand entry to swallow them whole.

Only the *demimonde* could behave thus. Wealthy wastrels and second sons, celebrity artists, actors, and authors. Enterprising entrepreneurs.

New money.

When one was as powerful as the Hammer, one didn't need shadows in which to hide. He was safest in the spotlight, where one had to step into it with him if one wanted to challenge his supremacy.

If he was feeling kind, he'd illuminate the skeletons in your closet. If he wasn't, then he'd leave your skeleton for me to dispose of.

I didn't feel ready to see him. When in the presence of such strength, such power and resplendence, I could hardly help but be both drawn to and repelled by it. By him.

Like with Night Horse, there was *that night* to address. And I didn't know if I could bury the hatchet, so to speak, with both of these men in the course of one eventful evening. I was already exhausted.

A spurt of anxiety invaded my belly as I approached the door and was surrounded by those clamoring for a look or a comment from anyone of prominence or renown. I needn't have worried as I was neither, and able to weave my way through without incident.

Almost.

Gathering my shimmering lavender gown at my thighs, I lifted the hem enough to take the few steps up to the grand landing. As one does, I looked down to make certain of my footing, and was impeded by a hand clasped around my gloved elbow.

Gasping, I looked over at a stranger—a disheveled man with a preposterous mustache—who released me at once to retrieve his pencil and poise it above a notepad.

"Are you anybody?" he demanded impatiently.

I stared at him in disbelief. Had I ever been asked a more outrageously insulting question? Surely not.

I knew what he meant. Was I anyone of consequence? Did I possess a name his readers would buy a paper or periodical to learn about?

Thousands of people were born and died every day in this empire, and were as inconsequential as a teardrop in the Thames. If they were on fire in the middle of the street, most Londoners would be angrier at the resulting inconvenience of traffic than the loss of life.

Unless... you were *somebody*. Someone noteworthy.

"Are you?" I snapped back.

He put up his hands in a gesture of surrender. "I'm just a teller of stories, madam, wondering if you have any good ones for me."

I could tell him things that would make his eyes bulge out of his head. The media frenzy over the Ripper was one unparalleled in our city, and if he knew I had been at a scene, handled a victim...

Even a few years later, he'd be desperate for every detail. It'd make the front page. That was how much power the Ripper's name still held over the city.

Instead of answering, I turned away and hurried up the steps and into The Velvet Glove, already planning my escape through one of the more discreet back entries.

Warmth enveloped me instantly, and I blinked against the dazzling opulence of the place. Though this was a house of ill repute, the grand ballroom might be any society party at first glance.

But upon closer inspection, the cracks in the façade began to show. Beneath the winking chandeliers, men *and* women milled about billiard tables. They watched

each other with lascivious eyes as people bent and con-
torted to make the best shot, exposing the curves of
their bodies in salacious poses.

Others gathered around artfully arranged tables
playing cards or chess, or drinking from the finest
crystal whilst flirting with each other in the open.

Women employed by The Velvet Glove wore luxurious gowns in one color: crimson. They matched the
damask walls and the hue of the lavish furniture. Not
the comfortable bohemian hodgepodge Bea offered her
patrons, but upholstered to bring to mind the one thing
for sale.

Sin.

I stood out of the way, surreptitiously scanning the
ballroom for a sign of Jorah, assuming he'd be holding
court on his throne by the grand staircase. The dais he
reserved for himself and only the most prominent of
guests was full of both partygoers and their paramours,
but the man himself was nowhere to be found.

Letting out a relieved exhale, I began to catalogue
the women on the floor, trying to ascertain if Sophia
was close by. Beatrice had given me a rudimentary description: dark hair and eyes, lean and tall, with elegant
limbs and a conspicuous beauty mark above her right
eyebrow.

A bevy of brunette beauties graced the room, but I
could not make out anyone with even a scant freckle.
Perhaps it was time to strengthen the lenses of my
spectacles.

"Would the lady like champagne?" A footman in
white-tie finery brandishing a silver tray of the efferves-
cent beverage appeared at my elbow as if from
nowhere.

"Thank you, no." I smiled politely, still searching the
ballroom.

"What would you like to order, then?" he queried,
his politeness far exceeding mine.

"Nothing, thank you. I'm neither hungry nor thirsty." I was famished, all told, but something wouldn't allow me to partake of what was offered at The Velvet Glove. I couldn't say why, exactly.

"No, madam," he persisted, this time with meaning. "I'm asking what your pleasure would be for the evening. Have you a requisition I could acquire for you?"

"Oh... erm..." I looked at him then, expecting eyes narrowed in judgment, and finding only a practiced air of patience.

"I'm happy to help you, madam, as one is not wont to patronize The Velvet Glove if one does not partake in its singular delights."

I understood him with no mistake. I'd have to spend money or get out. This was not a place for people to loiter and enjoy free champagne.

"Actually, perhaps you can help me. I would love to speak with Sophia. Is she here tonight?"

He brightened at this, though his expression arranged itself into one of most sincere regret. "Sophia is engaged at present. Is there something else here that might tempt you?"

The question irked me. Perhaps it was the way he offered *something* and not *someone*.

Even here, women were things. Not people. Requisitions.

"I'm only interested in Sophia," I said, my politeness cooling into barely crisp civility. "When will she be available?"

"There are three visitors ahead of you, madam, but as always, you are invited to meet the premium to avoid the queue, though another customer will have a chance to best your price."

My brows drew together, and I ended up reaching for a glass of champagne. "Like an auction?"

He flushed a little, frowning at me as if I'd personally offended him. "Just so."

"How much?"

The number he quoted caused me to choke on my champagne, and I did my utmost to keep the resulting coughs delicate behind my glove.

It occurred to me to ask for the Hammer, but it spoke to the intensity of my reluctance to see him that I'd rather pay the price than beg a favor.

Luckily, I had that much and more on my person, as I'd made the hasty decision to keep Night Horse's coin with me even after I went home to change.

"Very well," I said, then cleared the hoarseness out of my voice with another—more careful—sip. "I shall be happy to pay that and more."

I could only imagine that my face matched the scarlet of the walls. To this nondescript porter of people, I was placing an order for sex. With another woman.

Technically, this wasn't illegal. Oscar had once bemoaned the fact that criminal sodomy only pertained to men.

"Likely because the law was written by men, and men like the idea—the sight—of women with each other," he'd said. "No man in their right mind would prohibit that by law."

I'd giggled at his wickedness that day, yet mourned the unfairness of his plight.

The footman bowed and abandoned me to wallow in my own mortification, and I did so by draining the glass of champagne.

A man caught my eye.

I hesitated to call him a man, as he was undoubtedly younger than my nine-and-twenty years. Scandalously younger... by perhaps as much as a decade. Gold hair and tawny skin festooned a form so graceful and agile that I might have guessed him a young athlete at University.

As he chatted with a small gathering over a billiard table, his smile was easy, confident, and his blue eyes alight with interest and mischief.

His beauty was undeniable. Unrivaled by anyone in the room.

I stared so long without blinking that the light began to blur a little, as did his features, until a memory superimposed itself over reality.

A blonde university lad standing over a table full of loved ones, toasting the future.

Our future.

A going-away party seeming like practice for the engagement soiree we'd host once he returned from America.

Loose-limbed confidence bordering on arrogance as he twirled me in a reel... looking at me as if *I* were unrivaled by anyone in the room.

Kissing me in the dark.

Hands everywhere.

Promising me the world.

I hadn't realized I'd been biting my lip until a sting permeated my memories and I winced.

"You like what you see?" A dark whisper in my ear tinged by lush, Russian sobriety.

With a little *eep* of surprise, I jerked taut, but didn't turn, knowing whom I would find.

Jorah David Roth would stand taller than any man I knew, his lids heavy as he looked down his patrician nose at me in wicked analysis. Hair the color of desert soil darkened with pomade and arranged with a perfect part. Eyes as difficult to read as it was impossible to determine the color. Green? Grey? Brown?

All of these. And none of these.

He kept everything about himself a secret. His name to most. His age to all. His residence, provenance, and motives were nothing but fodder for intense speculation.

I'd given him every opportunity to avoid me tonight. Yet here he was, as if eons of pain didn't lie between us.

I blinked, and the blonde boy's face was his own again, as he sifted a hand through his hair in a gesture meant to call attention to the sensuality of his every move.

I suddenly noted the presence of a few men in the room mingling with others... rather than white or black, their neckties were blood red. Like the gowns.

He was employed by the house, this boy. Jorah surely catered to every taste.

"I was merely considering how brave you are, to offer men to other men," I said, proud that my voice sounded like my own, even in the proximity of such power.

"Look around you, Fiona—my patrons are not only men. That one is most popular amongst women, actually. Women like you."

What did he mean, *women like me*?

I refused him the satisfaction he'd glean from me asking that very question. "You—you don't say."

I stared at the golden god with a very different sort of interest. A man that beautiful could be bought?

"You could afford him." Jorah's breath caressed the shell of my ear as he read my thoughts. He was the Devil on my shoulder, in a place no angel would venture. "I know I pay you well enough—if he is what you want, I will fetch him for you."

I cleared the intrigue out my throat and threw a fractious glance over my shoulder. "I'd *never*."

His chuckle washed me in shivers as I found his face much closer to mine than I'd realized. I took a step forward, and then another, creating the space I needed to clear my head.

"Never?" The Hammer tutted down at me as he straightened, seeming not to notice or care that I'd retreated. "Does it disgust you that he could be bought?"

I shook my head. "Not at all. I just..." I paused, affording myself one more glance at the lad before I turned and gave Jorah my full attention. "It's not that I *couldn't* pay," I explained. "I don't think I could pretend —no—that I could forget that *he* was pretending. That he wasn't with me because he desired me, but because I paid him to act as if he did. I don't know how you men can pay for so many women and ignore that they don't care about you."

Somehow, when Jorah looked at me, he could seem both mild and avid all at once. Lean and predatory, he stood as erect as a yeoman, hands clasped behind his back in a most unthreatening posture.

His voice, however, was utterly dangerous as he said, "It is unkind to assign to me the attributes of most men."

I could think of nothing to say to that. In truth, he was like no one I knew or knew *of*. He was bold but not reckless. Neither young nor old, but somewhere in the middle. In that span of two decades considered prime and powerful for a man. He was ruthless but proper. Cruel but elegant.

A gentleman gangster, I often called him. An elegant monster.

"Follow me, Fiona." He gestured toward the grand stairs.

"Actually, I'm here to speak to someone..."

He was already walking away, as if he knew I would go along despite my protestations.

I hated that I did exactly that. However, the fact that the suddenly muted ballroom was paying us undue attention sent me scurrying up the grand staircase after him.

We didn't stop until he led me up two more stories

and down a long hallway into a room I'd only been in once before. The Shiloh Room, he called it. *Shiloh* meaning *peace* in the language of his people.

During the years we'd worked together, I sometimes had need to meet in the office he received in downstairs, decorated to match the blood he spilled and the people he sold.

Red. Always red.

Here, not a drop of crimson could be found. In fact, the walls were papered in gold, the carpets white and strewn with lush rugs done in tranquil colors. His furniture was so delicate as to be feminine, but for the imposing desk along the back wall and a few overstuffed chairs next to the fireplace.

Half study, half sanctuary—I understood that the Shiloh room was a place very few knew about, and even fewer had the privilege of visiting.

The last time I was here, I'd awoken from being accosted in an alley by a man pretending to be Jack the Ripper. The Hammer had stitched a wound on my neck with the precision of a physician, explaining that his father had been one in Russia.

"You'd only lie with a man if he desired you?" Despite the intimate question, Jorah had put the desk between us, spreading his fingers on the surface and leaning on them, rather than claiming his seat.

I shrugged, doing my best to seem unaffected. "Terribly unworldly of me, I know, but I suppose that would be part of the... excitement for me."

He returned my shrug with one of his own. "People want what they want. And you want to be wanted. Nothing unworldly about that."

"You surprise me," I blurted, claiming a familiar chaise in the middle of the room. Not close to his desk, but not far enough away to offer offense.

"I do not take your meaning." His brow furrowed with new lines, and I realized he appeared older than the scant few months since I'd seen him last. Paler, perhaps. Not diminished or ill. But tired.

It wasn't my place to wonder why. "You're a man surrounded by sex every day. I imagine you are privy to all sorts of deviancies and proclivities. Compared to most, I must seem absurdly unsophisticated."

"In my trade, I have learned that tastes are vast and varied, and change through time and experience. I think you are sophisticated enough to know your mind about an experience you've never had." As he spoke, he made a slow and lazy assessment of my person, his eyes lingering everywhere they ought not to. "There are plenty of men who desire you, Fiona. I can name a handful of my own friends and enemies."

I swallowed, finding myself incapable of meeting his gaze.

Did he know what transpired between Night Horse and me this very night? Had he any feelings about it one way or the other?

Why would he?

"We shouldn't be speaking of such things," I said, sounding as if I'd run apace.

"Why not? If desire is what you require... you need look no further than an offer I've made to you in the past." He straightened, running two fingertips over the glossy surface of his desk as he carefully made his way around it only to lean a hip against the front ledge.

Now we had no barrier between us but a few steps and the layers of our clothing.

"I owe you a boon," he said, his lids falling to half-mast. "One I could repay to you in my bed, if you asked."

For some inexplicable reason, moisture flooded my mouth.

And temper flooded my veins.

"You truly are ruthless," I said. My gloves made a

rude noise against the half-forgotten champagne glass I still clutched. "Ruthless and—and *audacious*."

His expression was all bemused innocence as he pressed a hand to his chest. "*Moi?*"

I stood, discarding my glass to a table so I could gesture at him furiously. "You'd get me to take you to bed, to give you my virginity, and then have the nerve to call it a favor *to me*? I'd laugh if I wasn't so flabbergasted just now. The utter cheek of it!"

His devilish chuckle washed me in chills. "Has it ever occurred to you, Fiona, that I'm just that good?" He began a slow, graceful advance as alarming as it was unthreatening. I was struck by his fluid, lithe beauty. By the perfection in which his suit molded to his body and the precision of his shave against his regal features.

They said Lucifer was once the star of the morning. That he was favored and brilliant and the loveliest of angels.

In that moment I believed it, as I was afflicted with awe until Jorah stood before me, over me, vibrating with masculine vitality.

"You saved my life, Fiona." He reached out, toying with a ringlet at my temple. "But you would see God before I was through with you."

Something so girlishly giddy happened inside me that my astonishment escaped on an incredibly unlady-like snort. "Oh please," I said, desperately suppressing my surge of hysterical mirth.

Did people actually say those kinds of things to each other?

Certainly not to me. *Me*. Possessed of round spectacles and rounder hips.

His frown turned into a scowl, then something infinitely darker. "A less confident man would be offended," he said drolly.

"No, no, please, forgive me." I rushed to recover myself as he turned his back and marched to the fire, fully aware that this man's displeasure—his offense—was often as deadly as the blade's. "I meant nothing by it, I just—I couldn't—" I couldn't finish a sentence. In fact, I was afraid to address the situation one way or the other.

Again, he seemed to read my mind. "You can be honest, Fiona, as your reluctance in this regard is more insulting than anything you could say to me."

I cocked my head. "How so?"

He speared me with a wolfish look I might have called *wounded,* if the flames didn't lick amber into his eyes. "Do you truly think I would hurt a woman for denying me her body?"

I lifted my chin. "I can't speak to what you would do, as I do not know you. To me—to the world at large —you seem capable of anything."

He leaned his head to one side and then another, as if weighing my words. "A fair assessment," he concluded before turning to gaze into the fire, his features like stone. "I absolve you of all offenses, then, and give you leave to speak freely without fear of reprisal."

If it was honesty he wanted, then... "I find that the more arrogant you are, the less attractive you become to me."

"I find that is odd," he replied. "And very probably wrong."

"I beg your pardon, but I know my own mind!"

"You can beg me for anything, but it is my experience that women do not get wet for an uncomplicated, vulnerable man."

I cleared my throat, determined not to be discomfited by his lewd language. "There are many forms of vulnerability," I said coldly. "And if men would learn to exhibit some of them, they'd have to *pay* fewer women for their favors."

He infuriated me by laughing, a deep, genuine sound

that transformed him completely and stripped years from his features.

The appreciation of the sight turned my mood from tart to sour. "Why is it, anyway, that a man wants to be the first to have a woman? I should think experience and skill to be much more favorable than inadequacy and hesitance."

The fire licked shadows into the grooves and planes of his features. "There is something about a man that makes him crave to tame the untamed. To discover what has been hitherto untouched. It makes us monstrous, but there it is. To have a woman look up at him —like you are doing now, your curiosity battling your better judgment. It's a heady thing to win that battle... I imagine."

I gulped. "You imagine?"

His mouth twisted into a wry smirk. "I'm not in the habit of deflowering virgins, though I'm offering to make an exception in your case. It's an offer you have no obligation to take."

Good, because I had no intention of doing so. "This isn't a social call." I was reminding myself just as much as him. "I'm not in a state of mind to keep up with your games."

"What makes you think this is a game?" His movements became sharper, more precise, as he adjusted his cuff links and checked his watch impatiently. "Do you think I would *play* with you, after everything that has transpired?"

A glint in his eye told me to proceed with caution. It seemed to bother him in the extreme that I should draw the conclusions about him that he encouraged to everyone else.

"I think we should keep our arrangement to business," I answered, lamenting how quaint and absurd I was.

"I find myself wondering what you're doing at The

Velvet Glove dressed like that, if pleasure is not your business?" His gaze turned wintery. "Aramis Night Horse and I agreed not to send you work out of respect. Because I am not the devil you obviously think I am."

"I've never intimated that you are a monster or a devil or anything else." *At least not out loud.* "I don't understand how you could take offense at something I have not said."

He yanked his jacket down his shoulders, discarding it to the chair with distaste. His cheeks were flushed, as if the fire had become too hot for him to bear.

And still he never left it.

"I hear what you do *not* say, Fiona. Your face is a fucking open book. Even a blind man could read it. I know that even though you fear me, you think yourself above me. You blame all your sins on me, on the Syndicate, because you hide the bodies for the demons who would hurt you if you didn't."

"That is not my opinion, that's the *truth*."

"A convenient truth for you. It helps you sleep at night."

"And how do you sleep?"

"Like a child," he snarled. "Being the monster everyone fears has its conveniences. Because, you see, you don't have to dread what goes bump in the night if that very creature is you."

Puzzled, I hesitated.

In one breath he claimed to be a monster; in another he claimed a thoughtful benevolence. This was not the Hammer I'd met on any previous occasion, the unfailingly suave and insouciant criminal with no room for shame or mercy. He'd always been casually cruel. Would order a death between dinner and dessert.

This city was a graveyard of his making.

Was I to understand that my good or ill opinion of

him now influenced his previously imperturbable mood? Surely not.

"What do you want from me, Fiona?"

Despite myself, the question tugged at my heart. Because for the first time in two years, the Hammer looked like a human—his face drawn, the whites of his eyes faded, expression bleak.

It was as if winter had chipped away a bit of his soul.

Like mine.

Why should I feel sympathy for such a merciless man? I could think of no reason. And yet here I was.

Aramis Night Horse had said that men who were broken hurt others. No one in the world would look at the man before me and see anything but a paragon of power and privilege. A broken man would at least convey a weakness in any regard, and the Hammer had none to speak of.

None that were known.

But I was beginning to suspect he didn't hurt people because he was heartless. Did he and Aramis work so well together because they were a similar sort of broken? Or was I simply searching for an excuse for this softening of feelings for him?

I went to him, putting my hand on his arm. He tensed at the touch and regarded my gesture as if he wasn't certain what to do with it.

"I want nothing from you, Jorah."

His gaze snapped to mine, but he said nothing, so I continued.

"You are the only one of us who considers you in my debt, and I'm not the sort to put a price on doing the right thing."

His jaw hardened, though his fingers reached across to trace the satin covering my knuckles. "Always so noble," he murmured. I couldn't tell if he was being sarcastic or sincere.

"I'm here on behalf of a friend," I began, unable to stand the intensity of his presence much longer.

He sighed. "And what does this... friend... want from me?"

"Nothing. If you remember, it was *you* who found *me* downstairs in the ballroom. I wasn't here to see you. I was waiting for Sophia."

He blinked. "Sophia? What would your... friend want with Sophia?" A lascivious look darkened his features. "Have I read you wrong this entire time, Fiona? Do you remain unmarried because your tastes tend toward the sapphic?"

I snatched my hand away. "Some women were murdered, *actually*, and they both knew Sophia. All I'm looking for from her is information. Knowledge."

He made a sound in his throat between a chuckle and a groan. "Have you switched careers in earnest, Fiona? Have you officially donned the badge of detective?"

"I hardly know what you're talking about." I crossed my arms.

"Surely you know you're one of the most meddlesome women I've ever met."

"That's not true!" My hands dropped to my sides, curling into fists. "I'd rather have my nose in a book than someone else's business."

"Unless the Ripper is whispered over a corpse."

"He has nothing to do with this," I said. "I'm merely doing a favor for a friend."

He nodded, and suddenly all trace of that vulnerability I read in him was gone. Perhaps I'd imagined it in the first place.

Good. It was easier to dislike and fear him than to sympathize with him.

"Am I to understand you are back to working, then?" he asked, going to his desk and shuffling a few papers.

"Evidently," I replied, turning away from him, needing the heat from the fire. "You're free to resume sending me your victims, if that's what you're asking."

I could feel his gaze like a cold dagger in my back, but I didn't give him the satisfaction of my reaction.

"I will send you Sophia," he said in a voice devoid of inflection. "But remember, Fiona, knowledge isn't always power—sometimes it's a liability."

"What are you talking about?" I asked the flames.

"I'm warning you, that is all," he answered, his long stride taking him to the door. "In my world, information is the primary reason corpses are delivered to your door for disposal."

Chapter Twelve

✦✦✦

As I waited for Sophia, I tried not to wonder how many customers she had to service before taking the time to see me.

The footman who'd assisted me downstairs ushered me out of the Shiloh Room and down a floor to a small bedroom done in greens and golds. It was neither lush nor sensual, but serviceable and neat.

Considering what might have just happened on the mattress, which was made and smoothed, I opted to sit on the trunk at the foot of the bed.

It was in these moments alone, with nothing to keep my brain occupied, that I was at my worst. Pervasive thoughts taunted me, swirling like dry autumn leaves against the wintry ground, fragmenting to litter the pathways of my mind with crunchy, untidy scraps.

The youth downstairs who resembled Aidan had shaken me more than I wanted to admit. I didn't just avoid thoughts or memories of him these days—I slammed the gate, lifted the drawbridge, and fled.

Tonight, that escape drove me right into the image of Aramis Night Horse. Where had he gone when he left The Orchard? Whose arms—if any—had he found himself in next? I knew our kiss aroused him, but did it affect him? Likely not, as he'd made it clear that a kiss held no meaning in his philosophy. Though he paid me his coin, nothing about the act itself felt like a transaction.

It had been... rather lovely, actually. One of the best I could remember. The Hammer had been right, in a way, when he listed the reasons why being someone's first was a heady experience.

It felt like a privilege watching a curiosity become a discovery.

Beyond that, I'd enjoyed Night Horse's company. And granted, he was not only easy to look at but extraordinary and intriguing as well. The scent, textures, and yes, *flavor* of him all enticed me.

But should they?

Decidedly not. He wasn't a man to trifle with. To expect anything from. I knew this with all of myself. I'd be an absolute idiot not to.

Wandering away from Night Horse led me to Jorah, as they were inexorably linked. He wasn't a man I dreamt about in my quiet moments alone, but in his presence, it was nearly impossible to conceive of another man.

And he wanted me. Not even Aidan had made that so outrageously obvious. There had been passion between us, but also restraint. Respect.

I didn't think Jorah respected me at all. But he'd promised to worship my body. I couldn't say I didn't wonder what that would be like.

And then there was Croft.

Was there Croft?

Forbidding, scowling, commanding, *irritating* Grayson Croft. A man on the correct side of the law who often did all the right things in the wrong way. He could be as violent as Jorah, as callous as Night Horse, and as stern as the Queen. I'd never taken a particularly close look at him, because he was gruff and cantankerous and hardly had a kind thing to say to me.

But there were moments when he looked at me...

I ran a hand over my face, scrubbing away these fanciful thoughts.

Lord, but Aunt Nola had been right. I was surrounded by dangerous men, and at any moment one of them might betray me. If I meant anything to any of them, it was as a pawn, a plaything, or a pain in the arse.

I'd do well to keep that in mind and keep my eye on what was important. I had an Aidan-sized hole in my heart, and I had to fill it with meaning. With strength and purpose, and perhaps the feminine rage that kept spinsters warm at night.

The door opened with such force that it crashed against the wall, making way for the raven-haired, crimson-clad whirlwind I assumed was Sophia.

I stood, ready to introduce myself, but she swept right past me.

"God's ballocks, I'd rather stroke a cock than a man's ego. It takes less fucking work, don't you think?" Stomping to the washbasin, she splashed her face with some water and snatched a cloth to wipe the cosmetics from dripping into her eyes.

Obviously, I hadn't the reference between the two, but I was ready to agree with her wholeheartedly. I opened my mouth, but she saved me from having to reply.

"Apparently, the boss has commanded I tell you everything I know about whatever you have to ask me, and that won't take but five minutes, as you can fit the whole of my knowledge in a thimble." Laughing at her own joke, she retrieved a chamber pot from beneath the bed and took it to the corner of the room.

She fluffed her skirts over it and squatted without so much as pulling the screen in front of her before a stream hit the porcelain.

Gasping, I whirled around to preserve her privacy,

168

then berated myself for doing so, as the woman seemed less than worried about it.

"Place this fancy has a privy and everything," she explained with a rough chuckle. "But the maid on this floor is a right bitch. I like to make her empty my pot."

I nodded, though I couldn't tell if she was looking at me or not. "My name is Fiona."

"I know."

Her stolid manner unnerved me somewhat, and I thought she enjoyed doing just that. "I don't want to take up too much of your time," I told the opposite corner of the room. "But I came to ask about Alys Hywell and Jane Sheffield."

"I knew Alys was fish food weeks ago, but what's this about Jane?" Her voice had hardened, and I turned back to her, mortified that I'd announced the death of an acquaintance while she was having a wee.

She'd finished, thank God, and was discarding her drawers to a laundry bin near the cupboard while looking at me expectantly.

"Of course, you haven't heard. Jane was found at The Orchard a couple of days ago. She was poisoned, they think."

Sophia chewed on the inside of her cheek, sizing me up with dark, calculating eyes. "Alys *and* Jane are dead, then? Interesting."

"Why interesting?" I asked. Why choose that word rather than *tragic* or *sad*—or *joyous*, if that was how she felt?

"Just is." She shrugged a bare shoulder and returned to the washbasin. Selecting a clean cloth, she dipped it in the water and scrubbed a floral-scented soap over it until suds appeared against the fiber. "You're not here because you think I had anything to do with it, are you?"

Well... I hadn't lent the thought a great deal of credence until I'd met her. "Actually, I..."

"And who are you to be asking, anyhow?"

"I've been employed by Beatrice Chamberlain to... look into their deaths."

"What are you, some sort of lady private detective?" She scoffed. "Old Bea *would* hire you over a man, God love her."

"You and Bea—Mrs. Chamberlain are on good terms, then?" I circumvented her question with one of my own, though I hated when people did that.

"Oh, sure. I've nothing against her whatsoever." Putting her delicate, slippered foot up on the bench I'd only just vacated, she reached beneath her skirts with the soaped cloth and began to wash herself—intimately.

This time, I forced myself not to look away. If Sophia's gaze could be unflinching and bold, so could mine.

"Why leave The Orchard, then?" I asked.

She regarded me as if I were a special sort of dullard. "Why does anyone do anything? Money, of course. The Velvet Glove pays half again what I'd make at The Orchard, and the clientele are toffs rather than the working class, and prone to show their favor with jewels and the like. Additionally, I get these accommodations as one of the premier girls." She gestured to the room. *Her* room. "Beatrice had a favorite brunette already. Though I don't know what she's going to do now..."

"You mean Alys?"

"I suppose." Finishing with her... ablutions, she tossed the cloth toward the laundry bin, missed, and didn't bother to pick it up.

"Can you think of anyone you'd suspect would want Alys dead?" I asked.

"I'd no complaint with her, but Alys collected enemies like some people collect pretty butterflies. Like she was proud of them, and all." Bustling to the trunk I'd sat on, she all but shooed me away so she could toss it open and retrieve clean undergarments. "I thought Alys's death was an accident or, you know, she went for a holiday swim, like so many others."

We shared a grim look for the many who dove into the Thames around Christmastime.

"There's some speculation regarding that," I said. "But what about Jane? Who would want her dead?"

"Besides me, you mean?"

I did my best not to gawk, as I certainly hadn't expected her to just come out and admit it.

She cackled at my discomfiture and stepped into her drawers, drawing them up past the silk stockings with the most intricate lace garters I'd ever seen.

"You know how men are like dogs?"

"Yes, but you'll have to narrow it down for me to catch your meaning," I said before thinking, which amused her mightily.

"I like you," she announced, chucking me on the shoulder. "I'm referring to how the smallest ones are the meanest. Jane was like that. Pretty manners, innocent face, tiny little thing with eyes big as saucers. Tear your heart out of your chest... right before she eats it. I was the only one at The Orchard not taken in by that manipulative cunt. Or maybe not, now that she doesn't have me to torment any longer."

"What do you mean?"

Moving to a messy dressing table, she spread her skirts to sit, arranging bits and bobs in order. I was behind her, so she met my gaze in the reflection of her mirror. "The Orchard has—had—three sparkling gems in its crown. Alys, Jane, and Indira. And now only one is left?"

Indira? I couldn't say why, but something in me didn't want to believe it. The woman was as regal as a royal and just as mysterious. Elegant, exotic, enigmatic. It was a potent mixture. Intoxicating, even.

But venomous?

"You really think she would be capable of murdering two women she worked closely with?"

Sophia paused from powdering her bosom to cast me a derisive look. "You don't strike me as simple, Fiona, but one would think in your line of work you'd know that just about anyone is capable of any kind of thing. One can never tell by looking."

"You're right, of course." We shared a bleak moment of understanding before she went back to preparing her face for her next customer.

"If you want my opinion, it's probable Indira needs to be kept safe. She's more likely to be the next victim than the murderer." Sophia looked over her shoulder at me. "She has too much class to get her hands dirty."

I nodded. "One of the other girls, maybe? Or what about clientele? Can you think of anyone in particular who would like to hurt Alys or Jane?"

Sophia snorted as she pulled her lips tight to apply rouge. "Men love to hurt whores. It's what they do best."

"I... I understand that."

"Do you?" she asked. "Do you, really?"

"I do." I met her challenge with preternatural calm. "I was best friends with the whore who was hurt the very worst."

One brow lifted. "You think so?"

"Mary Kelly."

"*Fuck.*" It was her turn to gape, a charcoal pencil frozen halfway to her eyes.

"Indeed," I agreed. "I still search for him in my spare time."

"So this... is personal for you?"

"In a way," I admitted. "I have no personal stake in what I'm asking you, though. I did not know Alys or Jane, nor am I much acquainted with Mrs. Chamberlain. So anything you say to me will not be regurgitated to anyone at The Orchard without your consent. I just... I want to know who is killing prostitutes. *That's* what is personal to me. That is why I was hired to help, because the detective inspector on the case isn't inclined to work hard on behalf of two dead whores, as unfair as that is."

"Only them out there—the privileged few—expect fairness." She gestured with her chin toward the door. "The rest of us know better."

"We do. But that doesn't mean we don't deserve justice."

"I don't believe in justice."

"All right, revenge, then." I allowed my frustration to escape in my tone. "I'm not the law. I'm simply looking for the truth."

For the first time since we'd met, she was quiet. Pensive. Dare I say chastised.

"It's Davies isn't it? The inspector?"

I nodded. "How did you know?"

"He had to have spent half his salary on Alys, if it was a penny. Obsessed, he was. When she went private, and refused him, it was in front of the entire brothel full of lads. I cackle about it still in some of my favorite moments alone." She smirked, but it faded quickly. "He's had it out for The Orchard ever since."

I plopped down on the trunk, exhausted by the notion. "A detective investigating his own crimes. He could get away with anything."

"The police are famously terrible at policing their own," Sophie pointed out, drawing a lid down so she could line it properly with the coal. "If you've already ruled out Charles Hartigan, then I'd say Davies is the next likely bastard."

"Charles Hartigan?" I echoed.

She sent me a queer look. "No one mentioned him to you?"

I shook my head.

"I suspected some of the girls were seeing him on the side. I heard Jane was one."

I was almost afraid to ask. "What did he do?"

"He was unnatural. Eerie and quiet, nice but clinical, like a doctor, but powerful strange."

"Strange because of what he did to you?" I asked when she seemed lost in an unpleasant memory.

"Because of what he wouldn't do."

I wrinkled my nose, trying to make sense of what she was saying.

"He only got to Alys and me in The Orchard. He would pose us. Force us to wear his costumes. Tie us up and the like."

"Doesn't that kind of thing... happen regularly?" I scratched at an imagined itch on my scalp.

She rolled her eyes. "Well, surely, if someone fucks us after. He never did. Just looked and took pictures. Didn't even touch himself. Now tell me what sort of twisted bastard does a thing like that?"

I shrugged, mostly because I didn't understand. She found this man odd because he didn't want to pay her for sex? Only lewd photographs? One would think that was easier than giving him the entire business.

"Bea was well furious, but even after she gave him the boot, we'd see him lurking about Fleet Street with his camera 'round his neck. Leering at us. Always kept a bit of rope on him, may the blighter hang himself with it." She brightened with an idea, or a memory. "I saw him talking to Alys once on the street, and she spat on his shoe. We both know men who would kill over less. Even the Hammer, who's not wont to raise a hand to us, might put us in the ground for such disrespect." She spritzed herself with a heavy fragrance as if she hadn't just said her boss might kill her for insulting him.

I wasn't the only one who feared such things from him.

I held my glove under my nose, fighting a mighty

sneeze. Once I'd beat it back, I asked, "Do you know where I could find this Charles Hartigan?"

She shook her head, somber for once. "And I wouldn't go looking, neither. Men like him, they go to church on Sunday and still have bodies buried in their root cellars and bones in their coal boxes."

"I have to look," I said, with just as much gravitas. "But I'll not go alone."

Standing, she smoothed her hands down her dress, looking fresh and lovely in the soft light. "He's close enough to The Orchard, has to be, because he always walked and never took a hackney."

"You think he works on Fleet Street?" I asked.

"Maybe. Prattles on about formulas and medicines. A chemist or a physician, like I said."

A chemist. Or a doctor. They'd know exactly how to administer a poison... or even a medicine that was toxic in large doses. I needed to go to the coroner, Dr. Phillips, and see what he thought of Dr. Bond's assessment of Alys's death.

And to ask if he would give me access to Jane's autopsy report.

"Thank you, Sophia—you've been *so* helpful."

"Wasn't nothing." She opened the door to usher me out, and we made our way toward the cacophony of the grand ballroom. "Will you give Izzy my best if you see her? She always seemed so young for her age, you know, sweet. I felt a bit protective of her." Sophia nudged me. "Just don't tell the others I have a heart after all."

"I will, of course," I promised with a genuine smile.

She paused at the end of the hall that would lead us to the grand ballroom stairs and looked down, reaching into her bodice to adjust her breasts. That accomplished, she threw her shoulders back and faced the grand ballroom head-on, taking in as deep a breath as her corset would allow.

"Sometimes I wonder why the sun bothers to shine

at all on this world." She said the bleak words in a sprightly tone, though she visibly fought to find her smile. "Ah well. There's work to be done."

"Always," I said with a conspiratorial wink.

She put a hand on my elbow, squeezing it softly. "I hope you find him, Fiona."

"I'll do my best not to let Alys and Jane down," I vowed.

"No. I hope you find him. The Ripper. For Mary, Elizabeth, Martha, Catherine, Annie... for all of us who are afraid to be done like them."

"I hope I find him too," I said, and my voice was as hard as I'd ever heard it.

"When you do, I remember that justice and revenge can be one and the same. I hope you do what needs doing. There's no call for a man like that to walk the world."

I looked after her as she stepped from the shadows beneath the glitter of the ballroom.

"No," I whispered. "No, there is not."

Chapter Thirteen

✥

I never saw him coming.

I was thinking of Charles Hartigan, Inspector Davies, and Jack the Ripper. About all the men who liked to hurt women, who enjoyed them tied and helpless or posed as supplicants in death, as Jack did. Men who behaved violently in the face of rejection, as if a woman's scorn was the greatest challenge to their masculinity. Their civility.

Their humanity.

How many women died because they'd made a man feel less about himself?

The world of men disrespected women every moment. The weights and measures of their standards were so physically impossible, we caged our ribs to meet it. They laughed at us constantly, patted our heads like children, and told us to sit down. They deemed our fears as hysteria, our needs as inconsequential, and our opinions as adorable or ignorant.

And though it irked us—at times enraged us—we did what we must to endure.

So much of our energy was expended just surviving men.

Burning with an ire that heated me against the frozen night, I marched from The Velvet Glove to The

Orchard in the wee hours. The intensity of my wrath melted ice crystals unfortunate enough to drift into my atmosphere before they even landed on my skin.

The Strand turned into Fleet Street at Chancery Lane, and I needed to be alone with my thoughts, so the length of the walk didn't bother me. Nor did I feel particularly unsafe at such an hour.

London was a city in which one was rarely alone, even on a night this dark and cold. We owed our lives to the denizens of these hours. The doctors and nurses. The midnight bakers. Watchmen on their fifteen-minute routes. The revelers. The lantern-lighters. Midwives. Even the lonely and those who offered them comfort, if only for a few minutes. They outnumbered the cutpurses and crooks by far.

Even so, I was always armed and usually alert.

After such an eventful day, however, I was both too distracted and agitated to sense the shift in the shadows until I was yanked into them.

Rough hands wrenched me off my feet like I was a rag doll and dragged me into the recesses of an alley where my assailant tossed me against the brick wall. The gap was so dark and tight, I hadn't known it was there.

I shrieked as he ripped my spectacles from the bridge of my nose, and again when I heard them land on the cobbles with a sickening crunch. A hand slammed over my mouth and nose, inhibiting my breath but saving me from the juniper reek of gin drenching the man.

He had no face.

At least here, where he'd drawn me deep enough into this crevice, this purgatory between the dazzle of Fleet Street and the shadows of Hell, I couldn't make him out.

He wore no hat, but I had the impression that a dark mask or cloth covering of some kind obscured his appearance. Thin enough to breathe through, but tight enough to distort any defining features.

With preternatural strength, he held me above the filthy floor of the alley with an arm dug into my ribs. I kicked and struggled like a fox caught in a trap. I was no rabbit, no animal of prey, but still my bones were delicate, and I had to rely on my wits and guile more than did predators larger than I.

The toe of my boot found his shin, and I dragged it down the bone, eliciting a growl of fury that could have been made by a bear. Instead of backing off, he bore down, using his entire body to imprison me to the wall.

I panicked then, fighting for a life that only had minutes left if I could not find some air. Bucking and pushing with all my might made little difference. I pounded on his shoulders, wishing I had no gloves on so I could claw his face. Frantically, I searched for purchase to bring my knee into contact with any part of him. The softer the better.

Except the part I found was not so soft, but hardening rapidly, and my struggles only seemed to make matters worse.

I went limp in his arms.

If fighting didn't work, there were creatures that would play dead until an opportunity presented itself, and *then* they would strike.

This was more difficult than frenzy. It took every ounce of willpower I'd ever cultivated to force stillness. Readiness.

"There's me good girl." Uncultured and uncultivated, it was the most garbled Cockney I had encountered.

The Irishwoman in me wanted to bite him, to spit and fight and flail.

I was *not* a good girl. I belonged to no one.

And he belonged to the Devil, which was where I

would send him just as soon as I could move and breathe at the same time.

"I seen you working at The Orchard, and I thought to meself... why do those idiots pay for a fuck when its easy as this to take one?" Keeping one hand over my mouth, he reached down with the other to gather at my skirts.

I no longer had to pretend.

Terror stole the strength from my bones and what little breath I had in my lungs. I hung like a marionette, my limbs trembling and the champagne roiling in my empty stomach, attempting to escape into my throat.

An insidious numbness swamped me, threatening to lift me out of my own skin. It'd happened before, when I was pulled into an entirely different alley by someone claiming to be the Ripper. I'd somehow stepped outside of myself, watched the man hold his knife to my neck from the safety of the street lamps.

I couldn't let that happen again. Not here. I had to keep my wits about me, or I would not escape this intact.

Or at all.

In a sudden moment of clarity, I remembered something my father, a policeman, had said to a thief who stole into our neighbor's home and held an elderly mother hostage. He'd offered him the contents of my mother's jewelry box as well.

And the moment the greedy bastard relented, Frank Mahoney bashed him over the head with it, wrestled him to the ground, and led him away in irons.

Behind the man's smothering palm, I nodded, hoping he'd read permission in the gesture. I arched my back, crushing my breasts to his chest. All I had to do was make a would-be rapist think I wouldn't fight him. That I would let him have his way with me.

So I could get to the knife in my boot.

It had the desired effect. At least his hands released

me, and he pulled away. Though I still couldn't see his face, I had the sense that I'd confounded him. I took the opportunity to crouch down and reach for my blade.

Just in time for his fist to crunch against the brick wall where my face had only just been.

I hadn't disarmed him with my submission... I'd infuriated him. The inhuman bellow of rage signaled that now it wasn't my virginity in danger, but my life.

Seizing the knife, I surged up and, with a vicious cry, buried it in his chest.

Or would have, had he not moved enough for the blade to only find purchase in his shoulder.

I'd never stabbed anyone before. Never perpetrated any such violence. The knife slid in with more ease than I'd expected. I gave a gasp of utter shock before it registered that I wasn't out of danger.

By the time I'd gathered my wits enough to realize I had to try again, the man jerked away with a grunt and a curse. He staggered backward, and now he stood blocking my escape to Fleet Street.

The alley was a nook, not a true passage between buildings, so my only option was to try to make it around him. Not easily done in dress boots and an evening gown, but I had little choice.

And he had my knife, should he retrieve it from his shoulder. A more seasoned fighter would have had the presence of mind to keep their grip, to pull the blade out and try again for an organ. Because anything less wouldn't fell a man of this size.

Recovering from his own shock, he loomed ever larger, his breath coming in great, pained gasps.

"And here I was told you were clever." He reached across his chest to grasp the weapon.

It was now or never.

He couldn't know that this was my greatest fear. Not rape, per se. Not even murder.

But what struck me with the most terror in the world was the thought of bleeding out from stab wounds in a dark London alley, discarded like so much rubbish. Like one of the Ripper's victims.

With a sob, I dashed forward, everything in me reaching for the gas lamps of Fleet Street beyond his hulking form.

The back of his hand connected with my face with such force, I flew into the wall.

The last thing I remembered was the sickening sound of my head as it bounced off the brick.

Chapter Fourteen

❧❧❧

Screams roused me.

In that dark place between unconsciousness and awareness, one of my most vivid memories plagued me like a dream. My mother, telling me not wander into shadows or put myself in danger, because a banshee might come for my soul if I died from a misadventure.

Or worse, I'd become one.

A woman who died in so much pain or suffered such indignity that her spirit was cursed to relive the torment, and to visit it upon others. Her very scream would age a man twenty years, or warn another woman of her impending death.

Had one come for me now?

Was it Mary?

Did she screech at me from the shadows, shaming me for not delivering her wronged soul justice before seeing me off to Hell?

I blinked rapidly against pinpricks of perception permeating my confusion. The taste of terror in my mouth, thick and metallic. A throbbing ache in my head a percussion to the cacophony around me. Foul-smelling grit beneath my back. Cockney insults. Rank, shocking curses from shrill female voices. Two of them.

Not Hell, then.

Just London.

With a groan, I tested the mobility of my limbs before struggling to roll to my side. Pushing myself up with weak arms, I saw rocks and rubbish pelting my assailant, driving him back toward Fleet Street.

An owlish swivel of my neck revealed none other than Indira and Izzy behind me, charging like infantry, hurling projectiles with the accuracy of any rifleman in the Queen's own regiment.

How the devil had they gotten here?

It didn't matter. I'd never been happier to see anyone in my entire life.

I sat, immobilized, as they drove my attacker out of that alley with their female ferocity. After snarling some of the ugliest words I'd ever heard in my life, he turned tail and ran, the outline of my knife still embedded in the sinew of his shoulder.

I hoped it hurt like hell. For *weeks*. I hoped the wound turned septic and killed him.

"Oh, Viola!" Izzy wailed, dropping to her knees beside me. "My God, when I saw him strike you into that wall, I was terrified he might have actually killed you. I'm so relieved." Throwing her arms around me, she squeezed me hard enough that I grimaced.

Everything vaguely hurt.

Indira gently disentangled Izzy from me, and I sent her a grateful look. Though my eyes had now adjusted to the darkness, her dusky features were a little more difficult to make out than Izzy's in the gloom of the alley. I couldn't read her expression.

"You're bleeding," she said with little inflection.

I lifted my hand to where the throbbing in my face had concentrated to my bottom lip. Gingerly, I tested the skin there and found it broken. Blood now stained my best pair of white gloves, along with whatever unthinkable filth could be found in this alley.

"Is anything broken?" Izzy smoothed her hands down my shoulders and arms, searching for injuries that couldn't be seen. "Can you walk?"

I moved one leg, then the other. "I think so," I answered. "Once my head is finished spinning."

"You poor, poor thing," Izzy said, taking my hands and giving them an encouraging squeeze. "I'll be grateful tonight in my prayers that we happened along in time."

Indira rummaged around in her purse, extracting a vial and a handkerchief. Covering her finger with the cotton, she tipped a small amount of the contents of the vial onto the cloth. "This will stop the bleeding." She lifted the handkerchief to my lip.

I flinched away, eyeing it with apprehension. "What is it?"

"Only cayenne and oil," she explained impatiently. "It will burn but will stop the bleeding and clean the wound."

"Indira knows just everything there is about everything," Izzy said with unabashed veneration.

"Were your parents healers or doctors?" I asked, turning my face back to Indira with some lingering reluctance.

"My parents were forced to harvest spices grown on the land taken from my family by a wealthy English merchant, who sold me to pay their debts," she answered matter-of-factly.

I could think of nothing to say that would properly contain the depth of my regret on her behalf. Luckily, she pressed the handkerchief to my lip, and the burning sting emptied my mind of all vocabulary.

"I told you it would hurt." I heard Indira's smile in her voice better than I could see it.

"Do you just carry this abominable concoction around with you everywhere?" I asked, my speech becoming a bit muddled due to the pressure of the handkerchief and a warm numbness settling into my lip.

"Not only is cayenne helpful for nicks and scrapes, but also for the blandness of British food." She capped the vial and slid it back into the velvet bag.

I couldn't help but think of Jane...

Spices were often herbs, and herbs were often used as medicines.

Or poisons.

"Thank you," I said, a sudden and intense gratitude overwhelming my suspicion. "Really. Thank you so much. I don't know what could have happened had you not come along."

I did know, of course, we all did, but it remained unspoken as they helped me to my feet and made certain I was steady before accompanying me toward Fleet Street.

I was about to ask one of them if they could look for my spectacles, but the crunch of glass beneath Izzy's shoe told me that she'd found them on her own.

I winced, but said nothing when she muttered about the rubbish littering the ground. I kept spare spectacles at home and was due another trip to the optometrist.

"Did you know that man?" Izzy asked, "Is he a customer?"

"Don't be daft," Indira answered before I could think of a reply. "She's not one of us, Izzy. She's been deceiving us from the start. Have you not noticed she suddenly has an Irish accent? That she never took a client last night after what Morag and the lot did with Night Horse? Bea would have put any of us back to work. But she sent this one home to lick her wounds."

Indira was canny indeed.

We approached Fleet Street with caution, peering this way and that in case my attacker lurked close by.

Finding no sight of him, Izzy turned to me with eyes as wide and moist as a hurt child's. "Is this true, Viola?"

Their faces glowed shockingly pallid in the street lamps, shadows dimming the delicate skin around their eyes, and lips tinged blue against the brutal cold. They looked like a couple of ghosts in long, pale gowns and winter coats.

I was certain I matched them, racking shivers beginning to overtake my own bones—they had as much to do with the aftermath of the violence as the cold's relentless grip.

I took the handkerchief from my lip and looked down at the stain of my blood before dabbing it against the wound again. Wonder of wonders, it barely bled at all.

"My name is Fiona Mahoney," I confessed. "I am a postmortem sanitation specialist, but Beatrice and Amelia asked for my help in ascertaining what might have happened to Jane and Alys."

Izzy brightened a bit. "Amelia Croft? She used to do Alys's dresses. I bought a few costumes from her as well. Should have known from that beauty you wore last night."

Indira ignored her, crossing her arms over her bosom. "You were investigating us," she said, leaning against the edifice of the solicitor's office in front of which we lingered.

"But that makes no *sense*," Izzy blurted before realizing she'd been a bit loud for the hour and glancing up and down the street surreptitiously. "Bea can't suspect one of *us*. We–we're family."

"Of course it makes sense." Indira rolled her eyes and lifted her velvet bag, extracting a cigarette case and a book of matches. "If someone's been murdered, it's most likely family what done it before a stranger."

"Not in our line of work." Izzy sniffed, though the moisture gathering her lashes into spikes had yet to fall.

"I was supposed to find out if anyone knew useful information they were hesitant to share with Bea or the police, that's all." It wasn't a lie, but a soft truth. "She's afraid for her girls."

"With good reason, apparently." Despite Indira's measured demeanor, her hands shook as she held the match flame to the edge of the cigarette paper. The blue at her lips was more visible against the flame, and I knew we needed to get out of the cold. It had begun to drive even the heartiest of night revelers inside.

"How did the two of you get into that alley?" I asked, peering into the mouth of darkness.

"This building is connected to a shop what stores produce," Izzy explained. "We cut through a small cellar sometimes on our way back from a job."

I nodded, immediately regretting it as my headache intensified. "But... I thought Bea didn't allow you to work outside of The Orchard."

I hadn't thought Izzy's eyes could go any wider. "Oh, please don't tell her," she begged. "Bea doesn't allow it because she can't keep us safe out here. But we were offered an amount we couldn't let pass us by."

Indira exhaled a plume of smoke on a long breath. "I'll do what I have to," she said in a voice made of iron. "I want out of the life."

Izzy turned those big, blue, heartbreaking eyes on Indira. "You mean you're leaving us?"

"Why do you think I'd take a job like this one?" Indira gestured back toward the alley from which they'd come. "It's not that I'm not grateful to Bea for giving us a good place like The Orchard to work. But this isn't what I wanted."

"What do you want?" I asked.

"My sister and I are saving to buy a spice shop. We almost have enough."

"That is a lovely idea," Izzy said wistfully, burrowing deeper into her coat. "I hope you get that shop someday, Indira."

"What about you, Izzy?" I asked. "What would you do?"

She giggled, but it was a hollow sound with no mirth. "Oh, I don't think I'll age out of the life, just have to charge less, I suppose."

"You mean you'll do this forever? Do you want to run your own house someday?"

She shook her head. "I don't think about the future much. Sometimes I feel like my grave is already dug. I'm just waiting to fall into it."

Suddenly I wanted to embrace her. To save her. To save every woman who *had* to make a living on her back or on her knees and give them a warm place protected from the men who would have them. Who would hurt them. Who would paint the matching haunted looks etching bleak shadows on both their faces.

"Postmortem sanitation specialist," Indira said, testing my title. "You clean up after the dead."

"I do. I'm not accustomed to investigations, all told. I don't even know why I thought I could fool anyone. I just... the thought of what happened to Alys and Jane— I couldn't let it be. I hope you're not too cross."

Indira dropped her cigarette on the ground and put it out with the heel of her boot. "You should stop looking for Alys and Jane's killer," she said gravely.

"I thought Alys drowned," Izzy said, apropos of nothing.

Indira ignored her again, stepping to me and checking the wound on my lip. "The wrong person is likely to find out you're investigating," she warned me. "You could be next."

At the serious, sinister look in her eye, the bottom dropped out of my stomach, and I had to force myself not to retreat from her.

"We would never want anything to happen to you," Izzy agreed, wrapping her arms around herself and giving an exaggerated shiver. "It's too cold to stand out here. We'll see if we can't find some proper salve for your lip at The Orchard, and you can have a chat with Bea."

"I'm supposed to meet Amelia there anyhow," I said, fighting a yawn to avoid stretching the cut in my lip.

"Let us be off, then." Izzy hooked her arm through mine.

"Amelia has already been and gone," Indira said. "Before we left."

"Oh, that's right," Izzy said. "Bea will still want to look after you, though. And it'll get you out of this horrendous cold."

"Actually..." I gently extracted myself from her grip. "... I think I want to go home. I have people there who will tend to me."

Indira nodded and raised her hand to hail one of the few hackney cabs still loitering in the main thoroughfare.

Izzy wrapped her arms around me, clutching me tight. I held her, too, this woman who was still a girl in so many ways, who seemed so lost and young.

Was I ever like this?

"I can't stop thinking about Night Horse," she said against my ear. "I would have fought Morag harder had I known..."

"Don't worry about it." I pulled back and attempted a strange, painful half-smile. "He and I are acquainted. Nothing happened."

"You certainly keep dangerous company," she added.

She had no idea.

"Perhaps you can convince them to be kinder to the next woman?" I suggested.

"Perhaps," she said, looking unconvinced.

Once I settled into the hackney, I waved to the women, expressing my gratitude once again for their help.

"What address should I give the driver?" Indira asked.

I didn't know why I recited the one I did...

Maybe because of something the giant in the alley had said before he struck me.

And here I was told you were clever.

Someone had *sent* this man to hurt me.

Which meant I was getting close to the truth.

Chapter Fifteen

❦❦❦

I was just stepping out of the tub when Grayson
Croft arrived home.

Amelia had taken one look at me, filthy and
trembling on her doorstep at half-four in the morning,
and pulled me inside. She forbade me to speak until
she'd poured tea, heated a bath, stripped me down, and
settled me in. She'd washed my hair as I scrubbed the
filth from my face and body, the water soaking the pervasive cold from my bones.

This was why I hadn't gone home.

Because death often waits until dark, a lamp was left
for me, a fire in my bedroom grate, and supper in the
larder.

But my house would have been cold and quiet.

Or worse, I'd have had to immediately concoct a
story to calm Aunt Nola, who might have woken little
Teagan with her hysterics. Mary would have drawn me a
bath, but between her daughter and my aunt, some of
the chaos would have fallen to me to contain.

I loved every soul that lived in my house, but I
couldn't face them all. Not tonight.

Amelia had explained that Croft was called away to
another scene where two men had conducted an illegal
duel whilst drunk. One of them had not survived.

Declaring my gown beyond hope, she'd hurried out to find something for me to wear. Not a minute had gone by before I heard the front door open and close and Croft's worried call up the stairs.

"Amelia? What's going on? Every light in the house is blazing."

"Don't come up," Amelia sang back down to him, her Northern accent thickening around her brother's.

"You have someone up there?" he asked.

"I'll meet you in the kitchen. It's not what you think!"

"Better not bloody be." I could just picture how he said this, out of the side of his grim mouth as he marched into the kitchen.

Amelia appeared in the doorway as I clutched the towel to my body. "Put these on and join us when you can, dear. I'll make sure my beast of a brother behaves."

I slipped on the high-necked nightdress, the wrapper, and the large knitted shawl Amelia had thoughtfully provided. No doubt she'd guessed that the gown would be a bit tight, as I hadn't her petite frame. She provided me the shawl to protect my modesty as she'd not brought me my underthings or corset back.

The gown dragged a bit on the floor, as I hadn't her statuesque height, either. After I violently worked the knots from my hair, I left it to dry down my back in frizzing waves and returned the brush to the dressing table.

All this time, I'd avoided looking in the mirror, but curiosity overcame my reluctance.

My bottom lip felt like it had distended to the heft of a tin of lard. The cut throbbed and stung, and I had to be careful not to make certain expressions or it'd begin to bleed again.

Unable to see much detail without my spectacles, I leaned in close to the dressing table mirror to examine my face.

It felt worse than it looked, really. Though the skin was still pink, and I was flushed from the heat of the bath, I could tell where the bruise would be tomorrow. My cheek was swollen as well, and I'd barely paid it mind. It hurt a great deal less than where my teeth had dug into the inside of my lip.

I appeared much younger than my nigh thirty years like this—my eyes dulled by a patina of exhaustion, but rounded with the shock of the day. My hair drying wildly. My lips pale from strain except for where the skin had broken.

I looked almost like Indira and Izzy had, but for the blue of the cold.

Venturing out into the hall, I could hear the cadence of their frantically whispered conversation as I made my way down the stairs in my bare feet. The fifth stair creaked, and the house fell instantly silent.

I hurried the rest of the way down, as I had no reason not to.

They were possessed of a perfectly fine parlor with a cheery fire crackling beneath the mantel, but chose instead to gather in the kitchen.

I realized why when I opened the door.

Amelia bustled about the kitchen adding leaves, berries, and seeds to a mortar. She looked up as I entered, and then swiftly over at the Arthurian table where Croft sat like a hulking sentinel.

He stood at my entrance, and I realized in that moment what the phrase "murder in the eyes" truly meant.

It was when green irises turned black with a rage so dark and lethal that it might overtake one's humanity with true demonic wrath. Croft *vibrated* with violence.

"Gray has agreed to *sit down* and be still while you tell us—me—what happened to you." She pulled a high-backed chair from the table and settled it next to the warmth of the cookstove before shoving a cup of tea into my hands. I didn't miss that she angled the chair away from Croft, so we could not see each other before she went back to her mortar and pestle.

Taking a sip, I winced at the heat on my lip, but sighed when the brew, sweetened with honey, made its comforting way all the way down to warm my belly.

She didn't look at me, and I sensed that she was giving me the space to gather my thoughts, which I appreciated.

"I was walking from The Velvet Glove to The Orchard to meet you and Bea when a man pulled me into an alley."

I heard a chair scrape against the floor behind me, and Amelia turned to pin him with a ferocious glare. "As far as I can tell, you aren't hurt anywhere but your lip and cheek, is that right?"

The bath, I realized, was an examination as much as it was a kindness. She was able to ascertain by the way I reacted, by the condition of the rest of my body, how much damage had been done.

Which, she'd correctly surmised, was none.

"What about the things that don't leave a mark?" she asked, more for her brother's benefit than mine, I thought.

I shook my head. "I was only hit once. But it was enough to put me out for a few seconds."

A foul curse colored the air behind me. "Tell me you found a constable. That they're out there looking for this dead man."

"Gray, you promised," Amelia said.

"He could be stalking his next victim," Croft argued.

I shook my head, feeling absurd. "I don't think he'll go after anyone else tonight. In fact, I'm certain he was sent after me... and I think that's because I asked someone the right questions about Alys and Jane." I looked at Amelia, who'd stopped grinding, to gape. Then over my shoulder to Croft, who was staring at the teacup in front of him as if he wanted to smash it with the tight fist he'd rested on the table. "Besides, I stabbed him in the shoulder with the blade I keep in my boot."

"There's my girl." Amelia flashed a victorious grin as she poured the ground herbs and such into a dish and unstoppered a vial with clear liquid, adding a few drops. "They make you bleed, you give them one better."

"What the hell were you doing at The Velvet Glove?" Croft asked, earning him a scathing glare from his sister.

"Visiting Sophia," I answered.

"Sophia?" Brows drawing together, Amelia brushed her hands down her apron and turned to me with the bowl. "What does she have to do with any of this?"

I sighed, searching a mind muddled by pain and fatigue. "I suppose I should start from the beginning."

"Put this on your cut first," Amelia dipped her finger into the bowl and brought out a paste that looked like something one might fish out of Teagan's diaper. "You'll wear it for five or ten minutes and wash it off. Have a care to not ingest it, even though you'll want to lick your lips. It'll send your stomach into an upheaval you'll not soon forget."

She reached for my lip, and I flinched back. "What's in it?"

"Best you not worry about that, but you'll wake up tomorrow and find most of the swelling magically gone. And the bruise will heal at least twice as fast." She winked.

I looked around at the charming and often lovely sprigs of leaves, bundles of flowers, and dried herbs hanging from every part of the kitchen. A few live ones still flourished in the anemic light of the window, hearty plants I couldn't identify.

I'd become leery of such things lately... because I'd seen the blood leaking from Jane's every orifice.

But this was Amelia Croft. A friend. I'd nothing to

fear from her. I was merely overtired and being ridiculous in my hesitancy.

Lifting my chin, I allowed her to dab just a touch of the strong-smelling stuff on my lip.

That finished, she began to scoop the rest of the paste into a familiar-looking vial. "I'm sorry whatever information you learned tonight came at such a cost. Are you truly all right?"

I checked for the truth, and found that I was.

Shaken, of course, but also glad. Not glad to have been attacked, but to have learned that I'd ruffled guilty feathers. "I'm better than expected under the circumstances. What's bothering me the most is that there are too many suspects. We'll have to narrow them down, and I've no idea where to start."

"Let's start with a detective." Amelia gestured back toward the table, and I stood, allowing Croft to move the chair so that we all sat around it.

"Let's hear it," he said—rather evenly, considering what his face had been doing this entire time.

"I talked to the girls at The Orchard, and they had more than a few things to say," I began.

I was careful not to disturb the poultice on my lip as I told them about Morag's jealousy of Jane and Alys, and her tendency to bully the other girls. I moved on to Indira's possible play for the premier spot at The Orchard now that her rivals were dead, despite her dream of a spice shop. I spoke of the Vicar Jewett, who'd spouted threats in the open with many witnesses. Of Charles Hartigan and his confrontation with Alys on the street and Inspector Davies's dangerous obsession with the same woman. I even mentioned that Night Horse had had... relations with them both, though I left out *our* specific interlude.

I didn't miss the tightening of Croft's jaw at the mention of The Velvet Glove, the Hammer, or the Blade.

What Croft didn't know... well, it was better for the both of us.

"Everywhere I turn, I find motive for Alys's death, but the only time I heard a word against Jane was when Izzy told me she and Sophia were enemies," I finished, motioning to Croft. "That is why I went to The Velvet Glove. Bea and I agreed that speaking to Sophia was important. And Sophia pointed a very strong finger at both Inspector Davies and this Charles Hartigan."

Gingerly, I touched the poultice on my lip, astonished to find that it was already drying.

"I just wish I knew who he was," I murmured idly. "Or, rather, *what* he was and where to find him."

Amelia held up a finger. "You never spoke of this Charles Hartigan to Beatrice, did you?"

I shook my head. "I hadn't the chance yet, what with..." I gestured in the general direction of my face.

I thought I might have heard a growl coming from Croft's direction, but I didn't look.

Amelia continued, "I remember Bea saying some time ago that she was having problems with a businessman in her area—a photographer, no less. She had to ban him from The Orchard because he would pay the girls to take explicit pictures and then sell them to line his own pockets. She was furious, not only because he spooked the girls and accosted them in the streets, but he was also making profits off her employees with another illegal business."

"She was angry not to get a cut?" Croft guessed.

"More than that." Amelia chewed her own lip. "She was worried that photographic evidence of indecency would bring the police to her door for her or the girls. Especially when she was beginning to cultivate a good relationship with the local detective through Alys." She turned to Croft. "This was when Alys and Inspector Davies were still banging the bed knobs. Before their relationship went sour and he turned against them all."

Croft's lids narrowed in miniscule increments. I could hear his brain churning, whirring like the cogs and wheels of Big Ben with a narrative that was beginning to feel just as complicated.

"Who do you think did this, Fiona?" Amelia asked me. "If you had to listen to nothing but your intuition?"

I thought about it, rubbing at my throbbing temples. "I think I agree with Sophia. I'm starting to suspect Inspector Davies, and I really think this Charles Hartigan is worth looking into. But what I can't figure is why they would kill Jane when, as far as I know, they only had motive against Alys. That's the missing piece here, I think. What does Jane have to do with all or any of this?"

"And who sent this man to... to what? To kill you, too?" Amelia shook her head. "I can't bear the thought."

I closed my eyes, letting out a breath. "You didn't see this man. I'd say he's bigger even than you, Croft. If he wanted me dead, I'd be dead. He held me above the ground and nearly smothered me with his bare hands. He grabbed and groped at me, but didn't actually hurt me until I stabbed him. And even then, he slapped me with the back of his hand, and I went reeling into a brick wall. I think an actual punch might have broken bones, all told."

Croft slapped the table, causing both of us to jump. "I have had e-*fucking*-nough of this. Do you hear me?" He stood, marched toward the stove, and then paced back. "I'm going to find this photographer, Hartigan, and question him properly." He cracked his fingers.

"I'll go with you," I offered. "Let's do it tomorrow—er—today after we've slept."

He jabbed a finger at me, his shoulders heaving against his jacket. "You are going nowhere except home. Not back to The Orchard, not to The Velvet *bloody*

Glove, and certainly not to see a man suspected of murdering two women."

My mouth dropped open, and for a moment, it didn't even hurt. I wasn't certain if that was the poultice or my sheer exasperation at his overbearing audacity. "I will go where I like, Inspector Croft, and we both know a woman like me could get more information than a menacing detective."

"Don't be ridiculous." He gestured sharply. "Getting information is what I do."

Amelia stood at my back. "He'll be on guard around you. But around a desperate, lovely woman in need of some... discreet photos taken? He's certain to be bold. He won't be able to help himself."

"You could be close by as a witness," I said. "Ready to arrest him should I find evidence of a crime, or," I added for his benefit, "the barest hint of danger."

"Brilliant," Amelia agreed with a satisfied smile. "That's settled. I'll dig out some cosmetics to help with your bruising."

"*No*," Croft roared. "This isn't happening, Fiona. How could you chase after this villain now? Look at what you've done to yourself already."

"I didn't do this!" I said. "It was done *to* me. Which means I'm onto something, don't you think?"

He didn't deny it, but a breath whistled through his tensed throat. "One of these days, you're going to get yourself killed, and I'd... I'd never hear the bloody end of it from Amelia if anything happened to you."

It was almost like he cared. "I'll survive, Croft. I always do."

He snorted. "Until you don't. And then what?"

"Isn't that everyone? Nobody gets out of this existence alive. *You* risk your life all the time to keep people safe, to find out who is dangerous. May I not do so as well?"

"That's different, and you know it." His jaw jutted forward, advertising his increasing stubbornness.

"Because I'm a woman?" I asked.

"Yes, dammit. Because you're a woman."

"Well... that's just too bad." I lifted my own chin, setting my jaw as I'd often done against seven burly brothers. "History is littered with women who risked—who lost—their lives saving others. They're not always as canonized as soldiers are, or generals. But women can be fierce and cunning and yes, even dangerous."

"Don't I know it," he muttered.

"I'm not going to war or anything, Croft. I'm trying to stop women from dying in the streets, because no one else will."

That poked at him, and I watched the fire flicker in his eyes before it banked. His face softened just a few increments, and it made breathing easier somehow. "You don't need to martyr yourself for them, Fiona. That doesn't help anyone, especially Mary."

As his ire died, mine kindled, and I clenched my fists at my sides, unaware that Amelia's shawl slipped from my shoulders. "Obviously, martyrdom isn't my first choice, and maybe, just *maybe*, I'll be successful in solving these crimes. Did that ever occur to you? How about this? I wouldn't have to put myself in such danger if men like *you* and Davies did their bloody jobs!"

"You seem intent enough to do it for them," he growled. "And don't you dare put me in the same category as Davies."

"I'm trying to *help* these women. And it's a damned shame your sister had to ask me to, when she has you in her back pocket. You're one of the best detectives in this city, and you can't be bothered to lift a finger?"

"It's not my case! I'd be putting my job—our livelihood—in jeopardy."

"But the man in charge of the case could be the murderer!" I gestured wildly, knowing full well someone might hear us on the street, and I didn't even care. "Davies is so dirty he could bathe in the muck of the Thames and come out smelling better. Tell me how any of these women will get justice when there's none to be had?"

He turned from me and jerked the kitchen door open, letting in a blast of cool wind. He stood in the doorway for a moment, skin red with rage, now visibly prickling with the cold as he took three slow breaths. "Where's your proof?" he asked the night. "What evidence or information can you provide other than the words of a few—"

"A few what, Gray?" Amelia's voice could have been lost in breeze of a moth's wing, but it landed like a hurricane.

He whirled, and it was the first time I'd ever seen Grayson Croft look afraid.

"Amelia." He reached for her.

"A few *what?*" She let out a dry sob, wrenching away when he would have taken her hand. "A few whores? Who would listen to what they had to say, right? Who would take their word?"

His features crumpled. "You know I don't think—"

"Fiona." Amelia's face hardened, her expression turning into something so forbidding, I wanted to flee from it.

She never looked at me once as she addressed me, but held her brother in thrall with the force of her gaze. "Be a dear and go to the washroom. Use warm water to clean away the poultice. I need a private word with my brother."

"Of course." I gathered the shawl before rushing out.

Croft was staring at the wall behind her as she laid into him.

I crept back upstairs to wash and was chagrined to find that their conversation was not private at all. Not with how Amelia's voice projected. I learned more about her past as I washed away the miraculous herbs she'd used to aid my healing.

I learned how young she'd been. How many times she'd come home looking just like me.

And worse.

He'd saved her life when he was old enough. He'd put men in the ground for her, or at least I thought that was what she alluded to.

I rinsed my lip and scrubbed my face, lingering until mine were the cleanest features in all of the world, and still she railed.

Croft listened. To his credit, he listened.

Eventually, I wandered back down the stairs, avoiding the creak of the fifth. I thought she knew I could hear. Or maybe she was so angry that she didn't notice.

I thought about leaving, but couldn't very well do so in a nightgown.

With a puff of my cheeks, I sank onto a chaise in the parlor across the hall from the kitchen and tucked my feet under me.

"You're going to that photographer's shop with her in the morning. You two will see Charles Hartigan. And you're going to help her find out if he slaughtered my friend and threw her in the river, do you hear me?" She should have been a warlord, fearsome as she was. Or perhaps a queen. I'd have followed her into battle.

Croft replied, but his voice was at such a low register, I could only make out two words.

Fiona. Danger.

Whatever he said brought Amelia's fury back to a manageable level. "She knows her mind, and she'll have you to protect her."

He said something else, but I caught none of it.

"Grayson," she said, with the hoarse bitterness of a thousand wronged women. "I do not ask you for much, and I never leverage anything I did upon you. But this... this is important, little brother. And you *will* do it. If not for Alys or for Jane, for *me*. Because I couldn't raise you both... and I chose you, Grayson. I chose *you*, and I need you to return the favor."

I knew what she was talking about.

The child.

The child she'd given up for adoption to Kathryn Riley.

I closed my eyes, swamped in grief and guilt. Somehow, I knew Grayson Croft was doing the exact same thing.

Grief, I had learned several times over, was the price we paid for love. For family.

I understood that as fervently as I knew that tomorrow, Croft and I would be paying Charles Hartigan a visit.

Chapter Sixteen

❦❧

Even on a winter's morning, where I had to squint against the light, Croft seemed swathed in shadow.

He still wouldn't look at me.

So we both stared across the street at our quarry. C.B.H. Photographer and Gallery was tucked into a market square off Warwick Lane, a comfortable jaunt from Fleet Street by way of Ludgate Hill. Some tidy residences and apartments mingled in and over specialty stores such as bookshops, tea shops, and even a cutler's livery and guild hall.

Inspector Croft and I loitered out of view of the frosted windows, bundled in winter wear and our own discomfiture in each other's company.

I hadn't meant to sleep the morning away in Croft's parlor. I'd planned to request a frock I could wear home beneath my soiled coat and meet him in the morning.

I'd have it laundered, of course, and send it back with compensation and my undying gratitude. However, I'd lost consciousness before the Croft siblings concluded their fraught interaction.

The smell of bacon had roused me a handful of hours later in the exact same position I'd tucked myself into on the chaise.

I told myself that thoughtful, observant Amelia had tucked the soft blanket around me upon noticing that I'd unwillingly surrendered my consciousness. That the scent of clove and vanilla only lingered because the blanket resided in the same house as inspector Croft and his pleasantly pungent tobacco.

He would have likely shaken me awake and stuffed me into a hackney. He wasn't the sort to abide un-wanted guests. And if his foul temper this morning was any indicator, he *clearly* wasn't in any mood for me.

Not that I blamed him.

He'd barely said a word around the late breakfast Amelia provided, and avoided us altogether as she deftly altered a gown and applied cosmetics.

I'd never worn much beyond a dash of color on my cheeks or my lips. Looking in the mirror after she worked her magic, I'd gasped at the sight of me. Her poultice had worked its magic and, though the cut still remained, no sign of swelling endured the night.

Bruises had disappeared beneath a heavy layer of powder she'd moistened to create a sort of... Well, I wouldn't know what to call it. Not a paste and not an oil. Something pigmented and perfectly matching my skin.

It even covered the freckles on my nose, and I found myself turning this way and that, appreciating a brief moment of the porcelain skin my vanity had al-ways coveted.

She led me downstairs dressed like a gentlewoman down on her luck.

I immediately convinced myself I wasn't affected by the sight of Inspector Croft scrubbing the dishes like they'd done him a disservice.

After a cursory glance, he'd grunted something that might have been approval as he rolled his sleeves down and cuffed them.

The next thing I knew, Amelia had bundled us

against the late-January weather and pushed us out the door with words of encouragement like a mother might with two recalcitrant schoolchildren.

A total of fourteen words, three grunts, and a sigh had been spoken between Croft and me since then.

Not that I'd been counting.

We'd backtracked to my house in Chelsea so I could retrieve a fresh pair of spectacles and check on Aunt Nola before leaving for Fleet Street.

The hackney fare would be astronomical, and I silently thanked Night Horse for the extra income. However, it was Croft who paid the driver and sent him on his way.

We'd been waiting almost half an hour outside of C.B.H. Photography for the shop to empty of customers. It seemed the fates worked against us, as one or two people always wandered inside, interspersed with two families dressed in their Sunday best, no doubt sitting for portraits.

I didn't realize how tightly I'd been clutching a spire of the black wrought-iron fence across the way until the cold seeped through my mittens.

"I don't know what I expected." My thoughts become tangible in a wispy puff of frigid afternoon air. "I suppose I thought to see a furtive, weaselly man with scores of young women traipsing through his shop. This all appears so... so normal."

I expelled warm breaths into my mittens and held them against my nose, which threatened to go numb. A curse escaped me as I remembered Amelia's warning about rubbing the powder off my skin.

"I suppose there's no convincing you that this is a fool's errand," Croft huffed, pulling his hat lower over his shadowed eyes. "No hope that you'll listen to reason and allow me to question him properly?"

I really did attempt to look apologetic as I looked up at him. "Did you not mention that if you shouldered your way in there and stumbled upon evidence, it might not be admissible."

"I did. But the police have ways around—"

"But if I found evidence that he showed me of his own volition, not only could I bring it to the police, but I could also testify against the man."

He grimaced. "So long as no one knew I'd accompanied you."

"That's a fact easily avoided," I said brightly. "I think this might just work. Perhaps the London Metropolitan Police should regularly employ people like me to act as spies in clandestine investigations. Now *there's* a thrilling prospect."

"If by thrilling you mean terrifying, then yes," he answered grimly, squinting over at the shop as if were he to try hard enough, he might see through the shades. "And facts—truths—should not so easily be avoided. There are laws and rules for a reason, often to protect the innocent from being entrapped by the police."

"I understand what you're saying, but you have to admit that not all innocent people are protected from the police."

His jaw worked to the side, and still I imprudently continued.

"People like Mr. Hartigan are protected, but not people like Alys or Jane, or even—"

He whirled on me. "What are you suggesting we do, exactly? Subvert the entire rule of government? Create anarchy? Abolish the institutions of law and order?"

I gulped, realizing I was woefully out of my depth when it came to the information I needed to engage in such a conversation. "I'm not suggesting anything, per se. Just making an observation."

"Well, I think—"

"Look!" I gripped a gather of his coat at the shoulder, motioning down the way where a well-dressed man held open the door for his wife and two children.

"Those were the only customers left in the shop. We should go."

Glad to escape whatever disparaging thoughts Croft might have been about to elucidate, I set off toward the shop at a brisk pace.

"Remember not to shut the door if you can get away with it," Croft said as he fell into step beside me. "And to disassemble any notification bells if at all possible so I can position myself inside if you go to the back."

"I know," I said curtly. "We went over this at breakfast."

"Photographers work in the dark, so he might have a hidden room somewhere. Whatever you do—"

"Don't go into it, nor will I let him lure me into a basement or an attic, I *know*," I finished for him. "I'm not an idiot."

"Life would be easier if you were," he muttered.

"For you, perhaps."

"Fiona." He gripped my elbow and didn't let go when I made to jerk away. The gravitas on his features actually cowed me into silence for a rare moment. "Do not endure any indignities for the sake of information, is that clear? The moment he touches you, you scream for me. You run. You strike him in the nethers. You do whatever it takes, understood?"

"I understand," I said, so he would release me.

But as I made the rest of the way toward the shop alone, I added, *I understand that I decide how far this goes.*

A small porcelain bell affixed to a Christmas ribbon jangled merrily from the door latch as I poked my head inside.

The actual shopfront was equal parts charming, gloomy, and small. The bronzed register sat on what might have once been a tavern bar next to several Christmas postcards. Behind them hung a wall of dark velvet drapes obscuring the rest of the building from view. A few waiting chairs littered a veritable gallery of photographs, upon which several one-way lamps shone to most appealing effect.

"I'll be right with you!" called a cheery, masculine voice from somewhere behind the curtain.

"No rush at all," I called back, tugging on the ribbon to no avail.

Bugger. How was I supposed to disengage it without garnering suspicion? Alas, why did Charles Hartigan have Christmas decorations still displayed well into January?

Having retrieved another knife from my home—this one of the kitchen filet varieties rather than the utility knife I'd lost to shoulder sinew—I now drew it from my sleeve. I silenced the bell against my skirts whilst slicing through the ribbon.

After returning my knife, I debated on what to do. I couldn't very well keep the bell on me. Nor could I put it outside, lest he get suspicious.

Struck with an idea, I lifted it above my head and let go.

It fractured against the parquet floor.

"Oh lands!" I called in mock distress. "I'm awfully sorry! Your ribbon seems to have given way and your bell is shattered. I do hope it wasn't a keepsake."

"It's nothing at all," offered the disembodied voice. "I'll fetch a broom. Mind you don't get cut. Please do look around the shop whilst you wait."

"You're too kind, really. I feel just terrible."

"Think nothing of it," he called back, his voice getting farther away. Presumably he was going to the back to fetch supplies.

Reaching out of the door, I made the agreed-upon gesture to Croft, who loitered on the walkway outside. He would listen in and enter only if we moved behind the curtain or to another part of the shop.

I leaned the door against the jamb, rather than

closing it, and thanked whoever was in charge of my luck that this'd gone so smoothly.

Well, *smoothly* would have been a brass bell easily taken from a ring, but this ended up all right in the end.

I wandered around the shop feeling giddy. A little like a war spy.

Charles Hartigan was very good at what he did. His portraits neither seemed too posed nor too chaotic. The figures were relaxed and well illuminated. It was like having an audience standing in his gallery. Scores of sepia eyes stared out of a frozen memory. Family portraits, most, with a few stills of important men in suits clutching their lapels. Or groups in costume or uniform. Of commemorative occasions and political ones. Some even of gardens, landmarks, and one of the sea. I wished fervently that the cresting wave were any color but beige.

I longed to visit the sea, and had a painting of the White Cliffs of Dover hanging across from my bed so I could wake to it in lieu of a view.

I preferred paintings to photographs, I decided. I needed color. A bit of fancy and whimsy.

Reality was often too like this... monochromatic.

"Here we are." The voice startled me from this side of the curtain, and I whirled to see a slender man of medium height holding a broom and a pan.

Whatever I'd expected of Charles Hartigan, this wasn't it. "I-I really am sorry. I'm forever clumsy. You must let me pay for the bell."

He seemed to interpret my breathlessness as embarrassment for my mishap rather than distress that he'd appeared behind me with nary a sound.

"Nonsense. 'Twas nothing but a paltry trinket. I think I even have another one in the back somewhere." For a man of indeterminate middle age, he was neither attractive nor unappealing. Sort of like the tones of his photographs, he was simply varying shades of beige and brown, all the way down to his suit.

"What brings you to my shop on such a gloomy afternoon?" he asked as he swept. "Have you children you'd like me to photograph? I've a catalogue of a variety of poses, and that wall over there is for babies all the way up to debutants."

"Is it?" I said, drifting in the direction he pointed. It unsettled me more than a little that he immediately seemed so keen to photograph children.

He paused to crouch down and sweep the leavings of the ribbon and the bell into the dust bin. I hoped he didn't mark the cleanly cut line of the ribbon. I hadn't really considered that one might look for a fray. "I do commemorative pictures of many ladies' societies, if that's what you're after."

"Indeed?" I made myself busy scanning the wall of children. Chubby cherubs in christening gowns were framed next to cricket teams with trophies and gap-toothed smiles. Little girls in Easter gowns stood next to their mothers, their eyes happy, if not their faces.

"Tell me, miss, what are you here for?"

I found the answer at the exact same time he asked the question with a bit more urgency than seemed necessary.

A familiar face amongst the youths. Dressed in a bonnet and braids. A cryptic expression that would put the Mona Lisa to shame.

The only time I'd seen her, those eyes had been leaking tears of blood.

Jane Sheffield.

"I—erm." I cleared the shock out of my throat. "I am looking for a certain kind of photograph, Mr. Hartigan."

Turning away from Jane's mysterious smile, I found him a bit paler than before, smoothing a hand over thinning wisps of light hair. "I don't think we've been introduced, miss..."

"Viola," I replied, using my moniker from The Orchard. "Viola Montague." I'd made my first mistake. There was no written proof that C.B.H. Photography and Gallery stood for Charles Barclay Hartigan.

He was wondering how I knew his name.

"I'm told you are willing to take... more interesting photographs than your workaday photographer." Adopting a sly expression, I peered up at him from behind coquettish lashes.

He gulped. "Where did you hear that, Miss Montague?"

"Oh, here and there." I ran my gloved fingers across the bar, inspecting them for invisible dust. "I've a few... coworkers who claimed you paid them for portraits intended for men of particular tastes."

When Charles Hartigan smiled, it was with the teeth of a shark.

Every single hair on my body lifted in warning.

"I think we might understand each other, Miss Montague. But I'd like you to expound upon the specific tastes you are referencing."

I peeked around us, as if looking for eavesdroppers, knowing there was one close by. "These particular photos, one might only find in the boudoir of a lonely man, if you catch my meaning."

It might have been my imagination, but his smile dimmed just a little.

"I see..." He drew out the word. "And how much coin are you looking to make?"

"The most possible, of course."

"I'd have to leave your face out of it, then," he said drolly.

I hoped he meant because of my split lip. Not that I *wanted* to be the sort of woman who posed for torrid photographs that were indiscriminately disseminated.

But something in me bristled at the idea of not being desirable enough to.

To add insult to injury, Croft had heard him say that.

I had to unclench my teeth to reply, "Whatever you say."

"Come in the back," he beckoned, sweeping the black drapes aside. "I'll show you my work, if you demonstrate yours. My clients are very discerning."

Giggling like I'd heard Izzy do several times, I took off my hat and coat and hung them on a rack by the door. "Of course I'll go in the back," I said in Croft's direction.

Turning, I glided past him as if I were not terrified to have his body in between me and escape.

To have him behind me in any respect.

His back room was a tidy chaos. A large camera on a three-legged stand posed before a backdrop of silvery drapes and furniture that was as well made as it was well worn.

He gestured for me to take a seat on the couch in front of the camera. It was still warm from where I assumed the family before me had sat.

"Are you always so pale?" he asked with avid fascination as watched me with predatory eyes.

My fingers twitched as I managed not to touch my face. "Is that a problem?"

His toothy grin widened. "No. No, in fact, it's a boon if you'd let it be."

"What do you mean?"

"We'll get to that later." He bothered around with bits and bobs on the camera.

"I'm anxious to see your work," I said.

"Have you ever done this before, Miss Montague?" he asked, never looking away from what he was doing.

"I—Not often, all told. I might need a bit of direction. It's why I wanted to see what you did for the other girls."

"The other girls," he echoed, in a voice becoming increasingly soft. He looked at me for a long time, and I gave what I hoped was a reassuring bat of my lashes. "Which one of them sent you, again? Which one told you to come seek me out?"

I swallowed, ardently aware of the knife in my sleeve. "I forget her name just now, but she and I met through The Orchard, if that helps."

"The Orchard?"

I paused a beat longer than I should have because something in his tone bemused me. I couldn't put my finger on it, but it felt dangerous. As if he wasn't questioning what The Orchard was, but that it would send me.

It was then I decided to be bold rather than careful. "Oh, yes, her name was Jane." That felt important for him to know. That, should he be the reason the woman was dead, she'd not disappeared from memory.

He cleared his throat and went to his desk, rummaging around in a drawer. "There are a great many women named Jane."

"Jane Sheffield."

Making a noncommittal sound, he extracted a key from the drawer, went to a cabinet along the far wall, and unlocked it. I saw a black case he unbuckled with the utmost care.

My father had kept guns in just such a case.

"Take off your dress, Miss Montague." It was less suggestion than order.

"I-I'm sorry?"

"You heard me."

I flinched when he turned around, but let out a relieved breath when I noted that he held only a smaller version of the camera he'd mounted and not a pistol.

Thank God.

"But we haven't come to any agreement," I argued, standing abruptly.

"And we won't until you're naked."

"I don't disrobe unless I'm paid."

"Spoken like a true whore," he sneered. "But I don't think you are one. And I don't think you know what really happens here." He marched toward me, baring his too many teeth. "I think this is a fishing expedition, and that I'm not a trawl you want to catch."

My heartbeat accelerated and sweat bloomed on my palms.

He was cleverer than I expected, and still it seemed that he might incriminate himself if I pushed him.

"I'm not fishing for anything, Mr. Hartigan, but I do wonder *why* Jane's photograph is hanging among your wall of youths."

He put his face close to mine, his breath reeking of pickled eggs. It turned my stomach. "If you were here for the reason you claimed to be, you wouldn't have to wonder. Now either take off this dress or get out."

"I will not—"

He grabbed me by my wrist, and I winced as the blade strapped there bit into my skin. I struggled against his grip, but Charles Hartigan was deceptively strong as he jerked my sleeve up and extracted the weapon.

I should have hidden it in my boot.

Gripping the handle of the knife, he held it to my jaw as he dragged me toward the black curtain. "You tell those tarts at The Orchard—"

His words died as he bounced off the wall of muscle and wrath that was Grayson Croft.

With swift motions and hardly any expended energy, Croft had his arm around Hartigan's throat. He pushed at a soft point of the man's wrist with his thumb, and Hartigan's fingers popped open, sending the knife clattering to the floor.

I snatched it up and brandished it at Hartigan. "You couldn't have waited one more minute?" I asked Croft. "He was about to say something important."

Hartigan clawed at Croft's arm with panicked fingers, his face turning an alarming shade of red as veins began to bulge.

Croft let him wriggle and squirm for a moment too long as he speared me with a look so dark, I clamped my mouth shut.

"You were supposed to scream if he touched you," he growled.

"I was *going* to. I just needed him to finish his sentence first."

He closed his eyes and took a breath, holding on to Hartigan as if he were an afterthought when what he truly grappled with was his frustration with me.

Eventually, he rumbled into the struggling man's ear, "When I let go, you're going to sing like a canary. And then you'll hand over whatever photographs you have in your possession that even hint at impropriety, do you understand?"

The mere effort of nodding seemed to make Hartigan's head likely to pop like a grape, and Croft released him with a rough shove.

Scrambling to the couch I'd only just vacated, Hartigan crawled into it like a toddler would his mother's lap, clutching at his throat. "Y-you're police?"

"Detective Grayson Croft. H Division." Croft reached into his coat pocket to produce his badge.

"D-did *he* send you?" The red drained from Hartigan's face until he'd turned a sickening shade of puce. "Because I gave him everything he asked for. Honest."

"Who?" I demanded. "Davies?"

"A-and Pulliver, Weston, Moore. They all received the goods, and then some."

Croft and I glanced at each other, and I read the disappointment in his eyes. He hadn't wanted this to be a stain on the police. I wondered what he would do now.

"Did you ever take photos of a woman named Alys Hywell?" I asked.

He nodded like one of those bobble-headed dolls one saw in the toyshops, almost overeager to speak in the presence of Croft.

The blasted investigator would want me to admit later how effective he was, in contradiction to me, I just knew it.

"I sold them all at a premium after she became fish food. To Davies himself." Hartigan looked between me and Croft with a pathetic, calculating gaze. "I have an understanding with M Division. I've their protection."

"Not anymore." Croft stalked to him, and Hartigan shrank away as he was grabbed by the elbow and hauled to his feet. "Because no one will protect them from *me*."

"I-I'll testify," Hartigan wheezed, his voice squeaking like an adolescent's. "I'll squeal on them if you'll let me go. I-I fell on a bit of hard luck, is all. And these whores, they talked me into taking pictures. They preyed on my weaknesses. Once the money started coming in, I was able to pay off my debts, see? I-I didn't see no harm in it. What's a few saucy images between lonely lads? No one's hurt by it."

"No one is hurt?" I scoffed. "Two women are dead! And you would blame them? You pathetic piece of—"

"Enough," Croft barked, and to my intense mortification, my mouth snapped shut.

He said nothing more as he turned back to Hartigan, directing him to of his desk and cabinets. "You'll turn over your stock to Scotland Yard, and you'll make a condemning statement to the police and the High Court regarding all of your customers."

"I will. I will in return for exemption from charge."

Croft nodded, the vein at his own temple pulsing with strain. "Start gathering, Mr. Hartigan. I'm sending for them now, and we're going to comb every inch of this shop."

Hartigan's eyes darted this way and that, but he ultimately relented.

I trailed Croft to the front of the store. "You're not going to question him about Alys and Jane?"

"Of course I bloody am," he said. "Go home. You can't be here when Scotland Yard arrives." He ran a hand over his features, drawing them further down into a dark scowl.

"Why aren't you arresting him?" I asked.

"Because," he explained, with more grim patience than I expected from him, "this *is* a fishing expedition. And as anyone who has fished can tell you, you use the smaller one to bait and catch the true prize." He held the door open for me, and I paused, feeling like there was something else that needed to be done. Like we were missing something, somehow.

"What are you going to do?"

"I'm going ruin an entire division full of filth," he said. "And when I do, I think I'll find a murderer of women among them."

Chapter Seventeen

✾

Are you being brave or foolish, Fiona? To
   bait me is folly.
None of you find my gifts anymore. You
   do not deserve them.
But you know what I do to whores.
Best not be one.
Yours
for now,

— *JACK THE RIPPER*

My legs gave out from beneath me, and I
landed hard on the soft bed. My limbs were
at once weak with shock and trembling with
readiness. I ate up every detail of the letter, chewing
the words as if I could taste the meaning both expressed and hidden in subtext.

Not that the message wasn't direct.

Every edge and swoop of the red scrawls was ap-
pallingly familiar to me. The Ripper had sent me letters
before. He'd known things about me, about the murders I cleaned up after, that he couldn't have known had
he not been alarmingly close by.

"This... this came *here*? Addressed to me?"

Beatrice Chamberlain inclined her head as she rested a hand on my shoulder. From my vantage, she looked like every merciful statue of Mary standing watch over Catholic graveyards back home. Round, pleasant features arranged in an expression of angelic benevolence.

I'd come to The Orchard after a late breakfast to tell her what we learned from Charles Hartigan. I found her alone, packing away Alys's things in the decadent room the woman had inhabited during the last months of her tragically short life.

Bea had produced the letter addressed to me with the red wax seal intact. It'd arrived with the morning post.

"Some hateful joke, perhaps?" she considered.

"I'm afraid not." My voice quavered. "I've received such letters from him before."

"My God." She plopped down next to me, scanning the letter with new interest. "So many of us in the business have spent years speculating as to the ultimate fate of the Ripper, wondering why he'd stopped with poor Mary Kelly. When or if he'd begin his reign of terror again. As time has gone by, we all assumed him dead, moved on maybe, or captured for other crimes... But this. This means he's still out there. That he knows you're looking for him." The pity with which she regarded me was hard to witness.

"He writes to me as if we are acquainted sometimes," I admitted. "His previous letters helped to solve a case to which I was too close to see the truth. He seems grotesquely fond of me and threatening all at once."

"It's just... vile." Beatrice rubbed a motherly hand along my spine, warming the frigid chills coursing through my bones. "You poor girl. Must be a terrifying prospect to know the Ripper is watching you."

It was.

But also thrilling. Because if he was close enough to watch, then he was close enough to be caught.

"Bea." I glanced around the room, feeling as if the ghost of the vital Alys Hywel drifted somewhere above the filmy bed curtains. "I don't like the fact that the Ripper's attention has been drawn to this place. To these girls. If any other tragedies befell The Orchard because I was trying to help... I'd never forgive myself."

She took one hand, and we both watched the letter quiver in the other. "That is good of you, darling. I wouldn't fear him so much if it was only me I had to look after, but the girls... I bear the responsibility."

I nodded, wishing everyone felt that way about those in their employ. I certainly did. "Inspector Croft is gathering evidence against Inspector Davies from Charles Hartigan."

I'd no need to ask if she remembered the man, as her painful grip revealed so much at the mention of the name.

"Charles Hartigan?" she breathed. "That man is a toad. Worse than that, he's—"

"We know, but I think he's arranging some sort of deal with the police to go after corruption in their ranks."

She made a face. "I detest that he'll be walking the streets free to indulge his deviancies. Doesn't seem right. If you were to ask me, he's an excellent candidate for your Ripper."

My Ripper? I certainly didn't want him.

"What makes you say that?" I asked. "Salacious photographs do not a murderer make, though he is being investigated in regard to the deaths connected to this. Apparently, he took photographs of both Alys and Jane."

"Have you seen the sort of photographs he took?" she asked, disgust gathering her lips into wrinkled grimace.

"I haven't. Croft has taken over now that the main office is involved. I'm not allowed near anything deemed to be 'evidence,' more's the pity."

"Perhaps that's for the best." Bea patted my hand and stood. "I'd hate to think of you being a target for both the Ripper and Hartigan. Men like them... they are the reason all women are afraid."

"I'm not afraid," I said.

"Are you not?" She lifted an eyebrow at my trembling hands. "Not after your attack? I'm afraid *for* you, my dear."

How could I tell her that my affectation might be just as vile to her as Hartigan's? Of course, I was possessed of a healthy fear of torture and death. But my guile overpowered that.

I trembled as much from excitement as fear.

Searching the letter one last time, I debated what to do with it. "The galling idea that the Ripper would live a full life when he's taken that from others... from Mary. Well, that is a world I don't want to live in. It is a revenge I am willing to die for. I don't know if he realizes that when he taunts me, he only renews my resolve."

Beatrice bustled about, opening drawers and emptying them carefully into a paper-lined trunk. I wondered where she'd ship Alys's things. Or if she'd store them.

"I wish I was like you," she said in a falsely bright voice. "Strong enough to swim against the current. Most of us... we know where the river is going, we expect to be swept away by it, and we just allow it to happen."

Tucking the Ripper letter into a pocket, I went to her. "Not you, though. You changed your path. Your very existence disrupts the currents, and you are a force to be reckoned with."

"Go on, you. What nonsense."

"I mean it. I respect and admire you."

223

Blushing, she flapped her hand at me. "Tosh. If you're going to stand here, you might as well make yourself useful and stop trying to flatter me."

With a fond smile, I opened the drawers on my side of the chest and lifted crinolines and bustle straps into the trunk. I tried not to think of the gravitas of the chore. Of the woman I'd never known, whose delicates I now handled.

I wondered if we would have liked each other, Alys and I.

After emptying the first drawer, and then the second, I found the third full of petticoats shoved in without order. Drawing them out in armfuls of frippery, I heard something fall against the floor.

I wrestled the layers of fabrics to the bed and returned to where Beatrice retrieved a bundle of envelopes from the ground. Tied with a single white ribbon, they bore no name or address, but were written on similar pale blue stationery.

"I'm almost afraid to read another letter today," Bea said. "What if they're dreadful?"

"What if they reveal the killer?" I asked.

She looked up at me with tears shimmering in her eyes.

I took the bundle from her frozen fingers and carefully untied the ribbon.

"I'm going to need a drink for this," Beatrice said in a shaking voice. "Wait here, and I'll pour us some brandy."

"No need," I murmured, scanning the first letter. "You'll want to read this."

She hurried to my side, looking over my shoulder for a moment, her breath close and heightened. "I can't make out such tiny scrawl at my age," she admitted, drifting over to the fireplace. "Read it aloud?"

"My love," I began as Bea idly poked at the coals with a fine instrument, rekindling a long-burning blaze.

"When you look at me across the room, the chandelier turning your hair into a waterfall of silk, I find I cannot say the words that fill my heart. And so, I am compelled to write them down or drown in them. My entire life, I've been told I was wicked, but I never knew how transcendent that word was until you. You are the divine and I am the profane. I worship you. And I live for the next time our bodies can move in reverence and with abandon. I cannot wait to begin our future together. You are a dream realized. And I am devoted to making yours a reality. Love always—"

I gasped, putting my hand over my mouth as grief drenched me.

"What?" Abandoning the poker to its place, Beatrice circumnavigated the bed, wringing her hands. "Who."

"Love always, your *Sappho*." I flipped through the stack of letters. "It looks like there are replies here as well." I skimmed a few of the letters, no less lovely in their language. "They don't sign their names..."

"Oh, Alys. Poor lamb." It was Bea's turn to sink to the bed, her knuckles turning white as she gripped the counterpane. A spate of coughs overtook her, leaving her pale and wan when she finished.

"Did you know?" I asked, handing her a glass of water I'd poured from the sideboard. "That she was in love with a woman? Do you have any idea whom it would be?"

She drank deeply, clutching the glass in her hand when she rested it on her knee. "No... we all lost Alys. We all wept for her. Or grieved in our own ways. But no one expressed any more heartache than the rest of us." Bea looked up at me, her dark eyes shining. "Did the other girls mention anything about this?"

"Not a word."

She made a caustic sound. Half laugh, half sob. "And here I thought all this time that Alys was shit at keeping secrets. This was one she didn't have to keep. I would have given them a safe place to love each other."

I put my own hand over hers, offering her a clean handkerchief. "Perhaps they were not ready to share their love with the rest of the world. Sometimes a love this powerful is more sacred than secret."

She nodded. "All I can hope is that God is kinder than the Vicar Jewett believes. That they found each other in eternity somewhere."

The vicar. I still needed to ascertain if Croft was going to investigate him.

"I really should go, Bea. The longer I'm here, the worse it is, I'm afraid."

She patted my hand. "I understand."

I looked around the pretty chaos of the room. "Why not pay someone to do this? One of your maids or a porter?"

She gave a shrug that only served to elucidate how deep her shoulders had sagged from a massive weight. "It didn't seem right that Alys's things were pawed through by strangers. I haven't found kin yet, but at least they can be looked through with care. With remembrance."

"That's lovely of you."

The sound of a door downstairs alerted us both.

"I thought you were here alone," I said.

"As did I."

"I'll go investigate," I offered. "If it's nothing, I'll see myself out."

"If it's something?"

"Then I'll call for you to go find a constable."

She nodded, smothering a few more coughs into her handkerchief.

Creeping out to the landing, I listened for more suspicious noises. Rain pelted the roof, gathering in gutters to noisily splatter onto the cobbles. The cacophony of the storm had all but been forgotten until the entire place seemed to hold its breath and listen.

A door opened and shut, and I went to the window to see Indira and... *Sophia*, of all people, scurry into the afternoon.

They were dressed well and properly, their coats long and fine as they shared a blue umbrella.

What the devil was Sophia doing here? With Indira? And in the middle of the morning when they might assume The Orchard was empty?

I couldn't tell if they were carrying anything, and my curiosity drew me to dash down the stairs, fetch my own umbrella from the stand, and follow them out into the rain.

They walked arm in arm for two blocks until, with a kiss on air next to Indira's cheek, Sophia pulled her shawl over her hair and ducked from beneath the umbrella, crossing Fleet Street to Blighting Circle.

I watched her go long enough to note the street, and when I glanced back to where Indira had been, I was hardly surprised to find that her umbrella was swallowed up into Fleet Street's ever-present traffic.

Decision made, I scurried across the road, only just avoiding collisions with hackneys, paper wagons, and a trotting horse or two. Ignoring some colorful curses, I turned down the tight alley, hoping it wasn't too late.

I almost collided with the back of a fine coach, and I ducked behind it to catch my bearings and my breath.

Peeking around a wheel rim, I could find no sign of Sophia in the nearly abandoned lane. I whispered a foul Irish word and stamped my foot in frustration.

"Fiona?"

I'd recognize that smooth voice anywhere.

From inside the coach, two pairs of eyes blinked down at me through the sheets of rain.

One belonging to Sophia. The other to the Hammer.

The door opened, and Sophia stepped down from the coach, having procured another umbrella from her solicitous employer.

"The Hammer will conduct you home." Sophia pulled the door wider, uncovering an interior in which only Jorah's long, dark-clad legs could be seen.

"I'm fine, thank you," I called.

"It wasn't an offer, nor was it a request," he said from the shadows. "Get in."

Chapter Eighteen

❧❧❧

I almost never saw the Hammer in the daylight.

When I did, I was struck by how preternatural he was. His eyes some impossible, unidentified color, his skin something between pale and dusky, and his hair a light shade of dark.

Sometimes it felt as if I were in the presence of someone—something—else pretending to be human. Something not of this world but sent to observe it before they claimed it for their own.

Men like him are the reason all women are afraid.

Beatrice's words echoed in my head as we sat in silence, swaying softly on the well-oiled hinges of his private, luxurious coach.

His legs were so long, he had to tuck them to the side to avoid my skirts. And he did so, as if he were a man who respected the rules of decorum.

When he opened his mouth to speak, I felt a slight swell of victory, as I'd outlasted him in this aloof game he sometimes played.

"This friend of yours, the one you mentioned you were helping when you came to The Velvet Glove, does she happen to be Beatrice Chamberlain?"

"She does."

"*Ебать Сука!*" he cursed. "Why didn't you tell me?"

"You didn't seem bothered by what Sophia and I needed to speak of," I answered testily. "Besides, the identity of my clients is none of your business."

"I make it my business, because *you and I* are in business."

"Not by choice, as we've already discussed." I glared at him, wishing I'd not capitulated to his order to get in the coach. What would he have done if I'd defied him, run me down in the street?

Doubtful.

"What do you have against Bea—Mrs. Chamberlain? I rather admire her."

"Why does that not surprise me in the least?" he scoffed, before his gaze sharpened like a viper's, waiting to strike. "She took something from me."

"What did she take?"

"A client."

I made a noncommittal sound. Must have been a royal client to rile the Hammer.

"Have you told her about any of our dealings together?" he pressed. "About how we are acquainted and what you do for me?"

"Why would I—"

He leaned forward, visibly vexed. "What did Sophia inform you that you reiterated to Beatrice Chamberlain?"

"Nothing but a bit of gossip from the past, that's all. It had to do with these two murdered women who worked at The Orchard, Alys Hywell and Jane Sheffield." I watched him closely for a flicker of recognition and found none. "Now that my investigation has led me to your carriage, I have a few questions for you, as well."

"Your *investigation*," he echoed with a derisive snort. "I'll tell you this once, Fiona Mahoney. You stay away from Beatrice Chamberlain."

"Why?"

"Because I'm warning you to."

"Are you afraid of her?" I was beginning to learn that a challenge often made him say more than he meant to.

He lifted a brow. "Excuse me?"

"You heard me. Are you acting like this because she is a threat to you?"

"You think I *fear* her?"

"Why else would it matter if I speak to her or not?" I examined my nails, so I wouldn't have to watch the rage gather in his tensing muscles. I might have lost my nerve. "It sounds like you are concerned. Dare I say anxious?"

"You think I have anything but pitying antipathy for that—that *Cuchka derganaya*?"

"I don't know what to think."

He made a dramatic gesture. "Tell me, Fiona, when does the fly ever eat the spider? What has the lion to fear from the gazelle?"

I really did *attempt* to keep my eyes from rolling. "You are so..." I didn't dare finish the sentence, having not meant to start it out loud.

"I'm. So. What?"

I stared at him.

He stared back.

"You are so insufferable—no—*infuriating* some-times." There. If he punished me for the insult, I would still take pleasure in the saying of it.

To my surprise, he laughed, but only with his mouth. The effect was chilling. "Perhaps, but being in-sufferable doesn't make me incorrect. I think that woman is a viper, and so should you."

Curious—I'd only just ascribed that word to him.

"Because she stole a client from you? Doesn't that sort of thing happen all the time?"

His eyes cut away.

This time, it was I who sat forward, drawn by his

retreat. "Wait a moment. There's more to this, isn't there?"

"It's complicated," he hedged.

"You've told me more than once that I'm clever. Perhaps even I could comprehend a complication now and again."

That glint. The one that made grown men wither into simpering fools.

I was treading on thin ice, as they say, and even though it cracked beneath my boots, I still couldn't bring myself to flee to safety.

To my utter amazement, he slumped back. "Essentially, she bought some debts of mine and had the gall to pretend it was an investment in my establishment. She desired a partnership, after a fashion. Then, when I would have none of it, she made a move on some of my investors, and I actually lost a few of them to her scheming."

"I see," I said. "You hate her because she's actual competition."

He tilted his head. "I wouldn't go that far, but I would sleep with one eye open around her. I bought back what she had, of course, and then plucked Sophia from her stock."

"Stock?" I made a face. "They're women, not cattle. Their lives have value."

"They're women," he agreed. "And they're assets. Value can be both immeasurable and counted in coin."

"So she is a viper because she almost outwitted you?" I asked. "Does that emasculate you in some way? To have a woman nipping at your heels? One who refuses to pay you homage? You keep one eye open, pricked to the thought that, like this empire, the London underworld might not have a king always, but a queen instead?"

A prominent vein began to pulse at his temple as he rested his elbows on his knees and let his hands hang between them. "That is where you mistake me, Fiona, I see her as an absolute equal and will crush her as such."

"I won't let you do that." I don't know where the whisper came from. Nor did I realize I'd said it until I watched it land.

But I meant it.

Men always tried to crush women like Beatrice Chamberlain. Women who didn't behave as they ought. Who dared to claim a piece of power for their own.

I'd had enough of it.

"I am intrigued by this new you," he said, apropos of nothing.

I pulled a face. "I don't know what you're talking about. I'm the same person you've known for these two years."

"You are not." He shook his head. "Something has changed since your priest died. You are harder, I think. Bolder. Is it because you are now truly alone?"

Was he being cruel on purpose? Or did he think his assessment of my person somehow insightful or charming?

Either way, I itched to slap the mild curiosity off his face.

"I am not alone," I insisted. "I have..." *Dependents*. "I have people—more people than I know what to do with, usually."

Instead of replying, he asked, "What happened to your face?"

I blinked at the abrupt change of subject but answered, "I was attacked in an alley."

"By whom?" His tone lowered. Darkened.

"I don't know. I was knocked unconscious."

"Did he rape you?" His voice had gone so flat that it was dead, and his features were carefully blank.

"What a terrible question!" I said. "What if he *had* done such a thing? I'd be destroyed. And you bring it up as if it's nothing. How dare you?"

"It is not nothing," he said, without inflection. "And you'd be distraught, but you are not so easily destroyed."

It felt like a compliment. But a dark one.

"He wasn't after me for that," I admitted, feeling that sense of relief all over again. "He made it seem like it might be, but someone sent him to hurt me. To scare me because I'm looking into the deaths of Jane and Alys."

"I see." He put a finger to his chin. "Apparently it didn't have the desired effect of frightening you away..."

"No. But *this* did." I took the letter from my pocket and handed it to him.

His eyes ate up the words in a few deft motions before he delivered his verdict: "The Ripper is watching you."

I sighed. "Evidently. And I've angered him by pretending to be a prostitute for one night to get in good with the others. Only for information, you understand. I did none of the... the work."

Nodding, he carefully folded the letter and handed it back to me. "He wants to fuck you."

I almost dropped it. "What is *wrong* with you today? You're being especially vulgar and dreadful."

He lifted his shoulder. "I am a vulgar and dreadful man. A fact of which you are well aware and enjoy castigating me for on a regular basis."

"Not everything is about sex," I huffed.

"It is for him." He thrust his chin toward the letter. "It's why he does the despicable things he does."

"How would you know?"

His expression shifted in miniscule increments from brutal to bleak. "I've known some people that would give your Ripper nightmares. I know what drives them."

The Hammer never spoke of his past. Of his Russian father and his Italian mother, both of whom were Jews. Of the reasons he'd fled to this country, and the blood that seemed to follow him everywhere.

"How ghastly," I murmured.

"It was. It *is*."

I wanted to ask more, and also, I did not.

"You're wrong, you know," I ventured, deviating from an even thinner patina of ice. "The Ripper—if this truly is him—he doesn't want to... to have relations with me. He wants to keep me pure. He makes that exceedingly obvious. He kills women who are loose with their favors."

"He killed women who *sold* their favors," the Hammer corrected me. "There is a very distinct difference. And he likes to assume you are saving your purity for him."

"I'm not saving it for anyone."

"Then give it to me." He leaned back against the velvet of the coach seat, his legs still parted indecently.

"Why do you say such things?" I threw my hands up. "When you know it makes me less likely to do so."

The smirk that made him appear both unthreatening and utterly treacherous returned. "I'm merely throwing my hat in the ring, as it were. I want you to not mistake my intentions when you're making your decision. I want the experience to be... memorable."

I held my hands up against him, my bodice suddenly too tight.

"You are surrounded by men who want to fuck you," he said blithely, then counted off on his long fingers. "Aramis, Inspector Croft, me, the Ripper, vast and various men in your sphere you wouldn't dare to imagine."

"Please, stop." I pressed cold hands to my flaming cheeks. "Why do you insist on being so absurd?"

He bared his teeth in half a sneer and half a snarl. "Because *you* insist on acting like you don't know. Like you can't feel the wolves sniffing at your skirts, howling to be allowed beneath them. It's as infuriating as it is arousing."

"What you are saying makes no *sense*," I argued, yearning for him to take it back, to stop this if it was a cruelty, and to change his mind—to see reason—if he were truly so erroneous. "While I understand men are often indiscriminate in their tastes and would be as happy to take me to bed as any half-decent-looking woman who would have them, I *don't* understand why you flatter me like this. I own a mirror, Jorah. I'm ordinary in almost every way. I am not a perfect beauty like Sophia or Indira. I'm just... I'm pretty enough not to offend people."

"What you don't realize is how boring perfection can be. You are a woman of contradictions. Soft and hard. Innocent and informed. Delicate and strong. Careful and brave. You are like a fox, Fiona. Not just lovely, but clever, mysterious, and nearly impossible to capture. Even if trapped, you'd chew your own limbs off before you allowed yourself to be kept. Men who are worth anything, who know anything, they can tell that once you discover the power you hold, the passion that is banked within you, you will be a true vixen." His gaze was enough to immolate me on the spot. "It is impossible for me to express how intoxicating that opportunity is."

I attempted a swallow, failed, and tried again. "I hardly know what to say to something like that."

"It is not a statement that demands a reply." He shrugged. "It just is a truth that I want you to understand."

I stared at him for an uncomfortably long time. Blinking. Breathing. Unable to do more than just that. "H-how... how would you speculate about someone like Croft and me? I can't think of a time when you've seen us interact. We generally dislike each other."

"You do not always know when I see you." That was

his disturbing answer. "And Croft has spoken of you to me. I could tell how much he wanted you then. He was like this Rottweiler I once knew, snarling over a treasure he found in a rubbish heap, warning everyone away from it."

"When was this?" Croft hated the Hammer, for reasons neither of them would reveal to me. I imagined all their interactions were tense, to say the least.

"I forget the exact instance." He waved this away.

I blew out a full breath finally. "Croft is heading up the inquest into Alys's and Jane's murders now. He'll be so smug that I'm not investigating anymore."

"As much as I hate to agree with that dullard, I agree that you should stop looking into these dead women. It has become too dangerous."

"Because of the Ripper," I agreed with a sigh, more disappointed than I'd expected to be.

"Dangerous before him, it seems." His eyes touched mine, astonishingly earnest as he reached for my chin and inspected the split in my lip. "But yes, you want to be chasing the Ripper, not the other way around."

"Why is he like this?" I lamented, the letter burning my fingers. "How can one take pleasure in such brutal violence? In such public degradation?"

Jorah frowned. "Why would you ask me? Because I, too, am a killer?"

My nod was a single dip against the fingers that held my entire being captive only by my chin.

The atmosphere around us shimmered, but I couldn't exactly identify with what.

"I do not think as the Ripper thinks. I do not kill as he kills. I take no joy in it, only duty. The Ripper is ruled by his passions. His compulsions." He traced a nearly imperceptible line over the edge of my lower lip, avoiding the wound. "I rule mine. And you should be glad of it."

"Why?" I yanked my chin from his grasp. "Do you

want to hurt me?"

"No. But there are other things I want to do. Impulses... yearnings, that even I do not understand. I want to capture you like a bird, sometimes. Hang your gilded cage from an ornate hook so I can watch you. Study you. The way you move. The way you sing. The way the light hits you at different times of the day and night."

Somehow my face was captive in his hands again, his fingers charting a searing procession up my jaw, toward my neck.

My pulse raced in places I'd never known it could reach. My blood stirred about, not knowing where to flow. My thoughts evaporated like a morning mist against the brilliance of a man like Jorah David Roth.

"I want to dress you in every color, Fiona, and then unwrap you like a present..." His head tilted, and I'd not realized I was leaning forward until I could feel the wisps of his breath against my skin. "You would not allow this. And if you did, you would be other than who you are."

"Would I?"

A rare genuine smile touched lips, devoid of sarcasm or cynicism. "I have women who would crawl into the cage and lock it behind them. They would sing whatever song I wished and dance however long I desired. But not you, Fiona." He inched forward. "I have learned that getting what I want is often not better than imagining what it could be. But I have a feeling..."

"I kissed Night Horse."

His eyes flew open, and he straightened as if he'd been struck. "What?"

Heart still pounding, I groped for an explanation. "He asked me to—*paid me to*—while I was at The Orchard. He said no other woman would kiss him, and that he would help me in my investigation if I did... and that felt sort of sad, but also helpful. So I did it. And—I thought you should know that in case that—changes anything. Because you two are—well, what you are to each other. And we are... whatever we are. Which isn't—um..."

If there was one thing I always hated about myself, it was my tendency to babble utter nonsense when I was anxious. Silence became the enemy, when in reality it should be my friend.

"I don't know why I told you just now," I said, wringing my hands. "But I suddenly thought you should know. Or wondered what would happen if you *didn't* know. And then we—Before you found out, and—"

A frightening darkness passed across his features but disappeared when he blinked. There and gone so quickly, I wondered if I'd imagined it. "Despite what I just admitted, you are *not* my concubine and I'm not your confessor. Should I be telling you what I did only last night and with whom? Is that knowledge you want to have?"

"Categorically not."

"Then..." He seemed to cast about for words, which was so odd for someone full of such inexhaustible wit. "What you and Night Horse get up to is no business of mine."

"All right." I sat back. "Well. Then... good."

"Do you have an understanding between the two of you?" he asked softly.

"A what?"

"An understanding," he repeated. "A contract."

"Contract?" My brows drew together. "Why would I—"

"Because it's how these things are done, Fiona." He pinched the bridge of his nose with his fingers. "God-damn every Catholic saint, must you be so naïve? You need papers between you so the terms are clear. So you are protected. I would never think of taking a mistress unless—"

"*Mistress?*" I shrilled. "Are you joking? Night Horse and I are 'up to' exactly nothing. I haven't seen him since that one kiss, and I don't intend to—to do anything else with him." I wagged my finger at him like a scolding schoolmistress. "And any... carnal relations I might have in the future certainly would *not* have paperwork involved."

"You mean to say you'll never marry?"

At that, my mind went blank. "Well, I—I never said that."

"Marriage is paperwork," he informed me with a bland sigh. "It's little better than a business contract that will take away all of your freedom and property and give it to a man for breeding rights. The contracts I draw up are better, kinder, transactional rather than proprietorial. The rights, privileges, and futures of the women are protected."

"I'm glad for them," I said icily, crossing my arms over my middle. "These women who are contractually obligated to you, and you to them. I'm sure it's mutually beneficial to all involved."

"It is," he said.

"*Good.*"

"Then why do you seem agitated?"

Why *was* I agitated?

Likely because for a second, he'd held me in some sort of thrall. He'd made that cage sound strangely appealing, so long as he was ensconced inside it with me. A man had never been so oblique and brazen at the same time. Never had anyone wanted me so... honestly.

Not even Aidan.

And I supposed I didn't realize it was a contract with terms Jorah had been offering this whole time. That any sort of passion we felt would be interrupted by bouts of legal jargon and rules as written and agreed upon beforehand.

I could think of nothing less erotic.

Nothing more contemptuous.

"I think I have to go," I blurted.

"But we're not to Tite Street yet."

"We are close enough." I clawed at the latch to the carriage. "I can walk."

With a deep inhale, he settled himself back into his seat as if it were his throne, all traces of the seductive fleeing before the tyrant. "Didn't you have questions for me?"

Damn him for making me forget them in the first place with his wicked distractions. My work as a detective was, frankly, appalling, and I needed to get back to my actual vocation and leave this disaster behind me.

And yet I couldn't stop myself from saying, "You're paying Sophia to get information from Indira about The Orchard."

"Was that supposed to be a question?"

"Well? Are you?"

"No, I'm not. I get my information through Aramis, not Sophia." He paused, his eyes shifting this way and that. "Or I did. Aramis told me last time he visited The Orchard, his regular sources had been unavailable. He never said a thing about two of three of them being dead. Nor did he mention any interactions with you."

We looked at each other, our thoughts undoubtedly similar. Night Horse was exactly that... a dark horse. A killer to his core. Could it be his proclivities were becoming perverse? Could the man I'd kissed be a monster... well, more of a monster than I'd initially realized?

I had so much to think about, but I had to ask the questions while I had the chance. I was not keen to seek out the Hammer soon, as I sensed a strange shift in our relationship.

"Sophia and Indira were sneaking around The Orchard whilst I was with Beatrice, and then I followed Sophia to your coach."

"Oh?" His brows retreated up his forehead in mock innocence.

"What was it all about?"

"I wouldn't dare speculate." He showed me empty hands.

"Obviously she was reporting to you," I said with a scowl.

"She was, but you have no idea what about, and it had nothing to do with The Orchard."

"I don't believe you."

That galling lift of his shoulder set my teeth on edge. "Ask her yourself, then."

"She'd obviously lie to me to keep your secrets. She's not a fool."

He studied me for a long time, his features again inscrutable. "I will instruct Sophia to be brutally honest with you, Fiona. But you'll need to be careful which doors you open. Some of them might never close again, even if you wish it."

When I would have asked what he meant, the carriage pulled to a rather abrupt stop. I had to clutch the velvet seat beneath me to keep from pitching over onto him.

Glancing out the streaked windowpane, I watched the rain drip tears of dark red over the bricks of my rowhouse.

He leaned in once more, but only to unlatch the door and swing it open. As stolid as a yeoman, he seemed unfazed by the deluge as he opened my umbrella, gently took my hand, and helped me down from the coach.

Before he released my umbrella to me, he kept an insistent pressure on my fingers as he pulled me close enough to murmur into my ear, "Best you are not in Beatrice Chamberlain's vicinity when I do crush her, Fiona. Lest you be caught beneath my boot as well."

Chapter Nineteen

✦✦✦

T he next time I saw Croft, he stood on my front
stoop clutching my post.

The shadows of Tite Street crept away
from the buildings as morning arrived tardy, as it was
wont to in January.

The inspector's dark hair glinted with moisture, and
he smelled of strong soap, vanilla, pomade, and his
clove cigarettes.

"What are you doing here?" I asked, barely recovering from the shock of finding a man of his size and
pulchritude on my stoop without warning.

"Startling your postman, apparently." He offered me
the stack of letters, and I took them, walking my fingers though each one, searching only for red ink and
the slanted, angry script of the Ripper's.

Finding none, I abandoned the post to the tray on a
table beside the door. I gathered my umbrella in case
the threatening sky should pour its contents on my new
hunter-green frock coat with the brown fox-fur collar.

"You look—smart," he commented. "Going somewhere important?"

I didn't want to answer that, so I deflected. "Are you
here to share any news gleaned from Scotland Yard's investigation on M Division?"

"Fiona Ina Muerinn Mahoney, that is no way to greet a gentleman caller." Aunt Nola descended the stairs with the regality of the Queen, though I was chagrined to note that neither she nor Mary had tidied her hair.

It was early yet, but if one wanted a show of how *not* to greet a gentleman caller, it would be looking like a woman who'd been blown off a widow's walk during a sea gale.

"I've an appointment, Aunt Nola. It wouldn't do to be late," I said over my shoulder, pulling the door as close as I could to block her from view. "Inspector Croft and I are just discussing some business and will be on our way now. I'll see you and Mary for tea."

"No, you won't be home for tea," she predicted, peeking over my shoulder like an obstinate child and shoving her way between my body and the door to get a better view of the goings-on.

"Go back inside, Aunt Nola, until Mary can arrange your hair," I urged, prodding her toward the kitchens by way of the black squares. "She's laid out breakfast and coffee on the sideboard."

"Is he here to inform you about the betrayal?" She clung to the door, squinting at Croft with a lack of recognition, though they'd met briefly before.

He wasn't a man one easily forgot. But neither was she of sound mind.

"No, he is not," I insisted, doing my best to gently pry her fingers from the doorlatch. "He's simply—" I paused. I still didn't know the reason for his arrival.

"What betrayal is that, Ms. Mahoney?" Croft addressed my aunt in a velvety voice I hadn't known he possessed. One meant for speaking to babies and praising animals rather than barking at criminals and antagonizing me.

Nola narrowed her eyes on Croft, inspected him from

teeth to toes. "The cards. The guides, man. They promised treachery, betrayal, ruin, deceit, a break of trust, and an unseen enemy. Someone beloved will be disloyal." She pointed a gnarled finger at Croft. "Or maybe who *you* love? In any case, *someone* will be in love, and then... *treachery*. Treachery will tear those who love asunder. Forever."

"Dear me," Croft said, placing a hand over his heart, still treating my enfeebled aunt with rare good humor. "I certainly hope not."

"It's already happened, Nola," I said, attempting to assuage her. "Your guides were right. Alys Hywell and Jane Sheffield were in love. And they were both killed, likely betrayed by someone they knew."

She shook her head. "Then why aren't they silent?"

They were never silent.

Desperate to get to my appointment, and hear what Croft was doing all the way in Chelsea when he was stationed in Whitechapel, I patted her on the arm. "Perhaps you could pull more cards? Might they clear things up?"

She put up a finger. "I'd have to clip some angelica from the garden first and set out a quartz."

"Then by all means."

Giving one last look to Croft, she pointed at him, but said nothing as she turned away and did a strange little hopscotch toward the back of the house.

"She's harmless," I said, stepping outside and closing the door firmly.

He didn't move away, and we crowded each other on the landing.

His scent.

I really wished he smelled like anything else. It was so pleasant. So comforting. So... so everything he wasn't.

It was I who made the retreat, nearly flying down the stairs to find a hackney. "You'll have to be quick, Inspector, as my appointment is in about twenty minutes."

"I've nothing I can divulge to you right now." He caught up to me easily and offered me his arm. "I thought I'd accompany you to the coroner so Dr. Phillips could update the both of us."

I gaped at him. "How did you find out I was going to see Dr. Phillips?"

"I *happen* to be a detective, you know." He tapped on his temple. "Finding things out is more or less what I do."

I made an exasperated sound and swung around on my boot heel, angling toward the main road.

"Let me summon a hackney," he called after me. "Surely you cannot walk to St. Crispin's Hospital in twenty minutes,"

"*Watch* me," I snapped, irritated in the extreme that he'd used his larger-than-necessary shoulder to shove into my day. My time with Dr. Phillips always seemed rather sacred to me. I couldn't say why exactly. He was a kind, eccentric gentleman who valued science and his own brand of logic over just about anything else.

Which was why he'd often show me reports and divulge things a mere laywoman like me wasn't technically supposed to know. We had an understanding, he and I. One in which he used my business to supply universities and surgeries with organs, cadavers, and skeletons for articulation and such. And I used him to disappear the bodies the Hammer or the Blade made it difficult to be rid of.

We arrived by hackney about fifteen minutes later, my mood no better than it had been when Croft arrived on my stoop.

"You could tell me *something* you know," I snapped at him as I jogged along the hospital's walk to keep up with him, taking two steps for every one of his. "Surely you understand how difficult it is to devote time to this and then put it by, allowing someone else to take over."

He thrust his hand toward the entrance. "You call *this* putting it by?"

I made an unladylike noise. "This appointment was made days ago, as you are apparently aware, and I thought that I might learn something useful still. Besides, I'm rather fond of Phillips, and he shares his best port with me."

"At half nine in the morning?"

"Coffee, then. Are you *really* going to keep your progress from me just to be mulish? I *bled* for this case, for your sister. Or have you already forgotten?"

I'd have liked to think myself above leveraging such things to get what I wanted, but here we were.

Croft's thick neck audibly worked over a difficult swallow. Likely his pride.

Or his principles, I thought a bit guiltily. I knew it was against every rule that made him a detective to share information about an active case. Still, I needed to know *something*.

He held the hospital door open for me, admitting one other elderly man who might be a patient or visitor, it was impossible to tell. Taking a surreptitious glance around the empty, echoing halls of the stately building, he gave a sigh. "On Charles Hartigan's word, we questioned Davies and his cohorts at M Division. We searched their desks and their offices. We found some nude photographs in a desk, but it wasn't enough to obtain a warrant from the courts to search anyone's home."

"How is that possible?" I asked. "You had testimony and you found evidence in Hartigan's shop! Surely that's enough to—"

"Because it's a bloody murky law to begin with, one hardly any court in the Empire wants to prosecute. Hell, I'd wager my salary that most so-called decent men have a few dirty photographs tucked away somewhere." We descended the stairs to the subterranean level, where the morgue and coroner's office would be found. "When we as police and the courts start to enforce these sorts of moral laws, fanatics will use the legal precedent to start silly wars. Before you know it, priceless paintings hung in museums, and homes, and the bloody palace suddenly become illegal contraband. Rioters will tear down the nude statue of Achilles in Hyde Park. Do you see what I mean?"

I did. And I thought the law rather silly myself. But in this case, it was something that could help. "Then why have these laws at all?" I asked.

"Mostly? To assuage the prudes in Parliament, and to sometimes have an extra indecency charge to slap onto a pimp, smuggler, or vice lord. It's helpful if children are being preyed upon, or if the images are too... explicit. If I'm honest, more of the women in the photographs get in trouble than the men who supply them or those who enjoy them. That never sits right with me."

"What do you mean by 'too explicit'?" I asked.

"Another grey area, really." A slight pink color rose above his collar.

I stopped him beneath the sign that advertised MORGUE by gripping the coat at his elbow. "So, what, Davies and his accomplices get away with possible murder and we're left with no more leads?"

"Trust me, Fiona, no one is more disappointed than I."

"I very much doubt that."

His hand froze on the door latch, and he whirled on me. "Do you have any *idea* what it does to a detective's reputation when he investigates his own kind?"

"Why would it, if they were doing something predatory and illegal?"

He sighed, pinching the bridge of his nose. "It's difficult to explain. Complicated."

"But..." I shook my head, stymied by this. "Policemen have a moral obligation to be better than the common man. If they're going to be granted the authority to enforce the law, they are expected to be beyond reproach regarding it."

"In a perfect world, yes, but when have positions of authority ever drawn men who are above reproach?"

My mouth shut so quickly, my teeth clacked together. Mostly because he'd made an excellent—if intensely demoralizing—argument.

"I know these things are rarely ever that simple," I said, releasing his arm. "I suppose I just hoped this wasn't all for nothing."

"It's a bloody mire." He reached out as if he'd a mind to offer me comfort, but shoved a fist into his jacket pocket at the last moment. "Inspector Davies claims he did not procure pornography from Charles Hartigan. The constable who was caught with pictures did mention that we should look more closely at both Davies and Hartigan, but then alleged not to have procured his photographs from either of them. Hartigan still points a finger at Davies—however, in order to take down a member of the police, it'll take more than the word of a desperate man caught out for his crimes."

"You're right, this is a mire." I nodded, doing my best to follow. "You have Hartigan, at least. So that's something."

A guilty mien distorted Croft's features.

"*Tell* me you have Hartigan."

"I made a formal offer of immunity for his information. I had to let him go."

I said a foul word that drove Croft's eyebrows higher just as the door to the morgue swung outward. With surprising reflexes for a man of his size, Croft pulled me out of the way before the heavy door knocked me out of my boots and onto my backside.

"Stand aside!" barked an orderly with a dark, waxed mustache. He and his apologetic cohort hefted a gurney holding a body enshrouded by the conventional white sheet. Theirs was not an easy load, judging by the girth of the corpse.

Dr. Phillips lingered behind them, wiping his freshly washed hands on a crisp white cloth. His apron, however, was anything but clean, though the only stain I dared identify was blood.

"Lend me a half-hour, lads, before bringing me the next—Oh! Miss Mahoney, punctual as always." He paused, bushy silver brows lowering over brilliant blue eyes as Croft was uncovered by the swinging door. "Inspector, did I misremember telling you I had my only morning appointment taken by Miss Mahoney?"

I leveled Croft a speaking glance. No detective wizardry after all. He'd gone straight to the source and then undermined a rejection by forcing his way into *my* appointment. I'd a mind to tattle to Amelia on him so she could box his ears.

"Miss Mahoney and I are looking into the same deaths," Croft answered, skipping over the subtext of Dr. Phillip's rebuke. "I figured you'd be able to share more with an inspector present, so I accompanied her as a favor."

The pompous bastard!

I'd been rendered speechless by many a ludicrous claim, but this one beat them all.

Croft, the smarmy git, knew exactly what he was doing here, and came to capitalize upon my good graces with the doctor. How dare he pretend it was otherwise?

Phillips gave the inspector a credulous glance before turning to me with a shrug.

"The inspector was kind enough to show up on my

landing, unannounced, and escort me hither," I said, with a smile that was more a baring of teeth.

Phillips nodded, scratching at muttonchops wanting a trim, and I was swamped with a warm wave of fondness for the man. Though his nose was prominent and his chin diminutive, he was a very pleasant man to look at because of how he comported himself. Much like my father had once been, he was a gentleman from a bygone era. Though he had the mind of a scientist, he had the soul of a poet, and his compassionate regard for both the dead and the living made him one of the most respected and liked surgeons in the realm. With his impeccable manners and expensive, if dated, suits, he would have been as welcome at court as in his coroner's office.

With quick, efficient motions, he untied his apron and abandoned it to a laundry bin on top of soiled sleeve covers as he led us to the wall of drawers in which the dead were kept on slabs of ice.

"Jane Sheffield, yes?" he asked, retrieving a Globe-Wernicke clipboard from his desk.

The question had been rhetorical, as he counted four drawers from the right and two rows down, opening it with the flair of a magician unveiling his trick.

"She'll be released tomorrow," he informed us.

"To whom?" Croft asked.

"To the pauper's graves, I'm afraid, as no kin come forward to claim her."

"Such a shame," I murmured.

"Such is often the case with these sorts of women." Dr. Phillips efficiently pulled the sheet back, uncovering Jane's waxen features, neck, and shoulders. Beneath the sheet, a Y incision over her chest would advertise his autopsy, the findings of which we were here to ascertain.

These sorts of women.

For some reason, it disappointed me that he'd spoken of Jane and women like her so dismissively. I supposed I shouldn't have been surprised—though Dr. Philips was a kind soul, he was still a man of prominence who considered himself so high above *these sorts of women*.

"Have you ascertained her cause of death?" Croft asked, staring down at Jane with grim solemnity.

Did he see Amelia's face superimposed over Jane's? A stark reminder of everything she risked when he was a boy?

"You would think I had by now," Phillips answered. "But I've spent hours in the laboratory, along with a few chemist colleagues of mine, and can't seem to pinpoint exactly what happened to the girl."

"What do you mean?" I asked. "She was not poisoned?"

"On the contrary. She almost certainly was." He patted his vest pockets for his spectacles, and not finding them, held the clipboard farther away from his face as he flipped through hastily scrawled notes. "Tell me, do either of you know if the victim had a history of thrombosis?"

"Of what?" I looked up from her eerily still features, as still as that photograph on Hartigan's wall. She looked nothing like the girl in the portrait. Animated and lively, young and deceptively innocent.

I'd have not recognized her like this. Hair and features frozen and discolored. Eyes pressed closed by weights.

"Oh, right." Phillips gave a self-effacing chuckle. "You're aware that when we're wounded, our blood builds up a scab over the skin to protect and heal it from the inside out. Well, sometimes when a wound is only internal, the blood will attempt to do the same out of confusion and clot in our veins. This clot, a thrombosis, will often dissolve on its own, but if it moves to the lungs, or the heart, or—God forbid—the brain, it's generally quite lethal."

"You think one of these... thrombosis killed her?" I queried.

"Actually, the opposite. Her blood was like water. Thinner, if you'd believe it. I've never seen anything like it. It's why she bled from her orifices. However, I did not find sufficient internal hemorrhaging to kill her, and her stomach had been almost petrified by a corrosive agent. Just not one I have identified as of yet. Some chemicals are difficult to test for when diluted in the blood or the stomach contents. Also, there are deadly agents that can be absorbed through the skin, or breathed in through the lungs, that could kill. It's such a mystery."

I shuddered, doing my best to forget that the world was such a toxin-rich environment. "So, you think two different substances were responsible for how she was found. Any idea what might have thinned her blood to such a degree?"

He shrugged. "New medicines are always making such claims, but we've not produced a tried-and-true thrombogenic anticoagulant as of yet."

"Then how are these blood clots treated?" I asked.

"Most often with rest and prayer." He grimaced. "Some physicians will prescribe silicates, but that wouldn't have caused Miss Sheffield's issue."

"That's unsettling," Croft, who'd been patient and quiet, muttered out of the side of his mouth. "With so much that can go amiss, how can you be certain to treat any condition with certainty?"

Phillips snorted, clapping Croft on the shoulder. "I've always said madness is a lack of doubt, my boy. Nothing is certain, and everything deserves a second opinion. We doctors are experts at *not* knowing, though few will tell you so."

"Comforting," the inspector griped under his breath.

I smothered a smile, though Phillips seemed not to have heard Croft's sarcasm.

"There are plants that are said to have anticoagulant properties," he continued. "But they've not been proven in any clinical demonstrations and therefore are the domain of those women I like to call kitchen witches."

"Kitchen witches?" I echoed.

"Midwives, neighborhood healers, herbalists both of ethnic tradition and self-taught, or worse, religious deniers of the scientific method and scholarship as a whole. They often dispense these remedies to either miraculous or more often disastrous effect. It all depends on variables out of their control."

"Same could be said for your lot," Croft pointed out, bringing to mind the veritable dispensary of herbs in his own kitchen. "And there are too many who can't afford a doctor's care that have nowhere else to go but to the neighborhood healer."

"Just so." Phillips regarded the large inspector with a speculation I couldn't identify. One that almost seemed approving. "Medicine is a practice, not a promise. We are learning new things all the time, and some of those lessons are hard. Such as when we find standard practice is actually more harmful than healing."

Female herbalists, I considered. Like Aramis Night Horse's mother. Like Amelia with her teas and poultices, and even Indira with her exotic spices used for both food and remedies. "Women used to be burned for the skill they had with herbs," I remarked. "Maybe because they healed the wrong people, or didn't poison the right ones."

"I'm the first to admit that medicine is often made from such herbal remedies. Distilled down or extracted in a lab. So many illnesses can be treated or cured with something as simple as mint, pepper, or ginger—how ever, I take issue with the untrained treating the sick. It's dangerous, and I see the effects in this office too often."

Phillips pulled the sheet back up over Jane's head, and Croft helped him to slide the heavy slab back into the drawer.

Though I'd become somewhat inured to death, I had to hide a part of me that was distraught at the sight of Jane disappearing. Of her being trapped in that cupboard alone in the dark. The next time she was released, she'd be put in the ground, haphazardly tossed onto a pile of unwanted bodies in a field to the north and dissolved with lye. Her name not marked with a stone, but on records somewhere in a dusty storeroom.

Her lovers—her customers—would move on to some other warm, willing girl, losing themselves in supplementary pleasures.

Who would miss her? Who else would remember?

"What was she to you?" Phillips was suddenly at my side, looking down at me as if sensing the maudlin direction of my thoughts.

"Where's Croft?" I asked.

"Popped to the loo whilst you were staring at the drawer like you might bring the girl back from the dead."

"Lost in thought," I said by way of explanation. "I didn't hear him leave."

He patted my shoulder, leaving the warm weight of his hand there. "I haven't seen you in months, my dear. Do you very much mind if I ask after your welfare? It's none of my business, but I did hear from Croft and Aberline that you'd lost a childhood friend in a fire."

"I received your flowers." I took his hand and pressed it between mine. "I'm sorry I was gauche and didn't send a note of thanks."

"Pish." He waved his other hand as if to bat my apology away while squeezing my fingers softly. "I'm just glad to see you interested in the truth once again, though I worry about the cases you're taking. This death has no sign of the Ripper, and I can see that you've recently been hurt. What are you up to?"

I told him about my dramatically short stint at The Orchard and my disastrous acting as a lady of the evening. About Jane and Alys, Amelia and Croft, and even Beatrice. I glossed over the bit about my attack and the Ripper threat, whilst leaving Night Horse and Jorah out the story altogether.

"I worry about the company you keep, though it's not my place to say so." He took a sip of the coffee he'd poured us both whilst I spoke, and I stared at the third steaming cup he'd thoughtfully prepared for Croft. We stood at a counter across from his medical implements, and I examined his domain.

Coffee tasted strange in environs such as this. The acid became metallic, like blood, and sometimes the aftertaste lingered with a hint of the chemical odors permeating the morgue. Better that than the cloying aroma of decay whispering around the edges of the more stringent scents.

"You're lovely to worry," I said, and meant every word. "The world could use more honorable men like you."

"We both know my honor has a price, and we split the profits, you and I."

I stared into my mug. "That's different."

"Is it? Honor is not always an advantage. Look at Croft, for example. For him, it is a liability."

"What do you mean?" I set my cup down abruptly on the desk over which we stood.

"He cannot live in the shades of grey that we do, and his stout heart would shrivel at certain truths." Phillips was staring at me with piercing eyes full of meaning.

A meaning I caught like a lance to the chest.

He was speaking of our business together, of my dealings with the Hammer and the Blade. Of the bodies I brought to him, the demise of which he never questioned.

It didn't matter if Croft desired me, as Jorah had claimed, as the heat of his own gaze sometimes suggested. Somewhere inside I knew I could kiss the ire from Grayson Croft's hard mouth. That I could melt his muscle with curious fingers.

But if he knew me, if he ever truly *knew* me... he'd likely see me hanged.

I had too many secrets—too many sins—for a man like Croft.

"Honor never did anyone I loved much good," I said bitterly, thinking of my brutalized father, of my murdered brothers, of the war that tore my family apart.

I swallowed all of that, slamming the door to the vault in which I kept my family.

"Your and my dealings together is not the only truth that would put a wall between Inspector Croft and me," I said. "His honor would be damaged by so much more than that." I was thinking, of course, of Katherine Riley and what she'd done to his nephew. It was a sword hanging over our heads. A blade I never wanted to slice him with, though it cut me every moment I kept it from him.

"Truth is a funny thing." Phillip's tone changed from somber to sprightly. "It's often difficult to pin down."

I wrinkled my nose at him. "I've always thought truth exists, whether we believe it or not, whether we've found it or not. And it's the one constant in the whole world."

"Debatable." The doctor tilted his head from side to side, as if weighing the options. "Does truth exist in the world or in the mind? Is it a constant or can it be bent to perception? Science softens these questions, and I find that consistently calming. But there are few truths I could claim are constant."

A headache bloomed behind my eyes, and I watched the door for Croft's expected return. I was unable to keep up with Phillips today.

"Did you find anything out about Alys Hywell?" I asked, changing the subject.

"I found something interesting in Bond's farce of a report." Phillips opened almost every desk drawer to find the document in question.

Dr. Bond, a noted behavioral expert and neuroscientist, and Dr. Phillips were forever at odds, and I found their bickering adorable.

Finally consulting his notes, he said, "Alys Hywell was a distinct color of blue, especially around the eyes and lips, which is to be expected of a body drowned in the Thames in January. However, there was a blue powder on Jane Sheffield's lips as I wiped the blood from her face. A cosmetic of some kind, oil-based, I gather. And another woman, as well, was found with the same unction on her face some time ago in Knightsbridge. Heavily made up, her lips tinted a bit blue around the edges... I forget her name, though I've sent for the records."

That had to be something. "What do you make of it?"

"I'm not sure." He tapped his chin. "Reminds me of a theater production I saw once, where women turned to banshees and other such vengeful spirits and killed the Romans. These women were ladies of the evening all. Perhaps actresses as well? It almost seems to me... Well, no, surely I'm being ridiculous."

"What?" I prodded. "Tell me."

"Well, it almost seems ritualistic, doesn't it? Like something from the occult."

Kitchen witch. Why did I keep thinking those words?

Why would women paint themselves to appear dead when they were not?

In their hearts, women were vast creatures, often darker than the world gave us credit for.

What if a woman had gone through so much trauma, she was no longer sane? What if she'd lost something, say a child, and it broke her?

I wasn't thinking of Amelia, was I?

She knew all the victims. Often had Alys to her home, and delivered remedies to Beatrice.

I gasped.

Bea! Beset by that cough that refused to abate... Could it be caused by something insidious?

"Did Dr. Bond check Alys Hywell for poisons?" I asked.

"It doesn't say here—"

"Could you do it?" I gripped his arm. "For me?"

"She's in the ground. I don't have enough to exhume her for examination; there's not even a case on her death. Bond ruled it a suicide."

"I think he was wrong," I said. "Can you talk to him for me? Ask him about this blue substance and see if he noted it anywhere? Perhaps it didn't make it into the final report because he didn't think it important."

"Talk to Bond?" He slumped his shoulders forward in a comically boyish gesture. "Must I?"

"Please? It could be the key to solving these murders."

He heaved a beleaguered sigh. "All right. If only because it'll keep you out of alleys with violent men and the back rooms of brothels. I'll call upon him this afternoon and get back to you when I can."

I had to stop myself from doing something untoward, like throwing my arms around his neck. "Thank you. Thank you for everything. I will be in touch soon, likely with business. It seems the Syndicate is done being patient with my mourning."

He opened a supply cupboard and extracted a clean apron. "Very good. But do try to stay out of trouble, Miss Mahoney. I worry over you from time to time."

I kissed him on the cheek as he bothered with the ties behind him, and he blushed from his collar to his pate. "I'll be careful."

"No, you won't, but thank you for humoring an old man."

"I'm going to try to sneak out before Croft returns," I said.

"I sent him to the visiting washrooms on the third floor." He winked at me. "There's often a queue."

Flashing him my most brilliant smile, I swept out of his office and gathered my hem so I could jog up the steps and avoid—

"Where are you off to now?"

The very man in question stood above me, backlit by the anemic light let into the windows of the hospital corridor. It drove his deep-set eyes further beneath his strong brow, turning them oddly demonic from this angle.

I couldn't meet his gaze. Not with where my thoughts had just been.

Cresting the stairs to the main floor, I swept past him, tucking my umbrella beneath my arm so I might pull on my gloves.

As he was wont to do, he fell into step with me, following toward the main entrance.

"Dr. Phillips is going to consult with Dr. Bond today about Alys Hywell's death. He's searching for more similarities and the possibility of poisons," I informed him.

"Good, I'll tell him to report it to me, since you are 'leaving it alone.'"

I congratulated myself for keeping my mouth shut, though I had a few choice things I wanted to say to him. I wouldn't give him the satisfaction in public.

He held open a door for me, so I opened the one next to it, letting myself out.

Though Croft was not a dramatic man, his sigh certainly was. "Are you going to tell me where you're off to or not?"

"I fail to see how that is any of your—"

A large shoulder bumped Croft's in the causeway, and he ricocheted into me.

"Oi!" His hands closed around my shoulders, stabilizing me as he called after the discourteous man marching toward the hospital.

"Sorry 'bout that, mate," the chap called over his shoulder.

That. Voice.

I whirled, recognizing the ogre at once. "It's him!" I pointed, jostling Croft. "That's the man who attacked me in the alley!"

My assailant looked back at me first, and recognition sparked in his gaze before he moved on, locking eyes with Croft.

Violence shimmered in the air for the time it took to take a breath.

Then both exploded into action.

Chapter Twenty

❦

I couldn't say what the man saw in Croft's eyes that made him turn tail and flee.

Even I'd underestimated his bulk in the dark of the alley, and it was evident now that he had a stone on Croft at the very least. And I knew he was capable of violence.

The second his muscle twitched, the inspector was after him like a hound let off its lead, his dark coat flaring behind his legs. He barked his credentials and ordered everyone out of the way, but it didn't stop the pursued man from bowling over a few smoking gentlemen like a gather of ninepins.

Making much slower progress in my skirts and heeled boots on the slippery walk, I noted the gentlemen were helping each other up once I reached them, so I followed as fast as I was able.

Before they reached the hedge, beyond which a bustling street might have been an optimal place to lose one in a chase, Croft dove at the blackguard's legs, felling him like an ancient oak.

By the time I caught them up, the man was secured with his hands behind his back and was mewling like a child caught beneath a school yard bully.

"I did no'fing!" he cried, more for the onlookers' benefit than ours. "I'm a gravely injured man."

"You're about to be," Croft snarled, standing so he could turn the man onto his side, presumably to pull him to his feet. "A gravely injured man doesn't run like that."

"Wait," I said. "If he's the right man, he would be telling the truth." Certain he was, I still couldn't help myself from poking at his shoulder with the point of my unused umbrella.

His yowl of pain was confirmation to us both. I'd stabbed this man two nights ago, and I still bore the marks of his brutality.

"I want my knife back," I demanded, staring down into features only frightening because of their ugliness. Pale eyes placed too close together over a potato-pocked nose gave him the appearance of a wombat I'd seen at the zoo once.

Later, I realized the comparison was a dreadful insult to adorable wombats everywhere.

He spat at me, but his pain and lack of breath hindered his aim, and he only hit the hem of my dress.

Croft cuffed him, and he moaned, most of his body going slack.

"What's your name?" I asked.

"John Johnson," he said, his lip curled back in a hateful leer. It was a farce of an answer, and everyone knew it.

"Have an orderly call for a police wagon," Croft boomed, his nostrils flaring and his eyes still bright from the stimulation of the chase. "I'm taking him to the Yard."

"You can't. Wound's gone bad," Mr. Not John Johnson rasped, moaning with apparent distress. "Bitch stabbed me! Arrest *her*."

"You will watch your mouth, or I'll relieve it of all

its teeth." Croft's own teeth didn't unclench even to provide the threat.

"Tell me who paid you to attack me," I demanded. "I know it was no random assault of chance."

"Fuck you," the man growled.

I held up a hand against Croft's physical response, and to my surprise, it worked. He merely held the man with his arms painfully secured behind him.

I saw the telltale bloom of blood seeping through the layers of Mr. Johnson's winter clothes. "I'll convince my friend here to go easy on you if you just tell me who hired you to hurt me."

"Weren't supposed to 'urt you none. Just manhandle you a bit. She said it was to scare you off somefing. But you were a right cunt, and I thought you needed a lesson taught ya."

I watched a strange transformation overtake Croft. Rather than exploding with a fiery rage as he sometimes did, he blinked, and a chilling calm settled over him like a mantle. He took extra care hauling the man to his feet, going so far as to brush little leaves and specks of grass from his shabby wool coat.

Then he leaned his face uncomfortably close to his captive and said in a barely audible voice, "I can't *wait* until we're alone."

To his credit, the prisoner didn't show fear. Perhaps he was even less intelligent than he looked, if that were possible.

She. A woman had hired him. An exhilaration overtook me, the particular elation of being on the precipice of piecing together the solution to a problem that was assumed unsolvable.

"Who was she?" I asked.

His eyes narrowed to impossible slits. "Don't know her name. Wouldn't tell it ya if I did."

"You'll tell me," Croft said before turning to me.

"Dammit, Fiona, check if someone's sent for the wagon. This piece of filth isn't fit to speak in decent company."

I ignored him, having seen at least a handful of people jump to follow his order to summon the police the moment he'd issued it. "Please." I wasn't above pleading with a piece of filth to get the information I so desperately needed. "Just tell me anything. Was she light or dark? Young or older?"

"She's prettier than *you*," he said, though it'd lost a bit of its effect due to his alarming pallor and the bloom of sweat on his brow. "Skinnier and sweeter, too. Offered to suck me cock for a penny after she paid me pounds. Took 'er up on it, I did. I like me whores young, fair-haired, and frilly rather than—"

Croft jostled him, jerking the arm on his injured side. "You were not born into this world, you were shat into it. And you will be nothing but the muck of ravens when I'm through with you."

"Izzy," I whispered, dumbfounded by the intensity of my hurt.

Both men stared at me with comically similar quizzical expressions.

"Isabelle James. She works at The Orchard. She was the only one who was kind to me. She gave me impression of a girl without guile."

Johnson, or whatever his name was, snorted. "No such fing. All whores are good at acting. It's how they make their money."

"Enough out of you." Croft shoved him forward, toward the street. "Amelia was to visit Beatrice with some tea and jams she'd made," he told me.

"I'm on my way," I said, dashing toward the street.

"No!" He could no sooner release his charge and chase me as he could stop me with mere words. "Fiona, you stay here. I'll go myself once they arrive to gather this human stain."

I already had my hand outstretched to hail a hackney, pretending I didn't hear him.

"Say nothing to anyone at The Orchard!" he called after me, intelligent enough to realize there was no stopping me now, though his voice became increasingly louder. "And if you see a constable, you take him with you. Understand? Use my name. And don't bloody confront any suspects! Fiona?"

I waved back at him. At least, I thought I did. My heart raced, each thump a painful bruise, my mind reeling with so many thoughts I couldn't seem to pin one down.

"I'm bleeding," my attacker complained. "Don't ya have to show me to a doctor?"

"Oh, you'll be bandaged," Croft answered, though the rest of his reply was lost to the cacophony in my mind and a late London morning.

Izzy. I'd considered her an ally, if not a friend. We hardly knew each other, but she'd demonstrated such a sweetness of nature. She'd been almost childlike in her interactions with others.

And it'd all been a lie.

I thought of the night I'd been attacked. She was one of the women to drive him away. Had that all been staged? Or was it Indira's presence?

Or perhaps because he'd been about to hurt me, and that wasn't what she'd hired him to do?

Regardless of this revelation, I intrinsically rejected her responsibility for the murders of two innocent women. I wanted an explanation. A good reason for her to do this terrible thing to me.

All whores are good at acting.

Her and Indira's faces floated before me in the darkness of that night. I'd had the thought that they resembled ghosts because of their pale gowns and their paler-than-usual skin.

I'd assumed they were walking out in the cold for

too long, because their lips had been tinted with the lightest shade of blue in the pallid lamplight.

Or had they been painted?

It was all connected somehow.

Ghostly regalia. Corpses with bleeding eyes. Poisoned prostitutes. Preachers. Pornographers. Photographs. Police.

Kitchen witches.

I do commemorative pictures of many ladies' societies, if that's what you're after.

Charles Hartigan's words fractured into a thousand pieces, echoing through my racing thoughts like ricocheting bullets in an empty room.

This very well could be bigger than Izzy...

What if, instead of one bad apple in The Orchard, the rot had spread to them all?

Chapter Twenty-One

❧❧❧

S hame struck me immediately upon finding Amelia in Bea's parlor at The Orchard.

I'd entertained dark suspicions about her. Looking at her now, I found the entire notion patently ridiculous.

Dressed in an airy lemon day gown, more suited to a spring morning than a winter's afternoon, she beamed at my entrance. If two streaks of silver did not emboss her glossy, dark hair, one might not have known she was over forty.

One look at me and her smile faded in slow increments.

Bea, on the other hand, seemed to notice nothing amiss. "Fiona, my dear, won't you join us for tea?"

Amelia's bright and statuesque grace only served to illuminate how weary and frayed Bea was in the light of day. Her jewel-red evening regalia, the crystalline beads shimmering in the firelight, made me certain she hadn't yet been to bed.

They sat across from each other in chairs drawn close to the fire, and I noted that there was no tea to be found, though I'd been offered it.

"What's wrong, Fiona?" Amelia stood, dispensing with pleasantries as she pushed a book, a blanket, and some discarded frippery around on the settee to clear a place for me.

"Does Izzy work today?" Manners dictated I sit when bade to, though I was too anxious to do aught but perch on the edge of the settee, ready to jump up at a moment's notice.

"She was supposed to." Beatrice waved a handkerchief she clutched in her hand. "But I haven't seen hide nor hair of her since last night." Finally, she seemed to notice my state of extreme discomfiture, and she blanched. "Tell me something else has not happened."

I shook my head, distressed to hear that Isabelle hadn't shown her face yet. There was no way she could know that she was suspected of anything, was there?

Croft had warned me not to divulge information to anyone, but surely he hadn't meant his sister. And I had to say something, hadn't I?

"I was at the hospital chatting with the coroner today," I began. "And I happened upon my assailant from the other night. Apparently, his stab wound had gone to rot."

"Oh God, Fiona! Are you all right? That must have been terrifying." Amelia reached forward and pressed my fingers between her hands.

"Serves him right." Beatrice knocked on the side table as if applauding with her knuckles. "Tell me you went to the police."

"Croft was with me, and he apprehended the fellow. Who..." I bit my lip, preparing myself to deliver bad news. "He intimated that Isabelle James commissioned my attack."

"Izzy?" Amelia gasped.

"*Our* Izzy?" Bea put the back of her hand to her mouth. "He must be mistaken."

Amelia released me to reach for Beatrice, squeezing her arm. "You said she hasn't arrived to work for the afternoon... Is she often tardy?"

"Never. And neither is she truant." Bea had yet to cease shaking her head. "I don't believe it. It had to be someone else using her name."

"It wasn't her name he gave me, but her description." I clasped my hands together, hating the distress pinching the older woman's face. She really did look quite unwell. "Can I get you anything?" I asked, feeling ineffectual and cumbersome.

"No, thank you, dear. Butler is bringing the tea."

I nodded, wondering what to do next. "Is Indira about? I think the police would want to talk to her as well."

"They'll be here looking for Isabelle?" Bea asked.

"Yes, they're on their way once Croft has my attacker secured in a wagon."

Bea let out a beleaguered sigh. "Indira isn't supposed to be here until this evening, but she left early last night, begging a terrible headache." Digging fingers against eyes beset with more wrinkles than they had only a couple of nights before, she said, "I suppose the headache is contagious."

Amelia hovered and tutted as if she was also at a loss for what to do.

"Could she be with Sophia?" I asked.

That got Bea's attention. "Whyever would she be with Sophia?"

I grappled with what I ought to reveal and which of my suspicions needed to stay only that. Could I tell Bea she might lord over a den of vipers, just waiting to poison their next victim? Should I say that I was afraid that victim might be her?

"I saw them together yesterday, Sophia and Indira," I admitted. I'd wait until Croft brought constables here, then we'd piece together the entire story.

"I never imagined they were close..." Bea looked into the middle distance, distracted. "I hated to lose Sophia, especially to that pompous arse. The Hammer."

She spat the name as if it tasted terrible. "What a ridiculous moniker." She paused, horror dawning on her features. "Do you think Indira and Sophia have fallen afoul of whatever scheme Isabelle is caught up in?"

Even now, it seemed, she didn't want to believe the worst of her girls.

"I truly can't say," I replied. "At this point, it seems as though anyone could be in danger."

Butler appeared at the door carrying a tray with a china tea service, as silent and sinister as ever. Heavy lids and a shaking hand told me he'd had as much sleep as the rest of them last night, and his suit was in dire need of a laundering.

Beatrice thanked him and ordered him to send the remaining girls home for the day, as they'd be closing.

He nodded and left without a reply.

"Izzy, what were you thinking?" Beatrice whispered as Amelia poured out three cups and garnished each saucer with a delicate biscuit from an accompanying dish. "I couldn't ever imagine... She's always been such a sweet thing. Simple, all told. I hardly believe she has the wits to choreograph your attack, Fiona. Let alone anything so insidious as a murder."

I put out a staying hand, in which Amelia set my cup and saucer. "We don't know that she had anything to do with it just yet. The police only want to speak with her."

"But why would she want to scare Fiona away from your investigation unless she had something to hide?" Amelia asked, stirring in two lumps of sugar and a healthy dollop of cream.

Bea clutched the handkerchief to her chest, and the lace settled into the wrinkles of her decolletage. "I can't tell you what this does to me. The betrayal I feel."

"I can only imagine," Amelia said.

We drank deeply for a moment, each of us lost in our thoughts.

Betrayal. I didn't believe in Nola's cards, but... perhaps this would satisfy her nonetheless. *I* wasn't the one betrayed by someone close to me. But Beatrice had just been betrayed by a girl she'd done so much to protect. She loved those who worked for her, I thought, and that fit nicely into the macabre reading.

"The police are coming, you say?" Beatrice asked, her eyes becoming blearier by the minute. "I'm not dressed to receive them." She fluffed at her hair, which had begun to escape its chignon.

Amelia finished her tea in two gulps and stood, abandoning it to the side table. "Let me help you, Bea," she offered, helping her friend to stand by the elbow. "We'll pick you out something respectable."

"Not too respectable," Beatrice said. "If your handsome brother will be stopping in." She laughed along with us at her attempt at levity, but each of us sounded hollow.

"Thank you, Amelia, you're such a help." She leaned heavily on Amelia's arm. "I was feeling rather weak and overwrought today, which is not customary for me. That tea has seemed to help."

"I gave something to Butler to add to it," Amelia boasted. "It helps with lung congestion and vitality."

I looked down into my cup, having only taken two sips.

Bea smiled over at her. "Oh, I *thought* I tasted something different."

So did I.

I couldn't say exactly what made me wary of the brew, but I put the cup down.

Bea turned at the doorway, swaying a little at the motion. "I almost forgot. Another letter came for you, Fiona, dear. Like last time. It's on my desk. I was going to send for you today, but it seems you came to me. You might want to read it and decide what to do before the police get here."

My heart dove from its cage into my churning stomach.

Another Ripper letter. Now?

"I'll be right up, then," I said, my head swimming with an entirely new set of concerns, the pace of my breaths elevated so much that I had to lean on the desk once I'd reached it to make certain I was stable.

Amelia sent me a quizzical look. "Post for you was addressed here?" she asked. "Should we stay? Is it something you'll need to share?"

"No, do go on, I'll be along." I shook my head and instantly regretted it as an ache bloomed behind my eyes. I suddenly wanted so intensely to be alone.

Alone with the Ripper.

When I looked up again from the unstamped seal, I realized I was.

Unlike the other letters, this one was sealed at the edges by some sort of paper epoxy. I was afraid to unfold it without it tearing.

I eased open the middle desk drawer and found nothing of use but some pens, stationery, some envelopes, and a few odds and ends. Next, I reached to the right drawer, looking for a letter opener, one I might even keep with me until this sudden and intense sense of unease around Amelia Croft abated.

"You didn't finish your tea."

Not Amelia's voice.

Just then, the cold glint of a blade caught my eye. A knife.

My knife.

The one I'd left in the shoulder of the man who'd been hired to scare me away from the case. From The Orchard.

From the truth.

What was it doing in Beatrice Chamberlain's desk drawer?

I grabbed for it, my fingers stiff and clumsy as they found the cold press of the lacquered handle.

When I whirled for the door, it took an astonishing amount of time for the rest of the room to catch up. I was going to be sick if the floor beneath me didn't stop swaying like a ship in a storm.

Her face came into focus.

Bea.

Strong and stern and... sorrowful.

"I wish you were less clever, Fiona," she said, still seeming wan and tired, but no longer weak. What I read on her features shocked me just as much as the revelation. Not only was there resignation there, but genuine regret. Her proud shoulders slumped forward and her mouth was drawn into a hard line, as though bravely fighting the wobble in her chin. "Such a blasted pity. I *really* admired you."

Admired.

Past tense.

I clung to consciousness with the claws of a raptor bird snatching at its prey.

"What did you give me?" I demanded. Or would have, if my tongue had obeyed.

Where is Amelia? I wanted to ask. Was she working alongside her, or was Croft going to have to identify both of our remains?

I couldn't let that happen. I had to fight.

In slow motion, the knife slid from my hands as I clutched the desk in one last desperate attempt to stay upright. I didn't want to go down. I didn't want to bleed from my orifices and end up naked on a cold slab in a drawer.

I couldn't die without knowing what the Ripper had to say.

Chapter Twenty-Two

❦

S omething had crawled into my mouth and subsequently died.

Or perhaps I'd licked a penny drenched in bog water. Metallic and decaying, my tongue was like sandpaper against my palate. The ground pressed hard against my back, the cold seeping through the layers of my clothing.

I needed water, something to reconstitute my mouth, my aching body and rolling stomach.

Prying weighted eyes open changed nothing. I blinked. Blinked again.

Only the scratch of my lids against dry pupils told me I'd been successful, but it remained as dark out here as when my eyes were closed. No seam of drapes or light peeking around a door.

It was as if I were in a cave with no entrance.

Or buried alive.

Amid an immediate surge of panic, my limbs flailed and caught nothing.

Not buried, then. At least not in a grave.

I lay there attempting to get my bearings, to catch and hold on to panicked breaths. What did I know? It was cold in here, but not like one would suffer out-of-doors in January, or below ground.

The air was thick with scents. I breathed them in, testing it. The metallic taste I'd initially noted was actually an aroma sharpened by chemical undertones.

Beneath me, the ground was rough, but not with earth—with fibers.

Carpets.

But not the kind one would find beneath one's feet at home. Industrial. Wiry. Abrasive to my fingertips.

All right. I was indoors. That was something. Now I needed to explore further.

When I struggled into a sitting position, the darkness spun and I had no point of reference to cling to, so I held my head at the temples, rubbing the throb of pain, waiting, hoping it would pass.

What had Beatrice given me?

Betrayal.

To become as mad as Aunt Nola was one of my greatest fears. Yet, in that moment, I was almost convinced to start giving her spirit guides more credence from now on.

If I survived this.

I'd been expecting betrayal, but from all the wrong people. From the bold and brilliant criminals in my sphere, craven creatures of the night that they were. From the desperate, desolate, or depraved. The greedy and the guilty.

But not Beatrice Chamberlain.

Not her.

Even now, I rejected the memory of her features twisted with malice, swimming over me as I fought for consciousness.

Lanced with an emotion I could only identify as hurt, I fought a prick of tears amongst my existential panic. I wiped at my eyes furiously, not allowing them to fall.

Right now, I needed to figure out the *where* and the *how*. I could consider the why later, after I escaped.

If I didn't escape... well, that was a grief avoided.

I couldn't begin to consider fatalistic outcomes just yet. Lest they become a reality.

That macabre thought galvanized me, and my first course of action was a scouting expedition. I needed more information, and if I couldn't see anything, then I was forced to rely on my other senses.

It is difficult to express the sense of dread one feels when using one's bare fingers to blindly explore one's vicinity. On my hands and knees, I made slow progress in a random direction. Keeping one hand on the ground, I reached out with the other in a wide arc. First at floor level, and then higher. Finding nothing, I'd put that hand down ahead of me and repeat on the other side.

An eternity passed before my hand encountered something: smooth lumber resting against the ground. I followed the shape with my hand, patting my way up what was obviously a furniture leg.

A desk? A table? Wait... a bench. *Above* the bench was a table.

I used it to haul myself to my feet. Splaying my hands on the surface, I took a moment to stabilize myself, to check that my legs, apparently now made of pudding, would hold the rest of me.

They seemed at least willing to try, though I didn't feel safe letting the table go just yet. Instead, I walked the length of the long bench, running my hands over oddly thick paper strewn about its surface. My little finger encountered a cold metal object, and I carefully found that it was a tray of some kind.

My fingers found cold liquid inside, and I gasped, snatching it back as if it'd burned. I waited for something to happen, for my skin to start melting off or some other such nightmare.

It didn't.

Bending down, I inhaled close to the liquid, testing the scent. Perhaps a little vinegar or something...

I was parched, and an instinct pressed me to drink, but I quelled it immediately. I trusted nothing here. I resumed my careful journey and would have tripped had I not still been steadying myself on the table.

A body.

I knew it the moment my shoe touched it. The give of flesh was unmistakable, even in the dark.

I dropped to my knees, my hands finding a corseted waist and then a shoulder. I felt down to the limp wrist and ripped off the gloves.

Warm. Still warm, thank God. She had a pulse, too. Strong and steady.

A primal relief drenched me with such ferocity that it was immediately followed by shame. Because it didn't stem from the woman's life, but from my own elation at not being alone to die in the dark.

We had each other to cling to.

"Wake up," I begged, testing her breath with the back of my hand and then shaking her shoulders. Gently at first, and then with more desperation. "Please. Please be all right."

"Fiona?"

My name croaked from behind me startled me so much, I clasped both hands over my mouth to keep from shrieking.

"Fiona, is that you?"

"Amelia?" My voice shook, as I couldn't exactly tell if she were friend or foe. "Where are we?"

"I don't know. Wait..." I heard some rustling about, and suddenly there was light.

Sort of.

The orange glow of a match illuminated the corner behind me. Amelia was slumped with her back against a bare brick wall, her knees pulled up to her chest like a child's as she held the feeble flame close to her face.

Our eyes met and held.

She looked so afraid. So young for someone who'd lived such a long and difficult life.

"What happened?" she asked, her tongue sounding every bit as heavy as mine. "I was on the stairs... then I was dizzy. I fell."

"Beatrice put something in the tea," I said. Because honestly, it was the sum of information I had.

"Not Bea," she whispered. "That's impossible."

I hadn't the energy to argue the point. "Are you hurt? Can you move?" I asked.

She nodded. "A little bruised, but everything seems to be working. Are you?"

"I'm wobbly, but well. Someone else is here. I can't wake her up." I turned back to the woman, but it went dark again.

"Bugger, match burned my finger." I could hear Amelia scuffle closer, careful not to waste a finite supply of light. Clever.

When she reached me, she rose to her knees and clutched me into a tight hug, one I returned with vigor. "I'm sorry you're here," she said. "But thank God."

I knew what she meant, *exactly*.

"Matches," I said, aching to see again. "I can't believe the luck."

I could hear her fumble around with them. "Grayson slips them into my pockets sometimes, just to tease me. To bother me for a light. If we get out of this, I'll never nag at him about his smoking again. *Never*. He can puff away in every room of the house. I care not."

She struck the match on a matchbook and held it between us. But for disheveled hair and a wrinkled dress, she looked no worse for wear.

We both bent over the body still slumbering on the ground, curled on her side. I moved a swath of dark hair away.

"Indira!" Amelia said. "Shit. Oh merciless Christ. Is she dead?"

"No," I said, shaking her again. "She's breathing, but I can't wake her. Indira?" I called, a little louder this time.

Amelia held the match higher, looking over my shoulder to the table. "Maybe there's something here that could—"

Her words died as if they'd been strangled before escaping her throat. I turned from Indira at the sound, and caught the ghastly look of horror on her face before the match went out.

She didn't strike another.

"Amelia?"

"Jesus," she rasped. "My God. My *fucking* hell." A sob, bleak and unbelieving, echoed through the darkness.

"Amelia, what is it?" I asked.

"The devil's been in this room," she keened, her husky voice lower than I'd ever heard it. "We're going to die here."

I reached out and encountered her elbow, gripping it to bring myself closer. "Amelia, light a match."

"I don't want to see," she whispered.

"Then give them here." This was where she and I differed, where I differed from many people. I wanted to see. I *had* to see. Not looking was impossibly more frightening to me.

Amelia surrendered the book of matches, and I folded the flap over the head of one and struck.

The devil's work in a dark room.

I was on my knees before it, looking on in horror, silent and still until the flame bit my fingers. I dropped the match and lit another.

I should have known it would be dead women.

Trapped in photographs strung wall to wall, their faces unearthly pale, their eyes and lips tinged with shadows. Some staring. Some eyes closed. All in variations of nudity.

Amelia averted her face and sobbed quietly.

I couldn't look away. Instead, I pushed myself to my feet and examined every single photograph.

I'd seen plenty of the dead, but not like this. Not arranged in seductive poses, or worse, submission. Some were tied with ropes; others had whip marks on their backs or backsides. A few were presented like supplicant angels on their knees, hands tied together. Still more with their legs open or bent over.

I recognized faces. Jane's. Izzy's. Indira's. I'd bet my life that if I'd ever met Alys, I'd recognize her as well.

But Indira wasn't dead.

I struck another match and studied a photograph of her strung over a bed, her dark hair a swath of ink on the white sheets, her breasts beaded against the cold, her eyes open and staring. Blank. Around her neck was a rope, and a dark substance trickled from the corner of her slightly parted mouth.

Even I couldn't tell the difference from blood.

This was where she and Izzy were coming from the night I was attacked in the alley. *This* was why they looked like ghosts in the insubstantial light. Because they'd been made up to appear dead.

Not for a theater.

But for pleasure.

Was this what some men wanted? Sex with death? A corpse was cold, yes. But she was still. Silent. She had no opinions or emotions or needs. No objections. She was just an inanimate object now. A dead plaything.

I swallowed the bile crawling up the back of my throat, thinking this was the worst thing I might ever see in my life.

Then I looked down at the table.

I was wrong.

Chapter Twenty-Three

❧

I wasn't at all surprised to see Charles Hartigan standing there when a niche opened in the wall. Because he was most definitely the long-limbed but unimpressive man doing such dastardly things to the women in the photographs strewn about the table. He'd been careful to keep his face out of shot, but his form was unmistakable.

As I stood there and stared into his beady eyes, so alarmingly close together, I actively hated that I now knew what his cock looked like.

It was knowledge I'd happily submit to a lobotomy to erase.

"We can charge more for those," he said mildly, holding his lantern aloft to get a better look at his handiwork. "They're not pretending."

I leapt away from the table as if it might bite me. I'd dropped the matches, but it didn't matter now; his lantern illuminated every corner of the small, dark room.

He'd said *we*.

No sooner had I latched on to the thought than Beatrice swept into the room behind him, her evening gown covered with a simple, dark frock coat.

"Bea!" Amelia choked out, taking a few unintentional steps forward before stopping herself. "What is this? What have you gotten yourself tangled into?"

The older woman wiped at exhausted eyes as she took us in. Beyond that, I read in her features something I hadn't expected to find.

Regret. True remorse.

"Amelia," she said, as if chiding a wayward child. "This was never a tangle until you interfered. Until you involved poor Fiona here."

Amelia's pain, her bewilderment, was a palpable thing. It vibrated through the air toward me and plucked my heart right out of its cavity.

Betrayal.

"I was trying to help you find Alys and Jane's killers," Amelia said. "I thought—"

"I know what you thought." Beatrice sighed, leaning her shoulder against the wall as if she needed to be propped up. "I've known you for fifteen years, enough to know you'd never suspect a whore of hurting another whore like this." Her features hardened. "But you always forget that I'm not one of you, and never have been."

"But you sell women," I blurted, my Irish blood heating me from the inside as it gathered rage from fear. "Don't imagine that makes you any better than they are."

"I *am* better, dear," she said with absolute conviction. "When I found my husband had squandered the money I brought in my dowry on his mistresses, on his whores, I could have murdered him. I went to the brothel to do just that, in fact, seeking revenge. What I found was an opportunity. The oldest profession in the world. Women selling their bodies. And if they don't walk the streets, they must rely on men to sell it for them. Men who keep the profits. I could not stand for it, and so I used my husband's name to start a business of my own."

"None of that explains this filth." I motioned to the photographs.

She shook her head at them, as if they offended her as well. "I had a complicated couple of years. Made bad investments. Ran afoul of a few dangerous men who hated the idea of a woman among their ranks. I was forced to search for additional avenues of revenue, which was how I found Mr. Hartigan here."

The man in question bowed as if being presented to debutantes, beaming with pride.

Looking at him made me physically ill.

Amelia shrank back as well, gripping my hand as if doing so lent her strength. "I know there are periodicals and publications full of lewd pictures, and that is always going to be the case, but this is something different, Beatrice. This is... this is..."

"I believe the term is necrophilia," Charles supplied helpfully.

"It's *disgusting*," Amelia spat. "No. Worse than that. I don't even think there's a word for the depravity. For the inhumanity. How could you supply such violence?"

Beatrice pushed herself away from the wall as if rejuvenated by her own growing ire. "Because violence against women makes men come. And men buy what makes them come. Sex is everything to them, once you get down to it. They are simple creatures of pathetic and predictable tastes driven by a hunter's instinct to fuck, maim, and murder."

"That isn't true," I argued.

"Oh? And how would you know?"

I swallowed, cowed by the condescending antipathy in her voice. I knew good men. And I knew a few bad ones, as well. All of them had mentioned they liked their women warm and willing.

And alive, I'd assumed.

"Sex is the urge to mate, and you can't reproduce

with the dead," I said carefully. "This feels to me like a very specific deviancy,"

"And a profitable one," Beatrice said.

"How dare you?" Amelia stepped forward, her grip on my hand tightening to painful. She trembled, but I read as much rage in her as fear. "You murdered Alys, *my friend*, so this sack of dusty shit could sell photographs of himself defiling her corpse?"

Beatrice put up her hand as if to stop her. "Oh, dear God no," she said. "No. Alys and Jane both consented to have these photographs taken. As did Indira here. They were all remunerated."

I'd placed my body in between helpless Indira and the rest of them. They'd have to go through me to get to her... but I rather thought that was what they meant to do.

"What did you do to her?" I demanded.

"Oh, it's just a bit of chloral hydrate," Beatrice said. "Same as you. She's a touch more sensitive to it, evidently. She should wake up any moment."

"Does that mean you're going to let us go?" Amelia asked without much hope in her voice.

"I'm afraid not." Beatrice sniffed as if holding back invisible tears as she turned to me. "I really am sorry you were caught up in this. I wish you'd been easier to scare away, and yet when you showed up with your wounds to warn me, I knew that if I didn't have to be rid of you, we might have been friends."

"You sent Izzy to hire that man to attack me," I accused.

"He took it too far, obviously." She held up her hands. "Isabelle, that idiot girl, probably misremembered the orders."

"She was only good for one thing," Charles leered from where he still blocked the doorway. "Well, two if you count the fucking."

My confusion must have shown on my expression.

"Izzy procured my models for me for a nominal fee," he added.

"Where is she now?" Amelia's voice cracked with emotion.

Bea rubbed at her eyes, stretching the bags beneath them. "Yes, but it was Alys's greed and her ego that did her in. She wanted a bigger cut, tried to leverage secrets to get them. To blackmail me. So I had Butler drown her in the river."

"*No.*" Amelia gasped.

"Are you saying Izzy is dead, too?" I asked, doing my best to keep talking in a pathetic attempt to elongate my life.

Beatrice turned her remorseful gaze on me. She appeared almost contrite. "Isabelle liked you as well. It didn't sit well with her, your attack. She began to have dangerous doubts... to talk nonsense. She should have learned from Jane's mistakes."

"Jane's mistakes? What did she do?"

"Jane went to the police, and, luckily for us, it was a cohort of Davies she confided in. He brought the matter to me, and of course I had to deal with it." Beatrice looked to us as if we would share her frustration, but she found no compassion between us.

Her idea of "dealing with it" was to poison the poor girl.

"Is that how you're going to take care of anyone who defies you?" I slapped the table, so angry I wanted flip it over, to scatter the photographs and stomp them beneath my feet. "You're just going to discard them—us —like so much rubbish?"

She shrugged. "I do what I have to. Just like you."

"You hypocritical bitch!" I snarled, the strength of my wrath intensifying my dizziness, which in turn fueled my anger.

The woman had the gall to look incensed.

"I can't believe I respected you," I cried, incandescent with rage. "I admired your grit and your savvy. I cheered when you chopped the legs from under men who would oppress you. I appreciated that you gave women who would do this dangerous work a safe place off the streets. Away from Jack's domain. Except they were *not* safe. Not from you." I stabbed a condemning finger at her but had to put my hand back down on the table to stop the world from swaying beneath me like a ship in a storm.

"They would have been safe, if they had any loyalty," she countered, venom stinging her every word. "But in this game, one does what one must to survive."

"Don't you dare think you've won," I warned her. "All these disappearances will lead to your doorstep, or do you not remember that the police are on their way to your establishment, if they aren't there already?"

"What sort of imbecile do you take me for? Of course I didn't forget. Which brings me to what happens to you..." She turned toward the door. "Charles, would you fetch the tray, please?"

The tray was already on something just outside their door, because he never left our line of sight to reach for it. Upon the silver perched three glasses of what appeared to be water.

Before Beatrice said anything, I already knew better.

"I am not a woman without a conscience. I find the thought of your suffering untenable. In here is a lethal dose of chloral. It will put you into a comfortable sleep and then paralyze your heart and lungs, so you slip away softly. You won't feel a thing."

"Yes," hissed Charles from behind her. "Nothing is felt by the dead."

I knew, without a doubt, that if we drank that poison, we'd be the next portraits he would take. I'd do everything I could to avoid such degradation.

"I'm not drinking that," Amelia said.

"That is up to you," Charles said with a pleasant, almost anticipatory grin. "But you'll stay in here regardless... and it'll take a day for you to be desperately thirsty. Three at most for you to wither away."

Beatrice fetched silk gloves from a reticule and began to tug them on. "I'm going home to change and bathe, which is where the police will find me after they search the empty Orchard. That business with Isabelle took up almost our entire night, and I'm knackered. Once they inform me that the two of you are missing, I will launch a search the likes of which this city has never seen. One that will lead us to Indira here." She motioned to the slumbering woman, still curled up on the hard ground. "I'll cultivate a fiction wherein she hurt Alys and Jane over sheer whorish jealousy. She wanted to be the premier courtesan and needed to get rid of the opposition. When you two ventured too close to the truth, she'll have killed you, as well, and then disappeared. Possibly back to India."

"Gray will not stop looking for me," Amelia warned. "Nor for my killer. You know how he is, like a hound on a fox hunt."

"Well, India is a rather large place, Amelia, and after all this tragedy, I'm going to decide to sell and retire to the Continent. We all know how Inspector Croft hates to step out of his boundaries..." She chuckled at her own joke, and it was all I could do not to claw her eyes out.

In fact, I realized, that was exactly what I should be doing: fighting for our lives. It was that, dehydration, or poisoning.

I lunged for her, or tried to, but I remained ungainly and slow, my limbs weak and feeble.

Still, I managed a swipe at her, grasped her coat, and held on like a barnacle, clawing my way up it even as she attempted to kick me off.

Hartigan might have come to her aid if Amelia hadn't followed my lead and launched herself at him.

I grasped her hair and wrenched her head back, finding a grim satisfaction when she screeched and flapped about like a demented corvid.

Amelia wrought havoc upon Hartigan, as well, but she'd yet to escape.

With a surge of strength I drew from devil-knew-where, I yanked Beatrice to the ground and narrowly avoided tripping over her flailing limbs on my mad dash for the door.

I made it.

I made it there.

Seven brothers had taught me to be scrappy and tough, but no one my size had a chance against a man like Butler.

He appeared out of nowhere, and with a bear-like paw, hauled me off my feet and slammed me into the wall.

The impact stole my breath, or I might have screamed. The pain blinded me. I fought to move. To breathe. But no part of me would follow commands.

I slid to the earth in a heap.

I heard a slap. A cry.

Amelia.

"I will burn this fucking place to the ground."

I opened my eyes to see Indira with the matches I had dropped. She held one to a photo of herself, paralyzing the room.

Her lovely amber irises reflected the flame, burning with feminine fury. "I remember you told me, Hartigan, that you have film in this building that is some of the most flammable material in the world. That these photographs will burn faster than paper..." She cocked her head. "Should we find out?"

Hartigan held his arms out. "Wait. This whole block will burn, this building with you in it."

"Do you think I care?" She dropped the match dangerously close to the table, and lit another before we watched the first one fall. Indira turned to Butler, who'd clutched Amelia in his enormous grasp. "Let. Her. Go."

He looked back to Beatrice, who still struggled to rise from where I'd knocked her to the ground. She nodded and motioned to the door with a jut of her chin.

Hartigan retreated, and Butler released Amelia to help Beatrice to her feet before standing guard at the door.

"Do what you wish, Indira," Bea said, wrestling the mess I'd made of her wiry hair out of her face, as if she could regain any sort of dignity in our eyes. "We won't be here to spit on the ashes."

With that, she turned and left, taking the lantern with her. The lock slid home, imprisoning us with nothing but each other, a swiftly dwindling book of matches, and three glasses of poison.

"Don't do it," Amelia begged Indira as she wiped blood from her nose. "Those photographs are evidence. They must see the light of day and indict these monsters. So these women will have justice. Alys, Jane... even Izzy. Everyone there whose names we may never know."

Indira lifted the corner of her lip in disgust before being forced to light another match. "Hartigan told me the police aren't even looking at him anymore. And you heard Bea, they're in her pocket."

"Not Grayson. Not my brother," Amelia insisted before turning to me. "Fiona, we have to find a way out of here."

"I can't... I can't move my arm." I gasped, the pain still too raw to consider much of anything. I was tempted to drink the bloody tonic just to get it to stop.

"Oh Christ." Amelia scrambled to me, her hands examining my cradled arm with the touch of a butterfly's wing.

And still, it was all I could do not to snarl at her, to warn her away.

"It's not broken, thank God," she announced. "But he wrenched your shoulder out of socket."

"I can set it," Indira said.

I wanted neither of them to touch it, but I swallowed the intensity of my fear and pain and nodded, bracing for the worst.

Indira wobbled over, handing the book of matches to Amelia before the one she held gave out.

When Amelia lit one again, she was bent over me, staring down into my face like an angel, her hair somehow still smooth and unruffled. Amelia braced behind me and Indira in front, her hands poised on my shoulder.

"It's nice to meet the real you, Fiona," she said with a sad smile.

Then she moved, and I screamed.

Chapter Twenty-Four

✿✿✿

After our throats ran raw from screaming for help, we used the last of the matches to search for a way out. The room was brick but for a door as thick as the wall. Hartigan had perfected the art of imprisoning women.

Canny as the three of us were, we'd yet to find a way out. We even ripped up the carpet to see if we could dig in the packed earth.

I found some corrosive chemicals on a shelf and considered trying to eat at the wood of the door, but these weren't solutions I used in my line of work, and I didn't know what the fumes would do to us in a room with no ventilation.

Without a fire, we grew increasingly frozen as the day died.

And thirsty.

We finally huddled together, wrapping our coats around ourselves, our brains thick with cold and the chloral, failing to imagine what we could possibly do next.

I could feel the hope draining from us all, and it was one of the most sobering moments of my entire life.

"Sophia might figure this out," Indira said through

an obviously dry throat. "I told her what went on here. What I was being paid to do."

That pricked my awareness. "What were you doing with Sophia at The Orchard the other day?" I asked. "I followed you both, thinking you might be in on something together, but Sophia only led me to the Hammer."

"You know the Hammer?" I could hear a slip of interest in her voice.

"Yes." I could see no reason to deny it now. "He's hired me from time to time."

"To clean the blood he's spilled?" Amelia's acerbic words reminded me that Croft and the Hammer had bad blood between them, and I didn't know its source.

"If I'm honest, I don't often ask who made the messes I clean up," I admitted. "After this debacle, I'm forced to admit it's a practice I should have maintained."

No one shared my wry chuckle.

"That surprises me, Fiona." The disappointment in Amelia's voice itched at me.

"When I took the first job, I was not in a financial position to turn him down," I explained. "And now—"

"I love Sophia." Indira interrupted my confession with one of her own. Even though I couldn't see her in the dark, I had the impression both my and Amelia's heads snapped in her direction.

"And she loves me. We fell in love at The Orchard... working together. She wanted me to go with her to The Velvet Glove, but I didn't want to work for a man, and I was so close. *So close* to being able to buy my way out of the life. It's why I let Hartigan take these perverse photographs. With this money, I could start my spice shop. But now..." The tears in her voice broke my heart and produced a few of my own.

"I found letters in Alys's bureau," I said. "I thought they might be between her and Jane... but they were yours? Yours and Sophia's?"

"Alys was a ripe cunt." Indira spat on the earth. "I'm sorry, Amelia. I know you were fond of her."

"She liked me because I wasn't competition," Amelia replied. "I always knew that."

"Sophia and I were looking for our letters in The Orchard that day. I'd had a key made from Bea's master copy, one that would get me into Alys's room to search it. But you were there..."

"I'm s-sorry you didn't get them back." I couldn't seem to get warm, even as close to their bodies as I sat.

"It's all right. I have them all memorized anyhow."

It was possibly the sweetest thing I'd ever heard.

Just as it was becoming too cold to speak, our throats too dry to swallow, a cacophony reached us through the door.

By the time we'd helped each other to stand, a body came crashing through the door and landed hard on the ground.

Someone screamed in shock. I'd like think it wasn't me.

Especially because Croft stepped over the threshold and gave Butler one more punishing blow with his baton before tossing him to the ground with a satisfied grunt.

It was too dark to see his face, as he was backlit by lanterns and the torches of the police who swarmed in behind him to clasp Butler in irons. It wasn't hard to imagine his expression, however, as menace rolled from him in palpable waves.

"Grayson!" Amelia flung herself into his open arms, and he folded them around her.

I felt his eyes on me, and I'd admit I drank in the sight of his shadow, unable to remember when I'd been so happy to see any person in my entire life.

"My God, you're cold," he said, around rapid breaths born of exertion. "There's a fire lit out here."

It'd taken four strong men to heft Butler to his feet

and drag him out onto the streets as Croft hauled his sister out of the room and to the hearth.

Huddling around the blaze, none of us dared to touch the furniture some of the officers had drawn closer for us to rest upon. We knew what had occurred on the soft surfaces in this infernal place.

Water was brought, and Croft made certain we sipped when we would have gulped, hovering like a large, intimidating mother hen.

"It was Bea, too," Amelia croaked after a few sips. "She killed—"

He held up a hand. "The moment I saw Butler guarding the door, I knew. Though Charles Hartigan is spilling his guts, so we would have found out either way. Beatrice Chamberlain is being arrested as we speak. This lot will hang."

"Your hand," I said, noting his right knuckles and palm had been dressed with a thin, clean bandage.

Amelia reached out to inspect both of his hands. "What happened? Are you all right?" The left knuckles were split and swollen enough to cause concern, but apparently not enough to bandage.

Croft looked at me, at the split in my lip and the sling of petticoats we'd crafted for my shoulder. His gaze was unnervingly dark even as a strange lift tugged at the corner of his hard mouth. "The interrogation of your attacker, Benjamin Hornby, went longer than expected," he said. "But I got what I wanted."

I felt like I'd swallowed glass as I inspected his knuckles again. Those gashes could have been caused by teeth. By bone.

"Why did you come back here?" I asked, turning my face to the flames. "Hartigan had been released."

"You have Dr. Phillips to thank for that," he answered. "Sent me a missive full of garbled jargon and chemical components responsible for Jane Sheffield's death, and what they were used for. The third one down was photography development. And then, I just knew... I knew you were here."

I'd have to thank Dr. Phillips properly. God bless his diligent mind.

We thanked Croft, all of us, rather effusively. Amelia kissed his cheek and ruffled his hair, and, for once, he didn't grimace at the affection. "I told them you'd find us," Amelia said smugly. "They didn't believe me, but they don't know you."

"I'd tear this city apart to find you."

He'd replied to her, but I looked up to find his verdant gaze already upon me.

"Pardon my intrusion, ladies." A wiry detective with an impressive grey mustache bowed to us as if presenting himself to a bevy of noblewomen. "I've a coach with warm stones and piles of blankets waiting to take you from here, if you'd follow this constable."

Indira stumbled after the young bobby, but Amelia clung to her brother for a moment longer, regarding the man with a look I couldn't identify.

"Amelia," Croft murmured. "This is Detective Inspector Martin Thackery... my superior. He'll take you to Scotland Yard, where I'll meet you. I promise you're safe with him."

Amelia slipped her hand into Detective Inspector Thackery's, and I thought I saw the blue of his eyes melt into pools of gentility. He had a kind face for one dedicated to such a vocation of violence.

Tucking Amelia's hand into the crook of his arm, he led her toward the door, deliberately placing his body between her and where Hartigan stood sniveling in irons.

I made to follow, but Croft's hand snaked out and gripped my elbow. Jumping away, I wrenched my elbow from his grasp, and made a guttural sound I hoped no one had heard. Least of all him.

He curled both his hands into fists before burying them in his pockets.

I wanted to tell him I wasn't afraid. Just... overwhelmed. In throbbing pain. I didn't want to be touched until I could bathe, until I could wash that room and its contents from my skin.

"Who hurt you?" he demanded. "Do you need a doctor?"

I said nothing. He'd already broken the skin of his hands on the bones of the last man who'd thrown me against a wall. I couldn't have him handing every brute in London a retribution that went beyond the law.

And yet I couldn't help but flick a damning gaze toward Butler.

I could tell myself that if Croft hurt him, it was for all the women, both alive and dead, in those photographs.

"Thank you," I whispered, wishing I could say more. That I had a reply to the multitudes of sentiment I read in his gaze.

But I had nothing.

Or maybe I would have done something daft, like given him everything.

I didn't know much about what happened between men and women, but I knew enough to realize that intense gratitude could feel like something stronger, like something I was too cowardly to define.

"Promise me something," he said. "In the future, leave being a detective to me."

It was a promise I happily made in the moment.

One I really did *intend* to keep.

But one knew where the road paved with good intentions led...

And Jack the Ripper stood at the end of mine.

Epilogue

❧❧❧

Jane Sheffield and Isabelle James were buried a few days later in St. George's Cemetery in Whitechapel.

I'd bought their plots and headstones, simple as they were, at a bloody premium.

I even put one in place for Alys, though no one could say where her remains had ended up.

I knew I didn't have to, but the thought of these women—flawed and even downright villainous as they'd been to some people—dumped into a pit of lye was untenable. Much of what they'd supposedly done or not done had been no fault of theirs. I thought they should be afforded what little dignity I could give them in death.

A few of the women from The Orchard stood in black against the merciless cold with me as a stolid vicar blessed their graves.

I'd met all sorts who claimed to speak to God, to speak for him, to know how to get you into his good graces and therefore into the paradise he offered.

For a price. Always for a price.

Always paid to them and their institutions rather than to those who were in need. The way I figured, God had no need of my money. I saw his chapels, his cathedrals, his vast entire cities of riches and holdings, and I thought... if he was on his throne in paradise, what need did he have for hordes of earthly treasure? What temples could we possibly build to impress him?

When his son was here, didn't he walk in the dust with the rest of us? With the prostitutes? Did not he ask us to give to *them*? To the widows and the orphans and the outcasts?

I didn't do this expecting any kind of redemption, nor because I'd meant to commit a cardinal sin this very night. I just wanted something real to mark an end to this disaster, and as I looked around the gravesite, I believe it worked for us all.

Across from me, Indira and Sophia stood hand-in-hand, shoulder-to-shoulder, sharing each other's warmth. To the untrained eye they might have been any close friends, but I could see the love between them, the genuine feelings that linked their hearts just as tangibly as their fingers.

My heart swelled as their foreheads met, drawing strength from the other.

Because Beatrice Chamberlain, Mathew Butler, and Charles Hartigan were all incarcerated, Indira had decided to put her dream on hold for the time being and try her hand at running The Orchard.

When the hackney had come to collect them today, I noted that the sign above the establishment now advertised THE SPICE SHOP, and I approved of the retitling wholeheartedly.

Morag, Brinda, Kya, Katherine, and Isobel all stood in a row of mourning, roses in their hands as they gave their fallen family a final goodbye.

None of us truly knew how culpable Izzy was in Beatrice's machinations, but everyone seemed to agree that she was a woman easily bullied, manipulated, and led about by her broken heart.

When someone died, especially young and under

such tragic circumstances, their sins were so often for-gotten by the living.

Thus it seemed to be here as, one by one, the women of The Orchard dropped a rose on Izzy's grave, as well as Alys's and Jane's.

Very little was discussed between us after we duti-fully said our *amen* at the final prayer and dispersed. The grass crunched beneath our feet, frozen in the fading light of day, as we wound through the stones and pillars marking the dead.

I missed Amelia at the memorial, but Croft sent a note to say that he'd bundled her in a train headed for the South of France to visit a dear friend there. She'd been shaken by the entire business, and though she'd never showed it, he was worried about a decline in her vigor.

I knew what that meant. She'd lost so many friends at once. To the ground, and to betrayal. I was sure she was crushed by what had become of Beatrice.

My hackney driver, bless him, leapt down to help me into the seat, as I still had my arm in a sling. I thanked him and paid him extra for his pains before giving him directions to the hotel.

The hotel where I'd stay the night, but not alone. I'd sent a note to a man. One I wished to join me there for the evening.

For a night in each other's arms.

There'd not been another Ripper letter. Only a fake glued together by Bea to taunt me whilst her brew eased through my veins.

Croft told me that she'd requested to speak to me from her cell, but I hadn't been able to bring myself to go to her.

I'd missed something in regard to her. I should have known, should have seen in her the sort of person who would cause other women such unfathomable pain. I read people rather well, I thought. At least I had before...

No, I couldn't think of Aidan now. *This* betrayal was nothing to that one, but it touched the same place inside of me. The one where hatred lived. Hatred of them for being capable of such evil. Of myself for not sensing it. Of the world allowing it. Feeding it with the constant cycle of temptation, yielding, and obsessive search for redemption.

Aidan had stood as a bastion of that salvation, a literal messenger of the Redeemer, able to hand out absolution from his very grace.

And he'd chosen to wield the power of condemnation instead.

Beatrice, on the other hand, was a purveyor of temptations. An enabler of surrender. Had I turned a blind eye to her because I'd turned my back completely on any hope of salvation? Because I'd still wanted someone to revere? Someone to rely on when a letter from the Ripper arrived? Or when a man made me feel small and afraid? Or I needed...

Needed what? A mother? A protector? A mentor?

Anyone that didn't rely on me... or wield power over me.

I'd ascribed to her that duty—when she'd never once offered it—like a needy bloody child, rather than a woman possessed of three decades on this earth.

I wanted her to be my Joan of Arc. My Boudica.

But I'd forgotten what happened to them in the end. What happened to all women who led the war against the status quo.

They were the first to be chopped down by their enemies. Or they were hated for their power and taken down by their allies.

So where did that leave me? I was no holy warrior. No barbarian queen. I had no desire to be.

I was but a woman. And that was enough.

I had power over nothing but myself. And in the knowledge of that, there was freedom.

And, I was hoping as my chosen lover knocked on the door to the bower... more than enough pleasure.

Also by Kerrigan Byrne

A GOODE GIRLS ROMANCE

Seducing a Stranger

Courting Trouble

Dancing With Danger

Tempting Fate

Crying Wolfe

Making Merry

THE BUSINESS OF BLOOD SERIES

The Business of Blood

A Treacherous Trade

A Vocation of Violence

VICTORIAN REBELS

The Highwayman

The Hunter

The Highlander

The Duke

The Scot Beds His Wife

The Duke With the Dragon Tattoo

The Earl on the Train

THE MACLAUCHLAN BERSERKERS

Highland Secret

Highland Shadow

Highland Stranger

To Seduce a Highlander

About the Author

Kerrigan Byrne is the USA Today Bestselling and award winning author of several novels in both the romance and mystery genre.

She lives on the Olympic Peninsula in Washington with her two Rottweiler mix rescues and one very clingy cat. When she's not writing and researching, you'll find her on the beach, kayaking, or on land eating, drinking, shopping, and attending live comedy, ballet, or too many movies.

Kerrigan loves to hear from her readers! To contact her or learn more about her books, please visit her site or find her on most social media platforms: www. kerriganbyrne.com

CPSIA information can be obtained
at www.ICGtesting.com
Printed in the USA
LVHW040043010322
712297LV00005B/418